GOODBYE, SHE LIED

AN ESBETH WALTERS MYSTERY

GOODBYE, SHE LIED

RUSS HALL

FIVE STAR

An imprint of Thomson Gale, a part of The Thomson Corporation

Detroit • New York • San Francisco • New Haven, Conn. • Waterville, Maine • London

THOMSON
GALE™

LIBRARY OF CONGRESS CATALOGING-IN-PUBLICATION DATA

Hall, Russ, 1949–
    Goodbye, she lied : an Esbeth Walters mystery / Russ Hall. — 1st ed.
      p. cm.
    ISBN-13: 978-1-59414-602-2 (hardcover : alk. paper)
    ISBN-10: 1-59414-602-0 (hardcover : alk. paper)
    1. Walters, Esbeth, (Fictitious character)—Fiction. 2. Women detectives
—Texas—Fiction. 3. Older women—Texas—Fiction. 4. Retired teachers—
Fiction. 5. Rest homes—Fiction. 6. Swindlers and swindling—Fiction. 7.
Texas—Fiction. I. Title.
PS3558.A37395G66 2007
813'.54—dc22   2007022629

First Edition. First Printing: November 2007.

Published in 2007 in conjunction with Tekno Books and Ed Gorman.

Printed in the United States of America on permanent paper
10 9 8 7 6 5 4 3 2 1

The person who tries to live alone will not succeed as a human being. His heart withers if it does not answer another heart. His mind shrinks away if he hears only the echoes of his own thoughts and finds no other inspiration.

—Pearl Buck

CHAPTER ONE

Her eyes sparkled, the most alert deep Mediterranean blue you could imagine, surrounded as they were by a deep-lined gray face, a halo of white hair, the off-white walls of the room, and sheets as ivory as the silk that lines a coffin.

Melba Jean stood beside the bed and glanced down at the open file she held. Mrs. Cravetts, ninety-three, had not had a visitor of any kind in three and a half months. The room smelled of disinfectant, starched sheets, and of that odor particular to the very aged she was around so much she no longer felt a small shudder as she entered the building each day. What riveted Melba Jean's attention was the yellow Post-it Note she had put on the page that reminded her Medicare ran out on the patient in two days. That can be the warning track in the rest home biz when the individual or family has not made sufficient financial provisions.

It is a downright shame how people get old, their bodies let them down, and so do their families. Melba Jean's own white-haired mother had once reposed in a bed just like this, staring, with little more to do than wait.

Who knew how keen Mrs. Cravetts was inside those sparkling eyes? Melba Jean knew she still felt like a fifteen-year-old inside her own head sometimes, especially when a hand was placed on her thigh after that second glass of wine.

The other bed in the room was empty for the moment, the patient off getting rehab; the divider was pulled snug against the wall and battened down. Melba Jean closed and locked the door, put the clipboard on the stand beside the small water carafe. She reached for the spare pillow, held it for a second or two, then lowered it toward those eyes that got brighter and wider as the pillow approached.

The patient barely twitched, strapped in for her own safety that way, and the nurse call button off to the side where Melba Jean had moved it. The hands clenched in a spasm and there was a halfhearted kick or two. Then it was quiet in the room.

Melba Jean lifted the pillow and yanked off the cover, briskly put on a fresh one. She put the call button back in the patient's hand. A nursing home, unlike a hospital, did not have all the sophisticated monitors, which was handy.

She avoided the staring eyes that had already lost some of their earlier luster and backed away from the bed, closed the file in her hands, and pulled off the Latex nursing gloves as she headed toward the door.

On the way to the ringing front doorbell Esbeth slipped on a pair of worn pink bunny slippers some distant niece or nephew had sent to an aunt they no doubt thought was dotty because anyone who lived alone in her seventies and on occasion helped solve crimes certainly must be.

Oh, sure. You find one arm in your flowerbed and decide to see who it belongs to, the objections of the local law aside, and right away you get a reputation as the nosy sort of amateur detective who most riles the official keepers of the peace. It was that not-so-endearing trait that had led the sheriff to hire her as a part-time dispatcher—so he could keep an eye on her. Well, he had only himself to blame for how that had turned out.

Often cranky on her best days this early, she half snarled as she glanced at her watch. Seven-thirty a.m. The sky was dim and a dirty puce. Who in great gobs of grits would be calling on her at this hour? She swung the door open without looking out the peephole first and there stood Boose with a can of Budweiser in one hand and a smoked-down filterless cigarette in the other. He was five-eleven, all lean rawhide muscle, not a speck of fat on him, faded jeans, stained white T-shirt, worn boots, hair speckled by gray and mowed in a buzz cut, with a face that looked carved out of rock by someone who was just getting a beginning feel for the rock-carving trade.

Boose was one of those pure-through sons of Texas soil she had encountered when she moved out this way from Austin. Folks out in these parts, though friendly, ran to a salty attitude and brash-talking lot, which was a jolt for her at first, and Boose was one of the saltiest. The way he had shared with her that an uncle of his had died was, "He blew a head gasket, only it wasn't in his truck." Word had it that as a boy Boose had made his after-school money running moonshine and breaking mules. He was handy as an adult with his hands and could fix about anything that was broken, except his own marriages—he'd had five of those before he did the world and himself a favor by stepping aside from the pursuit of matrimony, even though women seemed drawn to him by strange and mysterious forces. He was sure wound up today like a spring on a cheap watch, even though he looked calm on his exterior.

"Dint wake you, did I? You old coots get up way 'fore the chickens most times, I figure. 'Spose it's to kick their feathery butts into layin' good. Right? Folks your age love an egg of a mornin'. Right? Well, I got a problem's right up your alley."

Any questions in the early chatter were rhetorical, so Esbeth swung the door open while Boose crushed the lit end of the cigarette out with the hard, callused ends of blunt fingers, field-stripped the butt from habit and dropped the shreds onto her lawn, which had turned into a brown rice crispy texture from the recent sustained Central Texas drought. He followed her inside, shut the door, and had to step lively to catch up as she moved in swift deliberate steps through the small cottage of her home into the kitchen-slash-breakfast nook to yank a couple of pieces of toast out of the toaster and butter them. "Pot of coffee is there on the stove. Help yourself, Boose. Sorry there aren't any of those eggs you seem to expect."

She could have added that a person does not arrive at genuine "old coot" status for a few more years. She was still quite *compos mentis,* thank you very much, in spite of being retired from a career of teaching school math for quite a few years to a generally uninterested, unmotivated, and, hence, unenlightened a group of kids with equally difficult parents as ever passed through any public school system. That did not make her dotty, though she did despair for the whole human race on occasion.

She took the pot of coffee across to the breakfast nook table and they settled into its two seats on opposite sides of the small table.

"Do you still have that job with the winery, Boose?" She slid a saucer with one of the slices of buttered toast his way. He poured coffee into a chipped blue Spode cup.

"Yeah. They can't do without me, turns out. For a while there when the management changed I thought I was gonna have to go out and get me a job blowing buffalo at a nickel a herd, but the family come through and decided to keep me on a spell. Heard you lost your gig at the sheriff's, though."

Esbeth felt a frown try to steal its way onto her face. She wrestled it back down before it could appear. Boose was, after all, merely being Boose. For all his ills and foibles, those aside, she still found him a likeable cuss. She was fond of him the countrified way you would have for a horse that might well buck you in sport, but was loyal to the bone all the same.

"It wasn't much of a gig, Boose, just part-time dispatching until he finessed himself out of a job on that corruption charge."

"A rap you helped hang on him, if I rightly recall." He took a loud sip of his coffee and looked over the rim of the cup at her with squinting careful eyes.

"Any rap people get is one they've hung on themselves. Justice is on their trail, whether they see it or not, and it often catches up to them. In this case, I just happened to be the one to help nudge and poke to help justice catch up."

"Which brings me to yours truly. I hear you been dippin' your beak into solvin' cases again. Read where you was the one nosed out a meth lab right here in town. That must've blown some smoke up the new sheriff's skirts." He reached for his slice of toast and took a bite out of one corner.

"No, the new sheriff wasn't too thrilled, and I only got involved because a lady at my church was worried about her son. I don't go out of my way to dip my beak, as you so eloquently put it, into anything these days. I just scoot by from check to check the way most folks in retirement do. How's your momma, by the way?"

He tilted a wary head at her. One eye squinted almost shut. "It's what I came to jaw about, if you don't have nothin' on the front or back burner."

She didn't, but hesitated to tell him that. When she lived back in Austin it seemed something was popping up all the time, not that she went out of her way to look for it, though she did find it, like that time she found the arm in her coreopsis bed. Out here, in Fearing, though a county seat town, the usual activities included watching grass grow, when it didn't just turn brown in the heat, and watching paint dry, which it did quite well on the hot days.

Outside a dog barked, accompanied by the distant sound of a trash compactor and men who yelled back and forth in Spanish as the garbage crew made their early morning pass through the neighborhood. Esbeth left her toast untouched while she took in every detail of Boose, from the crust of mud on the end of one pants leg to the yellowed patch on the fingers he used to hold his toast as he finished it off.

"I didn't know you smoked."

"I don't. Just do now and again to give the aluminum poisoning a boost." He held up the empty beer can he had crushed into a small silver lump.

"Or when something has your shorts in a bunch?"

"Then, too."

"What is it you came to see me about?" she sighed. Inside, the flutter of slow excitement kindled as it did whenever she got wind of something where her skills might be applied, whether the local law wanted her to meddle or not.

"It's Momma. She's a pickle."

"You mean she's in a pickle."

"If you say so."

The only thing she could recall about Boose's mother, as she sifted back through the past couple of years she had known him, was a story he had told of a reunion trip he took to meet with his Navy submarine unit. He had caught a few wild boar shoats in a trap earlier, when they were only thirty or forty pounds each, and had raised two of the hairy black pigs until the boar was around five hundred pounds and the sow at least four hundred. They had thick pitch-black fur, curved razor-sharp tusks, and would eat anything and everything. Boose had asked his mother to feed them while he was away. When he came home he could not find her at the house, so he went out to the pen and there were the two pigs but no momma—in the center of the sty was a single boot of his mother's. He had raced through the house and to the four corners of his property, coming to rest in front of the house where he had yelled up at the sky, loud enough to be heard in the next county, "THEM HOGS'VE DONE ET MOMMA."

Esbeth finished her first cup of coffee and slid her untouched saucer of toast his way while she filled her cup and his. It wouldn't kill him, though it might take the edge off any beer buzz he had this early.

Of course, Boose's momma had not been eaten by those wild hogs that time. But he didn't know that for the better part of a day. She had gotten a boot stuck in the gummy mud and had to run for it when the hogs made a move on her. She had gone over to her place to fetch another pair of shoes, in this case the only other ones she had, her Sunday-go-to-meeting boots. It had taken a day to straighten out the confusion. Boose was usually calm under pressure, and was scrappy enough too that most males in the area gave him a wide berth, even though he was gnarly as rawhide and no heavyweight. The string of five wives that had passed through his life no doubt added to the toughness, though otherwise had no effect on him, unless you count his being barred from weddings at the First Baptist Church for using a slingshot to hurl rice.

"Now, what's this about your momma?" Esbeth settled back into her chair.

He drained the refilled cup of coffee as if it was a shot of bourbon and set it down. That allowed him to move his arms about a bit, which he was prone to do while talking.

"Well, you know 'bout me being the last kid, number twelve, and Momma callin' me Boose after a caboose, right?"

"Yes."

"Then 'long came Pearl after me, kind of a bonus there, number thirteen. For most her life Momma never done nothin' but raise kids."

"And your father?"

"Run off, runned over. Somethin' like that. Anyways, Momma never paid into no Social Security. Then she got this ostrich thing."

13

"Ostrich?"

"You know, where her bones go bad from havin' so many kids."

"Do you mean osteoporosis?"

"Yeah, that's the rascal. When she needed to go into assisted living at the rest home we put up her place for sale and all of us chipped in everything we had. I mean to tell you, we were doin' all we could to care, not like that Ben Joe Camper who put his momma in the deep freeze that time she died and kept her there for three weeks 'til deer season was over, or Buzzsaw Taylor when his momma runned off with a UPS man, still in his brown shorts and everthing, and Buzzsaw dint even notice for a few days—well, almost a month."

"If we can get back to the subject of your momma," Esbeth fought back the beginning of a frown, "how much was it you all managed to put aside?"

"Sixty-four thousand dollars. It was all she had with what we could chip in on, and it was gonna be enough to get her by for a spell. But then someone from the bank come by and talked to her."

"Let me guess. A bank inspector had a teller they thought was crooked and wanted your Momma's help catching the teller."

Boose jumped up out of his chair, his face flushed, and his arms raised, ready to scrap. "Who told you?"

"Oh, sit down and calm yourself. Don't let your mud flaps get caught up in the wind. It's just a classic bank con, one of the oldest grifts around. I feared that's the direction you were going."

"What d'you mean 'grifts'?" He lowered himself back into the chair.

"There are grifters who go around conning people all the time. There are the big cons, like the wire, the rug, and the pay-

14

off, and there are even more short cons, like the pigeon drop, the gold brick, the home repair rip-off, the fake charity, the foreign lottery—especially a Canadian one lately—even a pretty complex one about someone stuck in a Mexican prison, and then there's the phony bank inspector scam. There are more of them than I can name, and a lot of them are aimed at older folks these days. Did you go right to the sheriff with this? The rest home's county enough to be in his turf."

"Yes, and I'd like to tell you about this new one. He said he'd look into it, but he dint sound like he'd make it no priority. I couldn't get no satisfaction from that man. None atall. It's why I come to you."

"You'd better tell me everything you can."

"These con men, or grifters, work those things a lot on old folks?"

"Often these days they do. Old-time con men used to like to sting crooked men, mobsters and the like with the big cons, since they operate illegally and weren't likely to make a ruckus. But in recent years lots of the small cons target older folks, like your momma."

"Why would anyone pick on old folks to rip off, anyways?" The color rushed back into his cheeks and forehead and his fists clenched and unclenched without him knowing it.

"Boose, you have to remember that people who grew up when we did are more trusting, and the lonely ones are easy to approach. We all lived in an era where trust was readily given and it was normal to lend a helping hand. Another attraction of picking on older folks is that when they get stung they feel stupid, and lots of times they never even go to the law at all about it, or get kind of laughed at when they do. It's humiliating, and enough of life is so in those years without that."

"If you know so much about all this, how do you think they played Momma?"

"My guess is that someone posing as a bank inspector came to her and asked her to help expose a dishonest teller. I imagine just enough was hinted to her for her to be stewing real good with curiosity to know who it was, enough, too, for her to want to get involved in something spicy where someone would get caught being crooked. She was sworn to secrecy while the inspector got her to withdraw money from her account in order to check the serial numbers. Or, sometimes all the grifter needs is a blank check to raid the account. Most of them can't help putting some mystery and intrigue into the story so there's a temporary junior G-man spy sort of thing going on until the victim, like your momma, finds her money is gone. That about the way it went?"

"Yeah. It was a guy. He got Momma to call the bank inspection place and everything, though."

"With a number he supplied?"

"Yeah. Some gal there said he was who he said he was."

"Then there are two of them, a pair of grifters, at least. The sheriff say anything about it, have your momma look through any mug shots?"

"Just a halfhearted batch or two on a computer screen. He acted like these sorts pass through areas all the time and there's nothin' you can usually do 'cause they're long gone by now."

"That is a good possibility."

"Isn't there anything you can do to get her money back?"

"That is the sixty-four-thousand-dollar question. What do you think I can do?"

"Well, they've kicked Momma out of that assisted living spot at the rest home. They're pretty sensitive about anyone havin' no money. She's gonna have to live in my place, and Pearl's had to come tend to her days til we figure somethin' out. The lot of us don't have any more money to put in the kitty. Come to think of it, we couldn't even pay you for any diggin' around you do."

"Don't you worry your bony head about that. I sure as bob white don't make my living off any of the poking around I've ever done in that line. If I did I'd have starved a long time ago."

"No. You don't look like you're starving any," Boose said. He may not have realized how that sounded. Esbeth couldn't tell as he glanced around at her small, cozy cottage.

She had to admit as she shifted her comfortable bulk in her chair that no one was going to mistake her for being anorexic. She said, "These people at the rest home. Didn't you talk with them? Couldn't they be a bit more understanding, given the circumstances?"

"You don't know these sorts, all smiley when you're checking your kin in, when they've had a sniff at a bank account, or if you're gettin' Social Security, which, like I said, you gotta pay into before you get any out. Or maybe you got one of those extra insurance things, which Momma don't. No, those folks at that home have a careful nose about anything green, and right now Momma's just so much stale cheese to that lot."

"Now, Boose, I didn't mention some of the other cons going on just to make all this sound complex. But the fact is that people like the ones who probably did this often have a lot of these going on at the same time, are extraordinarily good at covering their tracks, and are on the constant move. It's not that local law enforcers don't care so much as it is that they're over their heads right from the get-go with the likes of these. The whole intent by grifters is to slip and slide, be all smoke and mirrors, to get lost among what seem more serious crimes like murder, rape, outright robbery with guns, burglary and the like. Cops rarely catch people like this, and my chances aren't any better than theirs. It leaves the law with egg on their faces and that's why they don't even enjoy talking about this sort of thing much."

"You sayin' it don't matter my momma's lost everything and has to lay on her back at my place with my sister tending to her, or that you're afraid of a little egg on your own face?"

"Neither, Boose. I'm just sharing the hard facts, such as they are. If I was to find these people, the ones who took your momma's money, what would you want done with them? Turned over to the law so justice can run its course?"

"No. You find them you just tell me where they are. That's enough." His teeth clenched in flexing rhythm to his hands this time. He stared off in hard, eager anticipation.

That didn't seem like an altogether good or safe idea to Esbeth. Boose may be no giant, but he had wreaked some havoc in his day. When one of the Coxway brothers, all of whose necks were even redder than Boose's, had made disparaging remarks about his sister Pearl, Boose had rolled up his sleeves and headed that way, even when that meant dealing with the older brother, "Tall Drink" Coxway, who got his sobriquet by being six-foot-five and over two hundred pounds of muscle. That hadn't slowed Boose. He took the lot of them apart like so many cheap erector sets and Tall Drink's new distinction became the only person in his thirties to go about using a walker for the better part of a year. People often underestimated Boose, but never more than once.

"Well, we'll see about that." The soft spot for Esbeth was that though she felt far too young to be retired, reality kicked in when she tried to do anything too physical, or went to another room and could not remember for the life of her what she had gone there for and had to come back to where she had started to remind herself. Getting older was no day at the beach, or even one at the crawfish puddle, and her heart went out to Mrs. Hargate, Boose's momma, or anyone who got ripped off by those slick, younger con artists. Still, it would mean dealing

18

with the new sheriff, and perhaps that director at the rest home, who for her money might very well be as crooked as a pig's tail, not far above stealing gold fillings out of teeth.

"Well, I'm sure you'll do what you can," Boose said. Some of his earlier confidence in her and expectations of her had slipped.

She responded with a not-too-confident nod. The one thing she had not shared with Boose was her own reluctance to go to the rest home at all; it was her greatest personal phobia. Living alone all her life had given her an immense appreciation for her own solitude and independence. As each year went by—as each day went by, for all that—she knew she drew closer to where going into a rest home might be the only course open for her, and the thought chilled her to the rattling core of her bones. The people crowded together, the loss of dignity, even the atmosphere, mood, and smell of the place had made her skin crawl like it was trying to get off in the one or two times she had had to visit so far. She hated to admit, even to herself, how personal the threat of it all was. It was worse to her than going to the funeral of a younger friend and facing her own mortality. None of this was going to be easy; but, then, it never was.

Melba Jean slowed in the hallway as she came to the door of the corner office. She cleared her throat and rapped gently on the walnut-stained wood trim. The door was open, but she gave him time to turn off whatever occupied his time on the computer screen, often a poker or solitaire game. After a count to five she pushed into the room, the file still under her arm. Torrence Furlong was turning to face his desk and pulled down the French cuffs of his shirt as she entered. Behind him, on the computer screen, a tiny white dot lingered in the center for a second, then flickered away.

"What is it?" He was a big man, with a long, square face highlighted by white on the temples of otherwise black hair.

Meeting him for the first time you would take him for an ex–football player entering his late fifties with unusual grace, and you would have missed to the good side by five or six years. On alternate days, he directed the Oakline Hills Rest Home as well as a neighboring county's sixty-four-bed hospital, Kessler Memorial—the rest home on Tuesdays and Thursdays. He exercised his grip with an authoritative look, though he had long ago learned to hire capable staff members and to relegate and delegate. Most of his time was spent, when not in one meeting or another, looking and acting dignified. He could have easily been a college dean or a congressman. Panache and polish was his battle cry and credo, and in a town like this it had carried him far. He had his shirts starched until they creaked, and each movement he made was slow and deliberate, as if stretched out in time like some Japanese Noh play, where ten minutes gets dragged out into an hour. His manicured hands lowered to the gleaming wood surface. The polished teak desk in front of him matched the other furnishings that included bookshelves containing only a few books—one a leather-bound copy of *Gray's Anatomy* that had never been opened—and the bric-a-brac of awards a community like this showers on its civic leaders.

"That problem we had . . ." Melba Jean let it hang.

"To which problem do you refer?"

"The one where we were a bed short for Mrs. Maxwell."

"Oh. What about it?"

"The problem's taken care of itself. Mrs. Cravetts just passed on."

A shadow of doubt crossed Torrence's brow, but flickered away as fast as the dot on the screen had. He had thought, of all things, about Thomas à Becket, of whom King Henry II had said, "Will no one rid me of this man?" His loyal followers did just that, with repeated blows on his head with the butts of their swords, somewhat to the king's regret. Torrence smiled. "It's odd, isn't it, how these things have a way of taking care of themselves? Give Karl at the Kendall-Williams Funeral Home the call. He's right for this. She's cleared for cremation, isn't she?"

"Yes," Melba Jean said. She didn't need to look down to the file.

"Then push it through, will you?" He knew that even if they had to go the casket and funeral route that Karl would never say anything about any bruises inside the lips, if any just happened to be there. All that was part of his being under a special retainer.

Melba Jean nodded and turned, with a slow smile spreading. She liked making Torrence happy, liked it very much. As she left his office he turned back to the computer on the teak credenza behind the desk.

CHAPTER TWO

James Calloway reached for the oval brown bar of soap, rubbed it with the thick Egyptian washcloth, and let the heady smell of sandalwood fill his nostrils. The suite had come with perfectly good French milled oatmeal soaps, but the trick of getting exceptional service was to make special requests. The concierge had sent one of the bellhops scampering off to the nearest mall's Crabtree & Evelyn or Caswell-Massey soap shop to get him the exact soap he said he needed if he was to stay. He took another deep breath. It had been worth the young lad's effort. Slight wisps of steam rose from the water around him, the underwater jets lining the sides of the oversized tub swirled the almost too warm water. The womb-like comfort of a hot bath of a morning gave him time to think, to appreciate the many aspects of his life.

He had a theory about the very rich. In a nub, it was that many of them are past being able to enjoy or savor anything. Money is either there or flows in at such a clip, with no real sense of achievement or having earned it at all, that it cannot be felt. Picture Bill Gates going out to shop and having to hesitate over a new suit or car to ponder if he could afford it—not very likely. The fact that many of the very rich who have old money or too much of it feel bored or depressed confirmed his notion. "Oh, dear, a bit low on caviar and champagne on the yacht. When will the pathos and tragedy end?"

Years ago, at a blackjack table in the Fox Resorts Casino near

Norwich, Connecticut, the largest resort casino in the world, one purported to benefit the Mashantucket Pequot Indians, he was having the absolute worst run of luck of his life. He could not believe how bad the cards were falling. The heat rose to his flushed cheeks and he knew that sooner or later a single hand had to be a good one; but none had been. It made no sense, absolutely no sense. As a former mechanic himself, once running a three-card Monte game, he would have spotted anything fishy with the card handling. But the cards slid out of the shoe in hand after hand of some of the scaliest cards he had ever been dealt.

A calm person, a logical person, might have stood from the table and walked away, said tomorrow would be another day. He had stayed. Sooner or later the cards simply had to swing back his way. They had not. Near the end there had been a hand or two, but that had not even been a Band-Aid on the balloon. He had lost and lost big, which meant he had to cut out from the resort in the middle of the night with an unpaid tab at the Great Cedar Hotel. They wrote it off to a comp, no doubt, given what they had squeezed from him. A lot he cared about their end of it. He was broke, or as near to it as he had ever been. It had taken him three years to get back the nut he lost in that one night. A shudder went through him yet, even in the steaming water of the Jacuzzi.

It was that exact moment to which he most often thought back, when the fear and embarrassment, the sense of having no control, the feel of being the same unblessed lad who had grown up in the flats of Cleveland, Ohio, hustling after lumps of coal from beside the train tracks, had washed over him. He used those icy fingers of fear to motivate. He would never be poor again.

A knuckle rapped on the door. "Are you a prune yet in there?"

"No, Miss Baron. Until I am able to pick up a pencil by

simply touching it I am by no means as pruny as I am able to get." Blasted girl. Leave it to her to spoil the setting of the 1,598-square-foot Presidential suite at the Four Seasons. She should be over gazing out across Town Lake or the sprawl of the southern part of Austin.

"Breakfast just arrived."

"Well, why didn't you say so?" He began to rinse himself off and reached for one of the largest towels.

He dripped onto the bath mat as he glanced at the mirror that covered the wall behind the sink. The reflection was half obscured by a haze of mist that clung to the glass. He took another of the towels and wiped it clear until he could see himself—a pale, rounded body that spoke of being generous to himself and demanding no trips to the gym. He admitted he was a hundred pounds away from being a threat to any woman. Most people find a circular fellow to be jolly. They trust him, and that was all to the good. His eyes had a tendency to become mean, narrow slits easy to anger when he let them, but with constant concentration he kept them as open and jovial as he could, and it was by his wit and concentration that he made his fortune.

When he had dressed he came out into the room where Silky Baron strolled beside the broad set of windows, headset on, speaking in a soft tone as she made her pitch. She had not yet touched the breakfast he had ordered, her Café Latte or Old-World Birchemüsli with nuts and berries on one side of the white linen. For him there was an egg white spinach Frittata with portabella mushrooms, roasted peppers, broiled tomatoes along with grilled asparagus. His beverage was a cappuccino. He sat at the table and placed one of the salmon-colored linen napkins on his lap.

"The starving children of war-torn Afghanistan thank you," she muttered with sincere-sounding appreciation. Silky could spot the button to anyone's generosity. The con is sales, after all, and she explored needs with the best and had no peer at knowing the right time to go for the jugular with a close during her presentation pitch. The cell phone from which she worked had been bought with cash, was untraceable, and would be thrown away before its time was spent.

She was quite a sharp bird, that one, a lucky find, by far the most apt pupil he had ever had, and she was not too bad on the eyes, either, for all that. She showed her long legs with black cuffed slacks and a crease that glistened like a knife, white blouse, red silk scarf knotted loosely around the neck, black leather sandals that looped back and forth up to the tops of her calves. It was an outfit that could be demure and businesslike one moment and seductive as dammit the next, depending on how her clever Machiavellian mind read the mark.

To hear her present her starving children pitch, or the church in need of help angle, you would never know he had first met her in a topless bar on the outskirts of Las Vegas. Exotic dancing establishment if he was to use her words. She had the shape for it, but more than that she had honed her sense for where the money was to a fine edge. Leave it to Silky to know, to the nearest nickel, what someone she only glanced at was worth, how much she could shake the mark for, and when it was best to leave someone alone.

She hung up the phone and sat down at her side of the table while he toyed with his Frittata and reached for the newspaper by his plate. Her eyes swept over his suit, the dark blue Armani. "You're going to be the bank examiner again today?" Though she had never said so, he knew she did not care much for his penchant for taking his pickings from the elderly. He often stated that they have it coming, those older folks. No one asked them to be suckers. If he did not take their money, someone else would. Anyone who knew anything would be fools not to fleece the elderly like so many stupid sheep.

"I thought you just ran that most of last week?" she said.

"And quite successfully." He touched the corner of his mouth to remove a fleck of toast, then lifted the Metro & State section of the paper he held and opened it to the obits. There are always gems to be mined there—a bereaved widow or widower fat with an insurance claim, just waiting to hear of an opportunity or from a long-lost relative.

"We weren't done discussing it," she said, reaching across the table to lower the paper so she could look into his eyes.

"Yes . . . we . . . *were*." Each word distinctive and crisp. "As I have told you often enough, risk is the essential difference between a plodder and one who is successful in this game. Knowing the measure in order to take the appropriate amount of risk and no more is the essence of greatness. To not know it, as you well know, is the measure of failure, something from which to learn and never repeat. Like it or not, old folks are low risk, fish in a barrel."

His upper lip drew firm, and his mouth shifted to a near pout. He sought once again to raise the paper, but she held it down with a firm hand. "What is our deal?" she said, "What you should never be?"

His eyes unlocked with hers, and he looked away. They had been together two years, and from the beginning he had known he had to establish dominance between them—that all relationships ultimately come down to power, that she should damn well recognize his leadership. It was hard enough to roll over the way he needed to in some cons without coming home to someone who by rights ought to wear black leather outfits and carry a whip. He would tame her in time, but she was not taking to the bit with ease—you could say that for her. He thought of the only thing that calmed him and reassured him in times like these, the little leather pouch of bank safety deposit keys; he had tucked back the majority of what they took in before he split with her. When she knew what the totals were he could not fudge, but there were numerous times when she did not. He had plenty enough to take him into his declining years, in the style to which he had accustomed himself, and that was a comfort.

"I know," he said, making his tone as demure as he could manage.

"Say it."

He hesitated.

"I said say it."

Damn her. He was the mentor here. But he knew she would be difficult all day unless he got her calmed down, so he said, "I am never a prat, a pimp, or a prig to be." He took his medicine, for all appearances, like a classroom chump from a stern teacher, though he was old enough to be her father.

"That's right, and that goes for being sententious at the breakfast table. Now, are you going to be civil?"

"Yes, Miss Baron."

She let go of the paper and turned her attention to her breakfast. She still had him fixed with one attractive though narrowed eye, but that lasted only as long as it took him to lift the newspaper section back up in front of him while picking at his food, and when he peeked next her way she seemed absorbed in ignoring him and eating.

Silky crunched her fancy granola and watched Calloway—at least the part of him she could see behind the stretch of newspaper. He took a tentative bite of egg white and veggie and rolled it on his tongue. Well, the man did savor life in a way few people do, on an intellectual level. Most men get swirled up in things, whether a football game or their temporary desires. Her years of parading on the runway in the altogether had convinced her of that. The secret of men, and some women as well, is that intrigue often outweighs knowledge. People are like cats with a piece of yarn given half a chance. They will do themselves in, if you let them. That was what had attracted her to the idea of working with James. He approached the con with the mental stimulation of a game, one that did not involve sex. He spoke of how confidence is some balance-beam moment between hubris and failure, some delicate nudge where the right risk leads to the foreseen reward. She differed from him in that she craved the big money, not this nickel-and-dime jive—one lottery-sized score, that was what using your head was for. Take the money and run. She didn't want to make doing this a career. In spite of all Jimbo thought he was teaching her, she was way ahead on the essential bits. She tucked one side of her lower lip between her bright white teeth and bit softly. What she wanted from him was to learn how never to get caught . . . again.

She once had thought herself ready for the big con, the kind where you take on someone more crooked than yourself. Of course, you need to wriggle out at the end so he is afraid anything he says or does will bring in the law or make him look foolish—classic sting. It should have worked, only it had not. She and Roy Dean Vanderhael—"Van" a budding grifter like herself—had set up the mark and had cooked a store. Tony "Two Chins" Petralia was ostensibly a made man, but that meant nothing to her, though it should have. Van said the main thing was that the person needs to be involved in enough criminal activities to be reluctant to go to the law, and Two Chins was all of that.

Other than a little time spent on the dip, and the badger game they ran on suckers from out of town, she had not put in any serious work as a roper. Van had assured her the skills were not too different from shaking the pockets loose in the topless places she had worked. They had rented the warehouse, an empty one out near enough the airport to make for easy in and out, and he had rounded up the actors from former star wannabe pals back in L.A. He outlined the steps for her, and she went through the motions as if she had been setting up the big con all her life.

She had scouted out all of Two Chins' usual haunts, established a pattern, and managed to bump into him and be memorable. He had been nothing like she expected, tall, slender, an impeccable dresser. The nickname came from a cleft in his chin, which unlike that of Tony Curtis, he had gotten from a knife when he was a boy. Silky had stayed coy at first, had dribbled out bits of information about making some easy money, had gained his confidence. Then she had steered him to her acquaintance, Van.

They had both seemed determined to keep Two Chins away from the action, which, of course, had the desired opposite effect. Without telling him what they were up to, they let him learn that they were sidetracking "whales" from the other casinos by sweeping them up at the airport and taking them right to the warehouse on the promise of an easy killing. Whales are the prize catch of casinos—big businessmen, wealthy foreigners, or anyone who shows a willingness to play for the highest stakes and can afford to lose significant sums. Casinos are always trying to steal the prize whales from each other, comping them with the best rooms and sometimes even shanghaiing them at the airport the way Van was doing. That part was credible, and Two Chins bought into the notion, not knowing, of course, that the whales were actors, too. Van and Silky let him see that big money could be made, "telling him the tale." He threatened them until they were forced to let him in on one of the next fleecings, as they had planned. He would have to front the money they used to let the mark win at first, though, and he was fine with that. They reluctantly let him in, and allowed him to make a big profit, "giving him the convincer."

Then they tried to back away, cut him out cold, said the next whale was their big payday, too big for them to share. That made Two Chins drool. He was in on it, he said, no matter what, even though more front money than usual was needed, a quarter mil, chump change for him, but it was going to be enough to send Van and Silky to Rio for a change of scenery. It nearly worked, too.

The cops who raided that night seemed real enough as they smashed in the doors and set off canisters of tear gas. Two Chins bought it, too. He left the stake money behind, which Silky and Van loaded into their car on the other side of the building. Then Two Chins recognized one of the cops, knew him from L.A. and knew he was not a Vegas cop—was never going to be with his record. So much for blowing Two Chins off and putting in the fix with the local law; the paper trail was fixed to show that he was the one who had rented the warehouse when the real cops arrived later to find any left-behind gambling paraphernalia.

Silky and Van got away, but had violated the cardinal rule of the big con. The mark must not want to come after the grifters with intent to do them serious harm, which was the word Two Chins put out on the street by the next day. With the airport staked out with his men, Silky and Van hit the highway and planned to split the money and go different directions by Oklahoma City. But Van jumped the gun and took off in the night with the money. Silky ended up in Dallas, then Houston, and now Austin. She had worked the con in each of those cities with the far smoother James, from whom she had learned much and knew there was more to learn, so she put up with his occasional stuffy spells. He was sure right about one thing when he said that in the real world you only lose if you make the same mistake more than once, but in the grifter life you do not get even that many chances to screw up. He glanced her way while he patted his smug mouth with his napkin.

He raised the paper again and she gasped out loud.

"Don't be so dramatic," he snapped. She said nothing, though he could hear her suck in a loud breath. He lowered the paper. She sat transfixed on the other side of the table, staring not at him but at the lowered paper.

"Whatever is it that is bothering you, Miss Baron?"

She did not answer, just reached and grabbed the Metro & State section of newspaper out of his hands, leaped up from the table, and ran across the suite to her bedroom, slammed the door behind her. She rushed across to her unmade bed and sprawled across it, opened the page again to the picture of Roy Dean Vanderhael, the man who had made off with her share. The caption under the heading called him Vance Kilgore, but it was her Van.

The headline beneath the story read: *WIDOW CONTESTS SUICIDE RULING IN DEATH OF FEARING MAN.* The poor sap had at least had the sense to change his name—not a bad idea since Tony Two Chins had sworn he would chase the two of them to the ends of the earth.

Her hands began to sweat and the ink from the buttery feeling newsprint stuck to her hands. When they were running from Petralia and his Vegas bunch she and Van had each taken out two $500,000 insurance policies on each other. It was a hedge against either being killed. When Van had cut with the money and run, she had often wished Two Chins success in that end of the hunt. She had kept up payment on the policies all this time, but there had been no word of Van, until just this moment. Now Van was dead.

She poured over the details of the story. Good lord, Van, you certainly got yourself into it, didn't you? The wife she could understand, though she had never allowed him to sleep with her, and he had not pressed, which was something she looked for in her men after years of parading around nude in front of the swine. The more she read on, the Medical Examiner's verdict of suicide made her head reel. Van, or Vance Kilgore had a job in sales at Dell in Austin, which meant a commute of an hour or more each way to work from Fearing. He had left home before six a.m., according to his wife Adele. Witnesses had next seen the Kilgore Mazda swerving on the road two hours later, heading not toward Austin but back toward Fearing when it had gone off the road and smashed into a copse of trees, head-on into the largest of them, killing the driver. Then the story took its bizarre turn.

The EMS workers who first arrived on the scene removed him from the vehicle and noticed strips of blood-smeared duct tape hanging from his wrists and ankles that looked as though the tape ends had been torn. It was hard to tell anything from the head, since a massive head trauma was what had killed him, but in checking him over they found both nipples had been cut off, as well as one ear lobe and the end of one pinkie finger, the latter a sign of satanic involvement in some circles. The autopsy confirmed, said the ME, that death had come from the fractured skull of the car crash, which led to the suicide ruling. The sheriff had gone along with the ME's report and had pushed the widow for a quick cremation and she had gone along, but now she was having second thoughts.

The wheels were spinning in Silky's head as she did permutations. Insurance companies do not pay off on suicides. She knew that, so she was out a million in addition to the money Van had already ripped her off for unless she could do something. What could she do? Her partner had said they would be leaving the state soon for riper pickings. If some of Two

Chins' men were the ones behind any murder and cover-up as suicide, and she got the attention of law enforcers shifted to murder, would that be wise? But, hell, he had already promised to chase down her and Van. Chances were it was him behind Van's death. The million, then, was just running money. She could not let James in on any of this, or there would be only half the million, or less the way he skimmed off her, the price she paid for the chance to learn under a master he said. Then there was the obvious, to not get found and killed by Two Chins herself. The cops who looked into Van's death were, no doubt, small-town rubes in over their heads. She had to get them to think murder instead of suicide, but how hard could that be?

CHAPTER THREE

Though it was still morning, Esbeth pulled into the parking lot at the Sheriff's Department late enough that the "shade hogs" had garnered all the good spots where there was the least bit of shadow or hope for any. She had to leave her car in the blazing sun, a mean yellow orb in the now cloudless light blue that looked like a bowling ball on fire. It may be edging toward the latter part of October, but no one had gotten around to telling the Texas sun to let up just yet. True winter does not come to the central part of the state until January sometimes, and what folks up north would consider an Indian summer was just business as usual for the local weather. No one felt at home if their eyebrows were not half melted off by each mid-afternoon.

She faced going to the rest home later, at a time she had been able to wrangle an appointment with the director, though the thought made her shudder in spite of the heat. For now she had to confront another personal hurdle, that of returning to the department office after being let go when she had caused the sheriff, Eldon Watkins, to lose his job. The interim sheriff, Johnny Gonzalez, won the subsequent election and had not extended an opportunity for her to come back as part-time dispatcher.

Before she could enter the building one of the deputies came out. He didn't hold the door open for her, just gave her a look that would have wilted hardier flowers. Chunk Philips, the former right hand of Watkins, had not said "no" to many chicken

fried steaks, and might have thought he was next in line to be sheriff. He bore no goodwill toward Esbeth and wasn't shy about sharing that.

"He's not here," he said, slipping on a pair of sunglasses that made him look like some large, round insect beneath the broad-brimmed smoky the bear hat. Like so many big men, he had a face that said, "Love me as I am," and said it as a dare.

"Know where he is?"

Chunk shrugged and kept walking, not looking toward her, as if to do so would give him more indigestion than he seemed already to have.

She sighed. It was hard to come to an area new, as she had just a couple years back, and make friends slowly only to feel ostracized by some of them, all for doing what was the moral and right thing, though not the good-old-boy-network thing, as it turned out.

Without going inside she turned back and headed to her car. She pulled out of the gravel parking lot and headed for the nearest gas station with a pay phone. There is more than one way to skin a possum, as Boose might say, and she was a detective, after all, if more often than not a reluctant one.

Next to a red *Texaco* gas sign she saw the smaller blue one that confirmed the presence of a phone. A couple of them stuck out from the outside wall beside an ice machine. One of them had an *OUT OF ORDER* sign, but the other, the one most in the direct sunlight, worked. She stood in the heat, feeling a trickle of sweat start down her spine. Notebook in one hand she dialed a number she had not used in a while.

"It's your dime, so get talkin'."

"Shiner, it's me, Esbeth Walters."

"Oh, yeah. The little, round lady. You workin' a case agin or somethin'?"

"I need your help. Do you have your scanner on?"

"Yep."

"I need to find the sheriff, Johnny Gonzalez. Do you know where he's at?"

"Sure enough."

She sighed. You had to be pretty specific when you spoke with Shiner. He drove the tow truck in Fearing and liked to keep a thumb on the pulse, to hear him tell it. Esbeth figured that like most people in a small community he was just plain nosy and didn't like to admit it. It was better to call than to go over to his service garage because he had no lowers and only one tooth left of his original uppers and it was green and half eroded at the root. Try as hard as she might, Esbeth could not take her eyes off it when he talked. It hypnotized her. She imagined the bite imprint it left on a pimento spread on white bread sandwich. The image appeared in her dreams and haunted her. It was better to stay away, though Shiner was friendly to the bone and the sort of fellow who would talk to a stump. "Well, where is he?"

"Over to the Kessler County wedge meetin' with Sheriff Gary. Texas Ranger's there, too."

The Kessler County wedge was where a piece of the neighboring county poked across the highway for a mile along the state highway that led in to Austin from out where you could swing a dead armadillo, if you had a mind to, in any direction without hitting man, woman, or a house, though you might bang the dead carcass into a mesquite tree, prickly pear cactus, or mountain cedar, likely as not.

Esbeth hung up the phone and got back into her car where its tired air-conditioning struggled to keep up with the day's rising temperature. She should just wring herself out and head home, but she was a person of commitment and when she said she would do a thing it got done, if it killed her in the process, which had nearly happened once or twice.

Outside the car's windows, the speckled green and brown of vegetation in the late stages of summer dotted the hills that rolled by. The sumac made for splotches of red and the china-berry added yellow to the palette. It was no drive through the deciduous forests of New England when the leaves are turning, but Esbeth made the most of enjoying it on the drive out until ahead she saw a cluster of vehicles pulled over and huddled like a football team at the spot where that Vance Kilgore fellow had gone off the road, right on the county line, making jurisdiction a matter of a coin toss.

She recognized the brown and copper cruiser Johnny Gonzalez drove. The black and white squad car was that of the Kessler County sheriff, Hank Gary. She knew the beige pickup truck with antenna whipped up along one side, searchlight, and tax exempt plates. That would be Tillis Macrory, the Texas Ranger. She didn't know the black Crown Victoria. When she got out of the car all heads turned her way, and that included the woman who stood beside a man in a suit despite the heat.

Hank Gary took his hat off and held it in one hand at his side and gave her a frown that looked like he had swallowed something very bad that was wrestling to get out. Johnny Gonzalez looked as neutral as a stone carving of what a sheriff should be, though his eyes glowed like obsidian chips of lit coal beneath the shade of his hat. Tillis Macrory, beneath his white cowboy hat as worn by all the rangers, struggled to suppress a friendly smile. Esbeth didn't know what to make of the other two, a man in a suit, which you almost never saw in this or any other part of Texas, and a short-haired blond woman in jeans, white blouse, and red cowgirl boots. They stood beneath the partial shade of the large live oak tree that had a huge gouge in its bark where the car had hit it. None of them seemed appreciative enough, Esbeth thought, of the fact that at least live oaks don't lose their leaves in the fall like other trees, thus still providing shade. People should be more thankful of the little things in life, and there was not much thankfulness of any kind in the heads turned her way.

"We're having a meeting here," Sheriff Gary called out, putting his hat back on. No love lost there. He had been a pal of Sheriff Eldon Watkins. He could smile nice when up for reelection, but left to his own devices he could be as mean as a seven-legged spider.

Sheriff Gonzalez's response was harsher, in that he turned away and gave his attention to the man in a suit, ignoring Esbeth. Tillis, who knew her better than any of the others, called out to her, "This is a bad time, Esbeth. We're in the middle of something here."

"Yeah, something important," Gary added, in a yell while she was still twenty yards away.

Esbeth couldn't imagine a colder reception, unless she counted the time her friend Blanch had passed gas as they were going up to the top of the Empire State building in an elevator crowded full with fellow tourists.

The woman among the men snapped alert and ran over toward Esbeth. She ignored whatever the man in the suit called to her.

"I'm Adele Kilgore," she panted as she came to a stop in front of Esbeth. She held out a hand. "I've heard all about you. Everyone in the county knows about you, and all you've done."

Up close her hair was more of a dirty blond, parted in the middle with bangs that fell to the left and right of her face like inverted commas. She had trotted over as if she was the sort of woman who knew how to throw a baseball or softball. Her outfit was the kind to make men stop and look. The cute, upturned button of a nose looked like it had gotten that way by falling on it, but the flaw gave her more personality, rather than less. Then she smiled. What a remarkable smile. Her face in repose looked serious, concerned, even anxious. When she smiled it was more than a beam of sunshine; it showed a mischievous, even impish side of her. Here was someone smarter than most people with whom she spoke. Her best conversations, no doubt, were with herself, and were probably filled with ironic wit.

Esbeth shook the hand, took in the assertive face of a woman in her thirties who was more used to getting her way than she was getting in the circle of thick heads out here. "I've had to retain a lawyer," she nodded back toward the man in the suit, "something new to me. But what everyone tells me is that what I really need is a detective."

"Oh, dear. I'm not that much of one. People overrate me by far."

"You get results, and you're clever, and you don't have some of the built-in biases of these men." She frowned back at the men of law.

"I've had a bit of luck, that's all, and I'm working on something else right now."

Adele's voice went up half an octave. "But I need you. You can do more than one thing at a time, can't you?"

"I'm not so sure about that."

"Look," Adele bent close and whispered, "you know how it can be with these men, even the lawyer I've hired. They have a story down they like, that my husband committed suicide. It's easy, and it's done. But it doesn't make sense. Vance and I had our differences, but he deserves better than this."

Esbeth felt her brow wrinkle and fought against it. "It isn't . . . you know . . . about the money, is it?"

"No. I get two-hundred-fifty-thousand if I just shut up and let things run their course. But I'm not standing for that. Besides, I have some money."

Esbeth tilted her head back a bit and took Adele in. No, she didn't look the sort who stood still for anything that did not go her way, and Esbeth doubted if the law enforcement convention going on just beyond their hearing was one of those things. The men were huddled, and the lawyer glanced this way as if trying to signal Adele to come back and be among them.

"Listen," Adele whispered. "He got a haircut the day before, took clothes to the dry cleaners that morning, ordered tickets for us to take a cruise together, and made reservations at a restaurant for dinner that night. He wasn't depressed or despondent, and he left no note or message. Does that sound like someone who planned to commit suicide to you?"

A dark car drove by and slowed, not as easy to identify as an unmarked law vehicle as Tillis' truck, but one Esbeth figured for it. It pulled over to the side of the road ahead of the other vehicles and a tall, dark, lanky man got out. Esbeth guessed it was a Hickey Freeman suit he wore, one of the favorites of the FBI, and a second later the man had his ID out holding it up to the others. "Special Agent Carson Billings."

"Have a hard time finding us?" Sheriff Gary asked.

"Not really." The agent glanced over at Esbeth, as if he knew all about her and had already bought into the party line of the other law enforcers. "It doesn't seem all that hard."

Esbeth expected the agent to be younger, yet up close his hair had the sprinkle of silver threads of someone closer to his fifties than not. He wore rimless glasses that did little to hide bright blue eyes that managed somehow to look sad.

"What's this about?" Johnny Gonzalez asked.

"Roy Dean Vanderhael, the man you know as Vance Kilgore."

Adele's mouth dropped open and her eyes were as wide as they could get. Her hand reached out and clasped Esbeth's tight. "This just gets worse and worse." She turned to stare at Esbeth. "Can you help me? Please." Then softer. *"Please."*

Esbeth felt the sick lurch in her stomach she had whenever doing the absolute wrong thing and was about to get herself in her way, and Esbeth doubted if the law enforcement convention going on just beyond their hearing was one of those things. The men were huddled, and the lawyer glanced this way as if trying to signal Adele to come back and be among them.

"Listen," Adele whispered. "He got a haircut the day before, took clothes to the dry cleaners that morning, ordered tickets for us to take a cruise together, and made reservations at a restaurant for dinner that night. He wasn't depressed or despondent, and he left no note or message. Does that sound like someone who planned to commit suicide to you?"

A dark car drove by and slowed, not as easy to identify as an unmarked law vehicle as Tillis' truck, but one Esbeth figured for it. It pulled over to the side of the road ahead of the other vehicles and a tall, dark, lanky man got out. Esbeth guessed it was a Hickey Freeman suit he wore, one of the favorites of the FBI, and a second later the man had his ID out holding it up to the others. "Special Agent Carson Billings."

"Have a hard time finding us?" Sheriff Gary asked.

"Not really." The agent glanced over at Esbeth, as if he knew all about her and had already bought into the party line of the other law enforcers. "It doesn't seem all that hard."

Esbeth expected the agent to be younger, yet up close his hair had the sprinkle of silver threads of someone closer to his fifties than not. He wore rimless glasses that did little to hide bright blue eyes that managed somehow to look sad.

"What's this about?" Johnny Gonzalez asked.

"Roy Dean Vanderhael, the man you know as Vance Kilgore."

Adele's mouth dropped open and her eyes were as wide as they could get. Her hand reached out and clasped Esbeth's tight. "This just gets worse and worse." She turned to stare at Esbeth. "Can you help me? Please." Then softer. *"Please."*

Esbeth felt the sick lurch in her stomach she had whenever doing the absolute wrong thing and was about to get herself in serious, concerned, even anxious. When she smiled it was more than a beam of sunshine; it showed a mischievous, even impish side of her. Here was someone smarter than most people with whom she spoke. Her best conversations, no doubt, were with herself, and were probably filled with ironic wit.

Esbeth shook the hand, took in the assertive face of a woman in her thirties who was more used to getting her way than she was getting in the circle of thick heads out here. "I've had to retain a lawyer," she nodded back toward the man in the suit, "something new to me. But what everyone tells me is that what I really need is a detective."

"Oh, dear. I'm not that much of one. People overrate me by far."

"You get results, and you're clever, and you don't have some of the built-in biases of these men." She frowned back at the men of law.

"I've had a bit of luck, that's all, and I'm working on something else right now."

Adele's voice went up half an octave. "But I need you. You can do more than one thing at a time, can't you?"

"I'm not so sure about that."

"Look," Adele bent close and whispered, "you know how it can be with these men, even the lawyer I've hired. They have a story down they like, that my husband committed suicide. It's easy, and it's done. But it doesn't make sense. Vance and I had our differences, but he deserves better than this."

Esbeth felt her brow wrinkle and fought against it. "It isn't . . . you know . . . about the money, is it?"

"No. I get two-hundred-fifty-thousand if I just shut up and let things run their course. But I'm not standing for that. Besides, I have some money."

Esbeth tilted her head back a bit and took Adele in. No, she didn't look the sort who stood still for anything that did not go deeper, but she said, "Okay, honey. I'll see what I can do."

At the edge of the parking lot, one with a large number of handicap parking spots, Esbeth hesitated and looked down the landscaped sidewalk that led to the front doors of the Oakline Hills Rest Home. Fierce butterflies were fistfighting away in her stomach and her nerves were doing cartwheels, all aflutter as she took a deep breath and forced her weary feet forward. Bright flowers bloomed in clumps along the walk, but the grounds were maintained by an outside service that swung through once a week early enough to roust the old-timers out of their beds with the sound of mowers, weedwhackers, and leaf blowers combining for a whining and roaring din. The flowers, though watered and beautiful enough in their own right, did not show the loving touch of those in a garden you see in someone's home. The lawn's landscape was planned and rigidly maintained for a calculated aesthetic look that was unemotional to Esbeth's eye. Some of that could be her apprehension about entering a place like this.

The door closed automatically after her. The air, antiseptic and cool, had the faint funky smell that sent an ice cube rattling up in a slow crawl along her spine. The lobby was empty except for a man asleep in the corner of a couch along the far wall, his head back and mouth open. He could be dead, if it wasn't for the rattle of his snore. A card table set up along the wall had a jigsaw puzzle half completed, with at least a couple of its pieces on the floor.

Esbeth crossed the burgundy rug of the lobby to the empty reception desk. A visitor's register lay open on the counter. Beside it was a silver punch bell, the kind hotels used to have to call for a bellhop. Esbeth gave it a tap. The sudden loud "ding" did not rouse the sleeper across the room, and she had time to sign in before a woman with the stiff back of an uptight marine drill instructor came down the corridor. She was in the process of shifting a frown into a phony smile as she came up to the desk. She ignored Esbeth long enough to read the register entry first.

"Oh, you're Miss Walters. I'm Melba Jean Hurley, the one with whom you made the appointment earlier. There won't be much time. Mr. Furlong is very busy. But we always try to work everyone in, no matter what the . . . um . . . reason."

"Gosh, thanks," Esbeth muttered as she struggled to keep up with the longer-legged younger woman who moved down the hallways like a participant in an Olympic event. Most of the doors were closed along the corridor, but through one or two that were open she saw eager expectant faces of white-haired people hoping that the visit was for them. From behind a couple of the closed doors came the sound of televisions turned on way too loud for residents who were hard of hearing.

Outside the corner office door Melba Jean stopped and knocked first, gave Esbeth a gratuitous smile while they waited for the "Come in."

Inside, Melba Jean stayed just long enough for a quick introduction before she bustled back out the door. Torrence Furlong sat behind the wide teak desk that had nothing on it, like some aircraft carrier that was out of planes. It was not the desk of someone as busy as described. He waved Esbeth to one of the smaller leather chairs that resembled his much larger one, with a head rest and on wheels.

There was no sign that her visit had interrupted anything, but the director managed to give her a look that said he was quite busy, that she was testing his kind patience, and that he would appreciate her cutting to the chase.

"I'm here about Ada Hargate."

Furlong nodded, but waited on her to continue.

"I understand you had to kick her out when someone took

drill instructor came down the corridor. She was in the process of shifting a frown into a phony smile as she came up to the desk. She ignored Esbeth long enough to read the register entry first.

"Oh, you're Miss Walters. I'm Melba Jean Hurley, the one with whom you made the appointment earlier. There won't be much time. Mr. Furlong is very busy. But we always try to work everyone in, no matter what the . . . um . . . reason."

"Gosh, thanks," Esbeth muttered as she struggled to keep up with the longer-legged younger woman who moved down the hallways like a participant in an Olympic event. Most of the doors were closed along the corridor, but through one or two that were open she saw eager expectant faces of white-haired people hoping that the visit was for them. From behind a couple of the closed doors came the sound of televisions turned on way too loud for residents who were hard of hearing.

Outside the corner office door Melba Jean stopped and knocked first, gave Esbeth a gratuitous smile while they waited for the "Come in."

Inside, Melba Jean stayed just long enough for a quick introduction before she bustled back out the door. Torrence Furlong sat behind the wide teak desk that had nothing on it, like some aircraft carrier that was out of planes. It was not the desk of someone as busy as described. He waved Esbeth to one of the smaller leather chairs that resembled his much larger one, with a head rest and on wheels.

There was no sign that her visit had interrupted anything, but the director managed to give her a look that said he was quite busy, that she was testing his kind patience, and that he would appreciate her cutting to the chase.

"I'm here about Ada Hargate."

Furlong nodded, but waited on her to continue.

"I understand you had to kick her out when someone took

deeper, but she said, "Okay, honey. I'll see what I can do."

At the edge of the parking lot, one with a large number of handicap parking spots, Esbeth hesitated and looked down the landscaped sidewalk that led to the front doors of the Oakline Hills Rest Home. Fierce butterflies were fistfighting away in her stomach and her nerves were doing cartwheels, all aflutter as she took a deep breath and forced her weary feet forward. Bright flowers bloomed in clumps along the walk, but the grounds were maintained by an outside service that swung through once a week early enough to roust the old-timers out of their beds with the sound of mowers, weedwhackers, and leaf blowers combining for a whining and roaring din. The flowers, though watered and beautiful enough in their own right, did not show the loving touch of those in a garden you see in someone's home. The lawn's landscape was planned and rigidly maintained for a calculated aesthetic look that was unemotional to Esbeth's eye. Some of that could be her apprehension about entering a place like this.

The door closed automatically after her. The air, antiseptic and cool, had the faint funky smell that sent an ice cube rattling up in a slow crawl along her spine. The lobby was empty except for a man asleep in the corner of a couch along the far wall, his head back and mouth open. He could be dead, if it wasn't for the rattle of his snore. A card table set up along the wall had a jigsaw puzzle half completed, with at least a couple of its pieces on the floor.

Esbeth crossed the burgundy rug of the lobby to the empty reception desk. A visitor's register lay open on the counter. Beside it was a silver punch bell, the kind hotels used to have to call for a bellhop. Esbeth gave it a tap. The sudden loud "ding" did not rouse the sleeper across the room, and she had time to sign in before a woman with the stiff back of an uptight marine

41

all her money."

"That's not entirely correct. There are other facilities better suited to her needs just now."

"You mean now that she's been forced onto Medicaid. The Hargates have little enough and it seems a little heartless to give her the boot as soon as she no longer has the green she had when she moved in."

"You're being harsh, don't you think? The reality is that we have few enough rooms as it is, and we have to reserve those for people with the means for the kind of care we offer."

Esbeth didn't answer right away. She tried to count to ten, but got busy inspecting the director up close. He looked like one of those fellows who spent time in front of a video recorder so he could see how he moved and minimize anything that might look too human or could contain anything like emotion. He was a big enough fellow, but she did not figure him for being strong the way some of the local men could be. She'd had hunches that were stronger. He projected a confidence that said if he could not do a thing he could darn well afford to hire someone who could. He was also one of those men who liked to sound like everything in life was a simple business decision of one sort or another, nothing to get too excited about. She glanced up at the numerous awards and the few books.

"Don't you feel any responsibility for folks who get robbed while in your facility? You were eager enough to take her on when there was money in her account."

He shook his head, as if no argument was needed. He was used to the occasional rant and she was hardly a breeze compared to some storms he had weathered in the past.

"What precautions are you taking to protect the residents? I didn't see any posters telling them what to watch out for, and the lobby's clear enough anyone could come in and roam around, like some of those phony religious types who aren't with local churches but just come in to shake money from people too glad to see any face come in their door. That's hitting a bit below the Bible Belt, if you ask me."

"Are you telling me how to run this establishment?"

"Only if you have doubts."

"I think I've been generous enough with my time. You had better go now."

"Or what? You have me tossed out on my roly-poly butt?"

She had not seen him press any button or ring a bell, but Melba Jean appeared inside the door. She held a clipboard and waited, giving Esbeth the "just ate a bad lemon drop" look.

Esbeth pushed herself up from the chair. "Don't bother. I can find my own way out." She had expected this to be something of a waste of time, and she had not been wrong.

When she left the office she realized it must be soundproof. She could not hear what Melba Jean, who had stayed behind to talk, was saying. But she could hear a moan that came from one open door while down the hallway someone else screamed, "That's not mine. Not mine. Oh, give it back."

Maybe it was the cool air that blew through the hallway from the overhead vents, and smelled of WD-40 and dirty diapers, but the chill from before rippled along her spine again. Oh, please, she thought, just let a big rock land on me before I have to live like this someday.

She hiked down the hallway, turned a corner, and nearly ran into a woman who stayed close to the wall and carried what looked like a basket of cookies. Esbeth was no giant, but this white-haired woman was smaller yet, and she jumped when she looked up and saw Esbeth, and dropped her basket in the bargain. "Oh, dear. You gave me a start. I thought you was Mrs. Hitler."

"Who?" Esbeth crouched down to help the woman as she

with local churches but just come in to shake money from people too glad to see any face come in their door. That's hitting a bit below the Bible Belt, if you ask me."

"Are you telling me how to run this establishment?"

"Only if you have doubts."

"I think I've been generous enough with my time. You had better go now."

"Or what? You have me tossed out on my roly-poly butt?"

She had not seen him press any button or ring a bell, but Melba Jean appeared inside the door. She held a clipboard and waited, giving Esbeth the "just ate a bad lemon drop" look.

Esbeth pushed herself up from the chair. "Don't bother. I can find my own way out." She had expected this to be something of a waste of time, and she had not been wrong.

When she left the office she realized it must be soundproof. She could not hear what Melba Jean, who had stayed behind to talk, was saying. But she could hear a moan that came from one open door while down the hallway someone else screamed, "That's not mine. Not mine. Oh, give it back."

Maybe it was the cool air that blew through the hallway from the overhead vents, and smelled of WD-40 and dirty diapers, but the chill from before rippled along her spine again. Oh, please, she thought, just let a big rock land on me before I have to live like this someday.

She hiked down the hallway, turned a corner, and nearly ran into a woman who stayed close to the wall and carried what looked like a basket of cookies. Esbeth was no giant, but this white-haired woman was smaller yet, and she jumped when she looked up and saw Esbeth, and dropped her basket in the bargain. "Oh, dear. You gave me a start. I thought you was Mrs. Hitler."

"Who?" Esbeth crouched down to help the woman as she

all her money."

"That's not entirely correct. There are other facilities better suited to her needs just now."

"You mean now that she's been forced onto Medicaid. The Hargates have little enough and it seems a little heartless to give her the boot as soon as she no longer has the green she had when she moved in."

"You're being harsh, don't you think? The reality is that we have few enough rooms as it is, and we have to reserve those for people with the means for the kind of care we offer."

Esbeth didn't answer right away. She tried to count to ten, but got busy inspecting the director up close. He looked like one of those fellows who spent time in front of a video recorder so he could see how he moved and minimize anything that might look too human or could contain anything like emotion. He was a big enough fellow, but she did not figure him for being strong the way some of the local men could be. She'd had hunches that were stronger. He projected a confidence that said if he could not do a thing he could darn well afford to hire someone who could. He was also one of those men who liked to sound like everything in life was a simple business decision of one sort or another, nothing to get too excited about. She glanced up at the numerous awards and the few books.

"Don't you feel any responsibility for folks who get robbed while in your facility? You were eager enough to take her on when there was money in her account."

He shook his head, as if no argument was needed. He was used to the occasional rant and she was hardly a breeze compared to some storms he had weathered in the past.

"What precautions are you taking to protect the residents? I didn't see any posters telling them what to watch out for, and the lobby's clear enough anyone could come in and roam around, like some of those phony religious types who aren't gathered up small Saran-wrapped bundles of cookies and put them back in the basket. Bent low and close like this it was like meeting the Easter bunny.

The woman bent her head sideways and peered at Esbeth. "You know, that Melba Jean."

"Why's she scare you so?"

"I'm not supposed to be in here anymore. They give me the boot. Hey, you're that detective lady, ain't you? Here, give me a hand or I won't ever get up right again."

Esbeth got herself upright and reached to help the woman up. She was frail and light, felt like she had the bones of a bird.

"I'm Myrna Mae. We'd best get scooting before we're caught out here. I'll be out in the parking lot quick as a greased weasel with a bruised rump if that one catches me in here again. Are you working on something, or just general nosing about?"

Everyone seemed to think that about Esbeth. If it was up to her she would be home in her housecoat having a slice of pie with a hot cup of tea. But, no, everyone wants her to poke about and the rest think the less of her for it.

"Reason I ask," Myrna Mae winked at her, an act that made her wrinkled pale face nearly collapse in on itself, "is because they's another one of you detectives lives here."

"Oh, really?"

"Yeah, come on. I'll show you." Her head bent, as if listening for footsteps to come down the carpeted hallway. She tugged at Esbeth with a burst of strength that was surprising. It was the kind of strength that comes from fear, the kind that lets little old ladies carry a piano out of a burning house.

Myrna Mae hustled her down the hallway toward an open door at the end. As soon as they started in the room's doorway a loud quivering voice called out, "Ah, and who today will be the winner of our disco tent?"

As soon as they were inside Myrna Mae shut the door behind

them and said, "It's okay. It's just us."

Esbeth stared at a man who wore a burgundy robe and leather house slippers. His thick grayish-white hair was combed and his face shaved. It was a long face, a Basil Rathbone of a face. All he needed was a pipe and some tobacco in a Persian slipper and you would have a Sherlock Holmes. The eyes that had been wandering about like goldfish in a bowl settled and grew alert and sparkled as he looked Esbeth over. In explanation, he said, "It's an advantage to be thought a bit dotty around here. There are few things as worthless as an old man who doesn't know anything but thinks he does. That's just the sort I try to seem to be."

"Myrna Mae says you're a detective. Is that right?"

One eyebrow raised and he looked at Myrna Mae. "Now, really. No. I was a forensic pathologist in my former life. I try not to make much of it here or I'd be a threat."

"Everyone here sure seems careful."

"That's the detective in you noticing that. Yes, I recognize you. Your photo was in the newspaper back when the previous sheriff was let go. You're Esbeth Walters, and I'm Gardner Burke."

"I can explain that business about the sheriff."

"No need to. He was corrupt. It was a mere matter of time. You just happened to be the instrument that hastened his fate. I'm sanguine it would have come about sooner or later; you just made it sooner."

Esbeth started to say something, but Gardner held up a long finger. "You two had best duck into the lavatory. Quick."

His head tilted, his eyes unfocused, and he made a low, crooning sound as Esbeth closed the door almost shut. Then she heard the door snap open from the hallway.

"Beware the bent-nosed swine," Gardner bellowed, "or you'll all die of tricky-noses."

The door snapped closed, and after a couple of minutes he called out, "It's okay. Coast is clear."

"I can't believe you all have to live such a charade," Esbeth said as she and Myrna Mae came back into his room.

Gardner shrugged and waved her to the bed where Myrna Mae had perched herself. There was no sofa in the small room, just the chair in front of the television, which was on with the sound off. The words being spoken scrolled across the top of the screen, though Gardner ignored it—just another prop. Esbeth watched the words *"Ambient music"* run across the top while an automobile commercial played.

"Tell me, are you working on anything?" His question was polite, but the sparkle in his eyes intensified. Here was a race horse, still able and chomping at the bit, anxious to hit the trail again.

"A couple of things. With one of them I'm in over my head and you might be able to help me. Are you familiar with the Vance Kilgore case?"

"I have followed it avidly. It's either a fierce example of bungling or something, I suspect, is bent all the way up to the state level. The ME was inordinately quick to come up with suicide. In addition to the obvious—duct tape, nipples cut off, and all that—there's the cell phone. The ME made part of his case that the man could have called for help if he'd just escaped from being tortured. But he hadn't. Then there was no blood on the outside of the phone, but blood on the inside when they opened it, and it had been wiped clean of any prints. No one ran DNA tests on any of the blood, either, to see if it wasn't his. There is just too much that needs closer scrutiny than I believe it was given."

"He's a doctor, you know," Myrna Mae said. "Despite the conditions he's fallen to at this time of life. He knows things."

Gardner seemed uncomfortable with some of that, but added,

"I do still have an active license in this state, don't you know. I could get copies of the reports, even see some of the evidence, if there's a need for that."

Esbeth felt her own eyes light up. "Are you free to come and go from here?"

His keen eyes swept up to the wall clock. "In a few minutes the shift changes. Herr Furlong likes to have a quick joint staff meeting each day he's here to share announcements and swap war stories before he dashes off to a golf course. I can get dressed by then and while they're all putting their heads together we can make a run for it. All we need to do is back date the register to show I checked out with my daughter."

"Do you have a daughter?"

"I had a son who went off to college and came home as one. It just shows you can learn to cope with about anything, if you try. He's off in California somewhere. I haven't seen him, or her, in years, but the staff here doesn't know that." He got to his feet with more vigor than Esbeth expected, and began to pull clothes out of the small dresser against the wall.

"How many people work here?" Esbeth asked Myrna Mae.

"About half of them," Gardner answered for her, adding a large wink. He slipped into the bathroom to change.

For a minute or two Esbeth glanced around the small claustrophobic room and thought of her own cozy cottage, which seemed immense and sprawling by comparison. She turned to Myrna Mae. "You said you're banned from being in here. Why?"

"Well, the staff that's here is made up of nurses and administration with a few volunteers to help out. I was one of those for a spell. My mother was in here and I wanted to do something. I got to know quite a few of the other residents before my mother died. Cancer. I stayed on as a volunteer, but lots of people had complaints, and when the administrators didn't listen I went in and spoke up for the folks. Got to be where I was the squeaky wheel, I guess. So they barred me from being here, wouldn't let me help out no more. Now I gotta sneak in if I want to bring cookies and cheer up anyone."

There was more Esbeth could have asked Myrna Mae, but Gardner emerged wearing khaki slacks, a navy blue short-sleeved shirt, and brown Timberland hiking shoes. He looked refreshed and ready for adventure.

"How'd you come to be in a place like this?" Esbeth asked.

"There were times when it got hard for my boat battery to take a charge, and on most days I could relate to that. But I've had plenty of time sitting in here to get fully charged now. Besides, the house was too big and I didn't have the money I'd had to run it. This place seemed fine then. That was before I came here and it made me begin to wonder if even God had Alzheimer's. The only residents here who like the place have Stockholm Syndrome, in my opinion. Are you ready?" He picked up a hanging garment bag and a small overnight bag.

"Sure." Esbeth wondered where she was going to put him up for the night.

"Then let's go." He poked his head out the door, checked each way, then was off like a hound on the scent.

"What about your wife?" Esbeth asked as Gardner climbed into the passenger seat of her car. Myrna Mae was putting her basket into the car parked beside Esbeth's.

"Oh, she was a fine woman—the original giddy-yuppie. She ran a travel agency and retired about the same time I did, all set to go to the four corners of the planet. Then she got cancer. Four years she fought the good fight, and it pretty well drained us." There was as much emotion in his voice as Esbeth had heard so far. "There wasn't much left by the time she was in remission, but we set off to do that world tour just the same. But we had a setback. She fell off a boat on a trip we made to

Africa. The crocodiles ate her before we could get her out."

"She loved nature," Myrna Mae said.

"And it loved her," Gardner said, a wry twist to his bittersweet smile.

Esbeth looked from face to face, to see if she was being strung along. Both were genuinely sad faces. She sighed and went around to the driver's side. It had been a long, busy day for her, but she was beginning to think the hectic part had only started. She waved goodbye to Myrna Mae and climbed inside, where Gardner grinned like a kid out on a school treat.

"Glad to get out of there," he said. "I was running out of things like 'Gecko-Roman wrestling' to yell out into the hall. Being thought dotty isn't as easy as people think, though some folks have a natural flare for it." He glanced at Esbeth, as if giving her far more credit there than she wanted or deserved.

Oh, Lordy buckles, she thought as she started the engine. What have I gotten myself into this time?

CHAPTER FOUR

"Does this mean you're too busy now to be workin' on Momma's problem, and mine?" Boose glared hard at Esbeth, his glower a sign of some real or imagined buffalo chip on his shoulder.

She set the dark brown, crackle-glazed ceramic teapot she carried onto the wooden picnic table that sat on the extension of concrete slab that ran back from her cottage—as close to a back porch as she had, and a good place to watch the birds come to the feeder. Boose shifted his irritated look to the cup of tea she was pouring him. Then he gave a sideways glance to Adele Kilgore, who sat on the same side of the table beside him, wearing a weekend outfit of pale blue brushed denim jeans and navy blouse even though it was a Friday; she had taken off from work at the daycare center where she spent most days. She had been uncommonly quiet so far this morning. The day before had been a grueling one for her, spent in the tangle of a meeting in Austin after learning the man she had lived with was not who she thought he was. She looked beaten up, but not out of it yet, just dazed, and the crisp morning air had not perked her back up yet.

It was the first cool morning in a while, somewhere in the low sixties, which is low for central Texas, and Esbeth intended to enjoy it, if she could. That meant hot tea, though she knew Boose was a "coffee in the morning" sort of fellow.

"You can keep that surly, kicked-dog look to yourself, Boose

51

Hargate. I can out grump you on any day of the week and twice on Sundays. You try sleeping on a couch two nights running when you're built more like the pumpkin than the princess and we'll see how you feel then. Now drink your ding-dong tea."

Boose picked up his cup like it was raw vitriol. Country-raised Texans can drink their weight in iced tea, but often act like hot tea is the work of the devil. But he took a sip. "Ain't you two bunkin' together? I mean to shake off the chill a bit?"

"No. Thank you very much for asking in your usual un-abashed way. He gallantly tried the couch the first night, but he's older than me by a stretch, and longer, too. It stove him up something awful. So I'm the one who's had to learn to make do, and it's as much for your sake as anything."

"I s'pose this Kilgore woman here's paying you more."

Adele's head lifted, but Esbeth snapped at Boose before she had a chance. "She's not paying me anything, and neither are you if I have to stir up that kettle of fish."

"But how can you . . . ?"

"Just close that flapping muzzle of yours a doggone minute, wipe that whomper-jawed look off your face, and listen up." By now Esbeth was steamed up enough she had forgotten to pour herself a cup of tea. A fly buzzed around the top of the open jelly jar beside the toast, too, and she didn't even pause to shoo it away, just stayed fixed on Boose.

"As much as you think of my acumen, the fact is that I'm a mere retired math teacher, an old-maid schoolmarm who has the sense to know when she's tromping briskly through the quicksand. You come to me and ask to find the con man who ripped off your momma, but you don't pause for a second to understand why billions of dollars a year are ripped off from the elderly. It's because the people who do this have the ability to outwit small-time police or sheriff crews and even some of the larger state and federal units. They sting for small enough amounts that it sails under the radar of most law enforcement outfits that could catch them. Grifters are intelligent people, smarter than most of all the other criminals who end up getting caught. You check your numbers and an embarrassingly few of them are ever brought to justice."

A mockingbird chattered at her from across the back lawn and such was her mood that she waved a warning finger at it rather than pausing to enjoy its stepping out bold as brass between the oleander and crape myrtle bushes she had planted just last year, with cocky uplifted tail and a canny eye that swept the lawn for any bugs in grass too brown and crisp to need mowing.

"What I was. . . ."

"You let me finish. I'm not done venting." But she realized as she said it that she was. Long ago she had figured out that there were few enough things to let rattle you, and that friends were more important than anything. It was best to learn to be forgiving, and that thought settled in as she reached for the teapot and poured herself a cup. She was just about to lower herself down onto her side of the table when Boose tilted his head a bit and looked up at her.

"You mean you two really ain't rubbin' the bacon just a bit?"

Her blood pressure shot back up into the lower stratosphere and she was about to light into him again when the sound of crunching steps came around the corner of the house. Gardner Burke strode into view and said, "I thought I heard voices back here. I'm back from Austin, Esbeth." His sweeping glance took in Boose and Adele, too, as he came around the corner.

I wonder how long he's been around the corner on the listen, Esbeth thought as she played back the conversation so far in her head. Not long, she hoped.

Gardner wore a suit, and one that had fit him a few pounds back. There was no doubting the quality, but Esbeth had helped him steam it the night before to remove wrinkles as well as a faint mothball smell. Once he had the suit on, Esbeth could believe he had been a distinguished doctor of forensic science earlier in his life. He had a detective's keen grasp of detail, too, like the way he sensed Boose's discomfort of the moment—the quaint sort where the more countrified Boose probably thought "barbarism" was people going around forcing haircuts on others. Gardner loosened his tie, tossed his small briefcase onto the edge of the picnic table and shucked off his jacket and put that on the case. He rolled up his shirt sleeves before he held out a big, bony hand.

Boose stood up and the two men shook hands, Boose wary at first, with a lingering touch of his surly, careful look and Gardner with the relaxed grace of someone who is not out to make a point of his being a few inches taller. He did wince a tiny bit at the vise grip of Boose's shake but he suppressed it well. He gave a curt bow to Adele and eased his long, lanky self down onto the opposite side of the table.

Esbeth went inside to get another teacup, and the three of them sat in a strained silence while she was gone. A flutter of warblers in a neighboring pecan tree made a twitter, though nothing but the wind tugging at one of the napkins disturbed the quiet around the table until Esbeth was back.

"How did it go with your meeting?" Esbeth said. She poured him a cup of tea and finally got around to filling her own cup.

"Aside from the DA being a supreme jerk, you mean? But I'll get back to that in a minute." He turned to Boose. "You don't have any need to worry. It's not all about Adele's mess. Esbeth here told me about your situation, too, and I promised to help with it to the extent I could. It's a bit trickier. We just have to find a realistic starting point."

"Hey," Adele sat up straight. "What about me? I'm ready to offer a fifty-thousand-dollar reward to anyone who can provide evidence able to convict those who tortured or killed my husband. It was no damn suicide."

"You make that sixty-four thousand," Esbeth said, "and you'll have Boose's undivided attention."

Boose brightened and glanced Adele's way. That would fix things for him and his momma. Adele shrugged, didn't say yes or no to the idea, and kept her attention fixed on Gardner, who seemed to be doing his best to hold something back.

Gardner took a sip of his tea and nodded to Esbeth. "Not Earl Grey. A Brazilian yerba maté, I would guess?"

She nodded, and smiled for the first time in a while.

"If we can gallop past the gore-met moment. I dint come here for that," Boose huffed. "What do you think we can do about Momma?"

"There are only a few options that suggest themselves." Gardner set his teacup down and leaned closer. Esbeth had a hard time believing this was the same man who had to yell inanities down the hall in order to be left alone at the rest home. "The law is best suited to do background checks on known cons and see who's operating around here. That's why your mother was asked to look through some mug books earlier, though with no success. That was no surprise. It's a futile exercise if your grifter's one who hasn't been caught previously, and I doubt they even bothered to tap the federal resources for con artists."

Boose started to surge to his feet.

"Sit down, Boose," Esbeth snapped. "Let him say whatever it is he has to say, at least."

Gardner ignored the outburst and reached for the teapot and poured himself another cup. For the faintest second Esbeth was reminded of the Mad Hatter pouring tea in *Alice in Wonderland.* "If we were working this right after it happened we could always hope for physical evidence. In that case, there might be the slim chance that your contact person left a latent print or even epithelials—small cells that would give us some DNA. But, even then, if your con artist has no record or wasn't in the armed forces, there may be no prints or DNA to match against. Or, if he was as clever as many are, he would have been careful to touch or leave nothing. As it is, in your case, any such evidence that would have been in that room at the rest home has long since been cleaned away and the room turned over to another waiting resident."

Boose's brow narrowed into rows of bent ripples and he gave Esbeth an exasperated frown. She held up a hand for him to stay calm.

"We may have to do a variation of what the law is probably doing—just wait and see if we get lucky. That is, hope your man and his accomplice get caught elsewhere and charges are filed, in which case you could add your claim to any others, though there may not be much hope of getting any money back. Professional con artists, as I mentioned, are quite bright enough to squirrel what they get away in places that would be hard to recover any money taken. The fellow who was nabbed not long ago by the feds in that Canadian lottery scam got only two years in prison and none of the money was recovered."

"You sayin' we have about as much chance as a June bug in the hen yard?"

"Something like that. All we have is a greater motivation than the police, more self-vested interest. That's about all any private investigator would have. Sometimes it's enough. But I won't lie to you and say it's a certain thing that we get your man."

Boose shot up so fast he knocked over his teacup and spilled its contents. Pausing to mop up the wet spot with a paper napkin dampered his fire until Esbeth could motion him back into a sitting position, though he was poised to jump up again at the drop of a hat.

"There's a more proactive way," Gardner said, "but it's riskier."

"If it involves a ball bat, I'm in," Boose said.

Esbeth wouldn't care to meet the look Boose was sharing in an alley at any time.

"No ball bat. Sorry. There may be some digging and intrigue, but it would be best for you if Esbeth and I do any cloak and dagger stuff, though we might need the help of Myrna Mae."

Esbeth's eyes were wider this time. "Where are you going with this?"

"I'm going to have to speak with you in private about that later. The fewer people who know anything the better for now, and perhaps later."

"Go ahead and tell me," Boose insisted. "I can take the truth."

Esbeth exchanged glances with Gardner. Young people say that a lot, but they don't really know what it means yet. By young she was thinking of jaspers in their thirties, forties, even fifties. They think they want the truth, but don't know it for the bittersweet pill it is. Only a few she had ever met seemed prepared to deal with the stark nature of it. It means not dwelling on hope so much as living each day to the dregs, accepting who you are, what you are, and the limits of your own capabilities more—the kind of thing that caused Aldous Huxley, in his declining years to say, "It's a bit embarrassing to have been concerned with the human problem all one's life and find at the end that one has no more to offer by way of advice than, 'Try to be a little kinder.' " In her honest moments with herself, Esbeth had to admit she adhered more to the philosophical level of that than living it every day on a practical plane. Her penance, perhaps, was comprised of these little detecting efforts to fix the plights of others. At her own crankiest moments, though, Huxley's sentiment was the sort of thing she used to try and rein herself in, and sometimes it came close to working.

"It's not that, Boose. It's that Esbeth and I have some arranging to do that is better left to us for the moment. Trust us. We'll be doing all we can."

"But will it be in time?" Boose grumped and started to get to his feet.

Gardner waved him back down into his seat with one large, gnarled, wide-spread hand. He looked down at him, as if getting the deep measure of his soul. "Boose, let me caution you about haste for its own sake. When I was a young lad, still in short pants, I had a friend my age, Danny MacGregor, who we all called 'Scotch.' Our families lived on adjacent spreads and each had a buggy for when we had to go to town or to the church. Each family had a horse, too, that we two boys thought was not only able, but fast. Like any lads that age we talked up our respective horses and in the end raced them, one against the other, each pulling a buggy. The horses were, it turned out, fairly evenly matched. We whipped them into a frenzy and were racing neck and neck along the ranch road that had once been an old stagecoach line when ahead we could both see the one-lane bridge that in those days spanned Three Antler Creek, a place where we'd gathered crawfish together and fished for perch. It was getting closer and closer, we looked across at each other and whipped up our horses all the harder. The bridge got nearer and nearer. Then, at the very last second, we both veered off the road, me to the left and Scotch and his horse and buggy to the right. We ran those rigs at top speed down into the mud and water until we were in up to our knees. We had the devil's own time getting those rigs out, and both had taken a pretty good wetting down. I believe he got the strap at home—I know I did—and I've always been more careful ever after."

Boose squinted over at Esbeth. When the story was over he got to his feet.

"Well, I'd best blow this popsicle stand and get back to work if I'm not to end up in some old folk's home myself." He paused. "No offense there, Mister Burke. Um, Doctor Burke."

Gardner shared a thin smile. Esbeth thought about how most of his savings had gone into taking care of his wife's health and now she was gone. It had landed him in a place like the Oakline, yet she knew he would do it again a hundred times over to have ten more minutes with his wife. That was part of the big picture that comes into focus or doesn't for people.

Boose was around the corner of the house headed for where he had parked his truck when Gardner said, "Which brings me to your case, Adele. I'm going to have to ask you some very personal questions, if you don't mind."

"I'll answer as best I can. What sort of questions?"

"Your husband's chest was shaved. Why?"

"He had a stress test at work. An area clear of hair needed to be prepared, he told me, for positioning the various prongs of the medical machine used."

"And for the itching that resulted, did he use anything?"

"His doctor had prescribed a cream for that. Vance had very sensitive skin."

"That would be a topical EMLA Cream, lidocaine. Does that sound like it?"

"Yes." Her answers had gotten as short as those coming on a witness stand.

"And maybe an injectable form, too, if needed? There'd be a paper trail for that in the form of a prescription filled. All it needs is checking."

"Yeah, that's possible, too."

Gardner glanced over at Esbeth.

"What do we have to work with?" she asked.

"I'm not quite there yet." He turned back to Adele. "When you spoke to the DA, how did he seem to you?"

"Snide. Uppity. He sat there with this smirk of a grin the

whole time."

"The ME, too?"

"He was as bad. He didn't smirk, but he just kept saying the same things over and over again, like a fact's a fact and why couldn't I get that through my thick head. I know my husband didn't commit suicide. There was no motive, no note, nothing."

"Where are you going with this?" Esbeth asked.

Gardner was fixed on Adele. "They told you about the presence of lidocaine in his system, though?"

"Yes, and I said he'd gotten it to stop the itching when he shaved his chest. What's this all mean?"

"The questions I've been asking so far aren't the painfully personal ones I mentioned. But I'm about to get into those, if you're willing."

"Fire away."

"Were you and your husband intimate?"

"What do you mean? We lived together."

"I mean did you regularly have sex, fully enjoy that side of a normal married relationship?"

"What do you mean by normal? Just because people choose not to have sex doesn't mean they're not normal."

Esbeth felt her own eyebrows shoot up at that.

Gardner's tone stayed low and conversational, though. "Do you think he might have ever gone outside the relationship— that is, to satisfy urges that he thought were normal?"

"He wasn't fooling around. I'd have known. What are you trying to say?"

"The problem comes down to at least two quite divergent stories, one believed by those in law enforcement and the other harder to pin down. If I'm to straighten out any of this in a satisfactory way I'm going to have to dabble about in the gray area and see if I can't shake some of the mist away. Are you with me so far?"

"I want you to get to the bottom of this, the truth, if that's what you mean. What do the police believe?"

"Let's have your version first. How do you see the events unfolding?"

"Vance left first thing in the morning for work like usual. Some person or persons unknown abducted him, held him prisoner, and tortured him. He got away and was coming back to me as fast as he could drive when in his pain he veered off the road and hit a tree."

"And the 2.4 milligram to liters ratio of lidocaine that the autopsy registered in his system?"

"I can only imagine that he was in great pain once he got away, that he had the tube in the car and rubbed the cream on the open wounds as he came rushing back toward the house where we lived. The pain's what caused him to veer off the road, too, and it's what killed him. It was no suicide."

"How about the cell phone? Why didn't he call?"

"You're the one who pointed out that there was blood on the inside of the clam-shell cell phone, but not on the outside. Someone wiped the blood off, maybe the ones set on calling this a suicide because it's easier to wrap up. Now, come on. What's their version?"

"A viable explanation, given the evidence they had to consider, led them to suppose that Vance Kilgore, or Roy Dean Vanderhael, if the FBI's account is to be factored in, may have had a sexual liaison with someone on his way to work. The chest shaving leads them to think along homosexual lines."

"Vance was no . . . nothing like that." Adele leaped to her feet, which is not all that easy when seated at a picnic table. The abrupt move knocked over her half empty cup.

Esbeth wondered if she just ought to stain the whole tabletop a tea color and be done with it as she mopped up the spill, the second so far this morning. Gardner eased Adele back to her seat.

"Let me finish," he said. "I merely share the objective conclusion they come to, though I should call it a hypothesis since no definitive answer is within ready grasp, by them or me."

"But he was. . . ."

"The psychological profile they arrived at, based on interviews from his workplace and from others, indicates someone who likes to be dominated, who is subservient by nature, but who has a passive aggressive side. He may, they think, have gotten tangled up with someone who was into some sort of bondage, someone who he thought he could trust, but who then went too far."

"That's absurd."

"Not at all. It neatly explains everything to a police mentality that's seen pretty much everything. For instance, they think in his remorse he aimed at the tree and didn't swerve away from it when he might have."

"But Vance wasn't like that at all."

"You didn't know he was Roy Dean Vanderhael, either, did you?"

"I thought you were going to be on my side?"

"I'm showing you how it is from their perspective. Why don't you tell me how you saw things unfold on the day of his death?"

"The last time I saw him was at five-forty-five a.m. that morning. He got in his car and left the house. I think someone was laying for him. They captured him and tortured him. He got away somehow, maybe tore the duct tape, and came rushing back toward the house. It was my day off from the daycare center so he knew I'd be there. He at least used some of the cream for the pain, but he was in such agony that he veered off the road and into a tree and died. The pain had to be excruciating. Witnesses saw him moving uncertainly on the road and then veering off into that tree. He was out of control and unable to swerve. That's what I believe, and it's as credible as him aiming for a tree on purpose. Now, are you on my side or not?"

Gardner was calmer than Esbeth expected, far calmer than Adele. But then, he had dealt rationally with death for many years. His was a slow, careful, scientific mind. He reached for the teapot, found it empty, and set it back down.

"I'll make more," Esbeth said.

He held up a hand. "Don't bother. That was just a reflex action. I don't smoke or I'd have spent the time making a fuss over getting my pipe lit." He put both hands flat on the table and leaned closer to Adele. "Now I'll tell you one or two things that don't quite fit snugly into either version."

He waited until the flush on Adele's cheeks had faded. "Go ahead," she said.

"His wallet was gone, but a money clip containing sixty-seven dollars was in his pocket. That could be a lot of things, even someone nicking his wallet at the scene. It's happened before. The phone had blood on the inside but not on the outside. That doesn't lend itself to ready explanation. But the blood inside was his. I insisted on the test for that. Two very black hairs were noted on the duct tape that was wrapped around his ankles; Vance had sandy hair himself. No DNA tests were run on them, but apparently they've gone missing."

"Aha."

"Let me finish. To get to the lidocaine level they measured in his body someone would have needed seventy-five to a hundred tubes of the cream he had, and then someone would have to wrap his body in plastic for at least twenty-four hours to achieve and maintain that level in his bloodstream. Maybe there was an injection, too. I was able to track down the prescription through Vance's physician, but no syringe or container was found either at the wreck, and there's no way to check him for an injection now."

"What . . . what does it all mean?"

"It means there are some anomalies to the story, to either story. I don't know why the toxicologists at the lab didn't pursue it except that they said they weren't asked to. I don't know why the blood inside the otherwise clean clamshell cell phone wasn't tested for DNA earlier, nor can I explain what happened to the black hairs found on the duct tape that went missing. I don't have the leverage myself to tinker with either the ME or the DA. I don't have the troops they have to follow up on where the lidocaine might have come from, at least the quantity that was present. And, we no longer have a body so I can't do a second-opinion autopsy. The physical evidence side of things is a mess, but mostly a historical mess at this stage."

"Can you do anything?"

Gardner's focus had been tight on Adele, and for the first time he panned over to Esbeth. "This is getting into your province. Any ideas?"

"If there was ever a 'shake the bushes' situation, this is it. I've got a reporter friend or two left in Austin. That FBI fellow who's fluttering around like some warped butterfly may not like it, but I think some air on the subject might help things along. If there's any kind of fix along official lines, taking the case to the public in a quietly leaked sort of way might be just the ticket."

"You know, you have a devious streak, Esbeth."

"Yes. Many people remark that as one of my more striking characteristics." She paused, tilted her head at him. "Let me guess. You have something along similar lines planned for Boose's problem?"

"Well, when one is shaking bushes, why not shake as many as possible? Who knows what is liable to fall out. I suspect some berries—perhaps even our much-beloved rest home director—aren't as firmly on their branches as they think. I have only one concern. It might well put you in the limelight, and in harm's way."

"I'm not a hard target to miss these days, but I've been there before."

"If we get a nibble we might well have to set up a con of our own."

"A sting?"

Adele stirred. "If you just line up the guy who did that to Boose's momma he's liable to take care of the sting end with a bull whip."

"That's what I'm afraid of," Esbeth admitted.

"He looks like the sort who can take care of himself. I wouldn't worry over him," Adele said. She glanced in the direction Boose had gone with what Esbeth could only read as a wistful look.

Esbeth shook her head. She knew of Boose's raw animal magnetism that had led to the five previous wives. Oh, Lordy buckles, don't let us get a romance stirred up in all this, too.

Adele looked more attentive, but also tired enough to fall asleep right where she sat.

"Why don't you go home, honey, and leave this to us for a spell?"

Adele didn't argue, just rose and started around the house headed for the front.

Gardner stood up, too and handed her his jacket and tie. "If you'll kindly take this inside I have an errand to run."

"Where are you off to like a speckled bird?"

"To pick up one of those inflatable mattresses and a pump."

Esbeth felt herself blush. She hadn't meant for Gardner to hear her grousing earlier about sleeping on the couch.

"There's no sense in your not sleeping in your own bed," he

said. "I'll have to go back to that hell hole soon enough, perhaps, but I want to savor my freedom for the moment. Unless I've worn out my welcome here and you want to send me back to that place."

"Oh, I wouldn't wish that on anyone."

"What is it that bothers you so about that place, and others like it?"

"Just personal. I've been alone my whole life, and all I've had is my solitude. It's come to mean more to me than it should. You live alone too long and you come to value privacy above almost everything else."

"Even human contact."

"Sometimes."

"I understand. The thought must chill you to the bone."

"I know we can't do much about this business of people conning the elderly out of their life savings, but I want to keep it as our top priority."

"Above the more colorful demise of Vance, Roy Dean, whoever he was?"

"That's a puzzle, but is more hopeful of being solved than the scam on people in rest homes. I just don't want to lose sight of that. You've been in there, and look how silly you had to act to get by."

"If you let your mind flow free you can come up with gems like: Bernice, your burnoose is loose."

"That one barely makes sense."

"Which makes it just right. You have to take into account the patronizing attitude of most of the staff—the notion that all older people are headed like runaway trains for their second childhood."

"Well, you can assume a more sympathetic perspective on my part. You can dismiss the need to yell out inanities here." There was more grouch in her tone than she intended.

"I'll try to not crowd you too much in your own place."

"It's good for me now and then. You can stay as long as you need to."

"Don't tempt me. Given the chance I might just not ever go back to that rest home if it was up to me."

"I think you were just running out of things to yell down the hallways in your dotty act."

"You know, I believe you're right. There is indeed merit in the opinions of those who respect your skills as a detective."

"I suspect some of them there will start missing your quaint sayings soon."

"Oh, I wouldn't worry over much about that. They always have Luther Banks, the resident poet laureate."

"His dribble is as striking as what you were using?"

"One of his better efforts was, 'Roses are red. Violets are bluish. I'm circumcised, and I'm not even Jewish.' "

CHAPTER FIVE

The door to the hotel suite opened and Jimmy Calloway entered, as suave and debonair as a nearly round individual can be, still wearing his dark banker suit, though he had loosened the red tie. He glanced around at the carpet, as if wary of stepping on a viper, then he came across the wide main room toward Silky, where she sat at the imitation Louis XIVth desk with several small piles of bills—twenties and fifties—and a notepad and Mont Blanc pen in front of her.

She had turned the radio on and tuned it to the local classical station, knowing it was a calming drug to him—though she knew his musical background was self-taught, not acquired at either the Sorbonne or Oxford, as he liked to leave open to suggestion. The expression on his face, as if his shoes were too tight, said something was on his mind, but he cocked his head and held up a finger. He stepped over to the mini bar where he extracted a small bottle of Tanqueray without making a sound. He opened the ice bucket and slid two cubes into a glass to make no sound before pouring the gin down the tilted inside of the glass. From across the room Silky could only hear the lilting strains of the music. Calloway kept an ear tilted to the nearest speaker and let a faraway gaze settle across his face. As soon as the music stopped he stepped close to the radio and turned it off.

"Pachelbel," he said. "Canon in D Major. A marvelous short Baroque piece. You know, I was in Regensburg once where he studied under Kaspar Prentz, back in the sixteen hundreds."

"I'd have taken you for younger than that."

He ignored her for the moment. "That's where he got his flair for Italian composition, don't you know, though he was born in Nuremberg and was a contemporary of J. S. Bach."

This was not a good sign. Whenever he went on one of his pedantic side trips she knew trouble lay ahead. She braced herself.

He tilted his glass back until he had drained the gin and the ice cubes banged against his teeth—an even worse sign. He was, by nature, a consummate sipper. This did not look good, not good at all. Silky looked down at her pad, as if going over the numbers again.

"Do you mind terribly telling me where you were this afternoon?" He was relaxed, his real self, with his eyes narrowed in his piggish face so that the jolly facade was gone and the mean-streak James was home.

Silky's eyes swept across the nap of the salmon rug to the poppy red leather couch. Textures comforted her when she was the least bit rattled, and right now she used every bit of her self-control to seem poised and calm. When working a mark she could be ice itself, but Calloway had a knack of picking through her defenses. She looked him directly in the eyes. "I was making us money, as even you can plainly see, Jimbo. While you were out speculating about cash I was actually raking some in." She had, in fact, had to dip into some of her own cold, hard money stash. Sometimes you have to spend to make.

His head moved back a quarter of an inch.

Good, she thought. The FBI agents use a three-part saying she found useful on occasion, "Admit nothing, deny everything, begin counter-allegations."

"When Mrs. Rasmussen called she said she heard street noises when you answered. You are supposed to be a secretary, in a bank, a quiet and stodgy bank. The verisimilitude of the moment was very nearly ruined. I had to do some fancy footwork and say there is construction going on at her bank, a contention she disputed since she had just been to the bank to put away her pearls in her safety deposit box. I was on the spot and had to be more glib than usual, say it had barely begun. If she happens to go to her bank she may discover what a thin limb I was forced out upon by your . . . your not sticking to the agreed upon plan. And I want you to know that not now or ever do I want to be called Jimbo, or Big Jim, or any other diminutive you can think up. I prefer to, at all times, be called James. Are we clear on that?"

"Sure, boss. Why don't you have another gin and calm your jets?"

He looked at her, his head tilted a quarter inch to the right. Being so full of oats was not like her most of the time. He was not used to anything like sass from her. The prickled heat of suppressed anger showed as a pink tinge that eased up his neck to settle in his taut jowls. "What was it you played at today—that is, when you should have been planted here waiting on my call?"

"Oh, I worked half a dozen of the oldies, the twenties, pigeon drop, everything but the gold brick. I wanted to keep my hand practiced at the quick short ones. You never know when you need to pick up a bit of change. You know, a bird in the hand."

"I'll have you know that Mrs. Rasmussen is probably good for a hundred large, at the very least. The appropriate groundwork needs laying. Your fault, Silky, is impatience."

"If you say so."

"And my cut?"

She pushed a stack of bills over to the edge of the table. He scooped it up and counted it as he headed off for his bedroom, without another word or a look back.

Imagine, at his age and he still thought fear was a better glue than respect for their partnership. A cool million, all to herself, Silky thought. Keep that in mind. Focus.

As soon as she turned the corner and saw halfway down the block, Adele knew she had visitors—official ones. What could it be this time? Her foot eased up on the accelerator pedal and she took a moment to turn the rearview mirror and glance at her face. She eased up beside the two cars, one unmarked, though clearly her tax dollars at work on a federal level, that agent's car; the other vehicle belonged to Sheriff Gonzalez, and she bet he waited in the house, representing the department in person. There had to be another warrant. The neighbors would have fresh material for gossip, if the newspapers and other media had not already given her far more limelight than she wanted.

She parked across the street since one of their cars blocked the drive. The front door stood wide open, too, as she walked up the front sidewalk. A deputy stood outside the door, and though he yelled something into the house when she got out of her car he did not say anything to her as she went by him. He didn't look at her, either, but glanced away as if something on the far side of the street caught his fancy for the moment.

Inside, both the men stood in the living room and waited on her; the FBI agent tugged off the white rubber gloves he wore; the sheriff gave her his usual carved of stone look. They looked to be ready to leave. The lanky, tall agent was not young. He had a quiet dignity that told her she would have a hard time getting much out of him.

"Mrs. Kilgore," Agent Billings said, and waved her along as they all three walked toward the door. Sheriff Gonzalez nodded to her.

"I thought you'd gathered all the information you needed by now," she said to the back of the agent's head. He didn't stop to respond. She followed along until they were outside, the deputy going over to the Sheriff's Department car to wait on Gonzalez while the two men turned to face her, out on the sidewalk in the glaring sunlight.

If she expected cowed or embarrassed looks she was disappointed. The agent looked smug, and the sheriff didn't look like his expression had changed, or could.

"A few things have turned up that made us retrace our steps and dig a little deeper. You didn't mention that you had hired a detective and a forensic pathologist on your own. Is there anything else you're trying to hide?"

"Good grief. How do you stand yourself?"

"You seem to forget that capable law enforcement officers are already looking into the case. There's no need for you to muddy the waters by bringing in others."

"The same capable men who ruled suicide after my husband was bound and tortured? I can imagine you would want me to stand by and keep still, but you'd best get over expecting that."

"A hostile witness, wouldn't you say, Johnny?" The agent looked to the sheriff and talked as if she was not there.

She turned to the sheriff and caught the usual cold, cautious glitter of those black eyes beneath the shadow of his hat brim.

"Are you both done here?"

"Just a few questions."

She sighed and tried to see around them to glance into the house to see what they had moved, messed up, or broken.

"Which of you usually dealt with the mail?" The agent looked at her this time, as expectant as a lawyer who asks a man if he still beats his wife.

"We both did. When I was home, I brought it in. But often he got home before I did. I work at a daycare center, or did until all this mess started. I'm off for a week right now. Why?"

"I want to know if you were aware of these?" Billings held up plastic envelopes that contained white pieces of paper that formerly had been folded to fit into a #10 business envelope.

"It depends on what they are. Do you intend to keep that a mystery, too? You take things out of my house and then act like it's some childhood game, make me guess what. If you've got anything to say, say it like a man."

"Hostile, you see." He spoke to the sheriff again.

"Look, you tromp around like only the things you touch, or say, or do have any significance in life, for anyone. I just lost a husband and you've been as insensitive a horse's pattoot as I've ever met under any circumstances. If I knew who to write to I would, telling your superiors you need some sensitivity training. I don't know how you're let out on the street, much less allowed to deal with the public."

Billings straightened as if she had slapped him across the chops. He glanced to the sheriff, but something he saw there didn't reassure him. He cleared his throat, and for the first time since she had met him spoke in a civil and courteous way. "These letters we've found. Are you aware of them?"

"You're going to have to be more specific than that."

"They're anonymous letters, warning your husband about someone who is after him."

"No. I've not ever seen or heard anything about them. Let me look at them."

"I'm afraid they have to go to the lab first."

"Don't be afraid," she said. "Let me look at the damn things if you say they're important."

He did not respond, other than to glance toward the sheriff again.

"Well, what do they say?" she snapped.

"They mention only one name, someone called 'Two Chins.' Are you aware of anyone in your husband's past who went by that moniker? Did he ever mention the name to you?"

"No. Never."

"You're certain about that?"

"Good grief. Don't you think I'd tell you? Getting the stigma of suicide off his death is my only concern. If I knew a Mr. Two Chins, or whatever, don't you think I'd tell you all I knew? You are positively thick. I swear."

A battered pickup truck pulled up across the street and parked behind Adele's car. It was as faded blue as a robin's egg, though the door on the driver's side had been replaced with one that was either painted orange, or had rusted to that color. The door opened and Boose stepped out and squinted into the bright daylight like some night creature caught out of his element.

"What's he doing here?" Agent Billings asked.

Adele didn't know, so she didn't answer. Boose came up the sidewalk to them with a sailor's shore leave confident stride.

"Are these two peckerwoods botherin' you any?" he asked.

"That's no way to talk to officers of the law," Sheriff Gonzalez spoke for the first time.

Boose spun toward him and glared up into the shadow beneath the hat brim. "I dint vote for you last time, and I won't the next, so it's no use you sweet talkin' me. Now, if you're done botherin' the lady, why don't you remind your feet how they work and use them getting out of here."

The sheriff glanced to the agent; they both seemed to agree on something, took hard looks at Boose, gave curt nods to Adele, and then headed out to their separate vehicles.

"If they were looking for a suspect in a murder case instead of trying to ram this into being called a suicide I think you'd have done yourself a bit of harm just then. As it is, I don't believe you've endeared yourself to those men any," Adele said, as the agent's car pulled away, followed by the sheriff department's patrol car.

"No. Never."

"You're certain about that?"

"Good grief. Don't you think I'd tell you? Getting the stigma of suicide off his death is my only concern. If I knew a Mr. Two Chins, or whatever, don't you think I'd tell you all I knew? You are positively thick. I swear."

A battered pickup truck pulled up across the street and parked behind Adele's car. It was as faded blue as a robin's egg, though the door on the driver's side had been replaced with one that was either painted orange, or had rusted to that color. The door opened and Boose stepped out and squinted into the bright daylight like some night creature caught out of his element.

"What's he doing here?" Agent Billings asked.

Adele didn't know, so she didn't answer. Boose came up the sidewalk to them with a sailor's shore leave confident stride.

"Are these two peckerwoods botherin' you any?" he asked.

"That's no way to talk to officers of the law," Sheriff Gonzalez spoke for the first time.

Boose spun toward him and glared up into the shadow beneath the hat brim. "I dint vote for you last time, and I won't the next, so it's no use you sweet talkin' me. Now, if you're done botherin' the lady, why don't you remind your feet how they work and use them getting out of here."

The sheriff glanced to the agent; they both seemed to agree on something, took hard looks at Boose, gave curt nods to Adele, and then headed out to their separate vehicles.

"If they were looking for a suspect in a murder case instead of trying to ram this into being called a suicide I think you'd have done yourself a bit of harm just then. As it is, I don't believe you've endeared yourself to those men any," Adele said, as the agent's car pulled away, followed by the sheriff department's patrol car.

plastic envelopes that contained white pieces of paper that formerly had been folded to fit into a #10 business envelope.

"It depends on what they are. Do you intend to keep that a mystery, too? You take things out of my house and then act like it's some childhood game, make me guess what. If you've got anything to say, say it like a man."

"Hostile, you see." He spoke to the sheriff again.

"Look, you tromp around like only the things you touch, or say, or do have any significance in life, for anyone. I just lost a husband and you've been as insensitive a horse's pattoot as I've ever met under any circumstances. If I knew who to write to I would, telling your superiors you need some sensitivity training. I don't know how you're let out on the street, much less allowed to deal with the public."

Billings straightened as if she had slapped him across the chops. He glanced to the sheriff, but something he saw there didn't reassure him. He cleared his throat, and for the first time since she had met him spoke in a civil and courteous way. "These letters we've found. Are you aware of them?"

"You're going to have to be more specific than that."

"They're anonymous letters, warning your husband about someone who is after him."

"No. I've not ever seen or heard anything about them. Let me look at them."

"I'm afraid they have to go to the lab first."

"Don't be afraid," she said. "Let me look at the damn things if you say they're important."

He did not respond, other than to glance toward the sheriff again.

"Well, what do they say?" she snapped.

"They mention only one name, someone called 'Two Chins.' Are you aware of anyone in your husband's past who went by that moniker? Did he ever mention the name to you?"

73

Imagine, at his age and he still thought fear was a better glue than respect for their partnership. A cool million, all to herself, Silky thought. Keep that in mind. Focus.

As soon as she turned the corner and saw halfway down the block, Adele knew she had visitors—official ones. What could it be this time? Her foot eased up on the accelerator pedal and she took a moment to turn the rearview mirror and glance at her face. She eased up beside the two cars, one unmarked, though clearly her tax dollars at work on a federal level, that agent's car; the other vehicle belonged to Sheriff Gonzalez, and she bet he waited in the house, representing the department in person. There had to be another warrant. The neighbors would have fresh material for gossip, if the newspapers and other media had not already given her far more limelight than she wanted.

She parked across the street since one of their cars blocked the drive. The front door stood wide open, too, as she walked up the front sidewalk. A deputy stood outside the door, and though he yelled something into the house when she got out of her car he did not say anything to her as she went by him. He didn't look at her, either, but glanced away as if something on the far side of the street caught his fancy for the moment.

Inside, both the men stood in the living room and waited on her; the FBI agent tugged off the white rubber gloves he wore; the sheriff gave her his usual carved of stone look. They looked to be ready to leave. The lanky, tall agent was not young. He had a quiet dignity that told her she would have a hard time getting much out of him.

"Mrs. Kilgore," Agent Billings said, and waved her along as they all three walked toward the door. Sheriff Gonzalez nodded to her.

"I thought you'd gathered all the information you needed by now," she said to the back of the agent's head. He didn't stop to respond. She followed along until they were outside, the deputy going over to the Sheriff's Department car to wait on Gonzalez while the two men turned to face her, out on the sidewalk in the glaring sunlight.

If she expected cowed or embarrassed looks she was disappointed. The agent looked smug, and the sheriff didn't look like his expression had changed, or could.

"A few things have turned up that made us retrace our steps and dig a little deeper. You didn't mention that you had hired a detective and a forensic pathologist on your own. Is there anything else you're trying to hide?"

"Good grief. How do you stand yourself?"

"You seem to forget that capable law enforcement officers are already looking into the case. There's no need for you to muddy the waters by bringing in others."

"The same capable men who ruled suicide after my husband was bound and tortured? I can imagine you would want me to stand by and keep still, but you'd best get over expecting that."

"A hostile witness, wouldn't you say, Johnny?" The agent looked to the sheriff and talked as if she was not there.

She turned to the sheriff and caught the usual cold, cautious glitter of those black eyes beneath the shadow of his hat brim.

"Are you both done here?"

"Just a few questions."

She sighed and tried to see around them to glance into the house to see what they had moved, messed up, or broken.

"Which of you usually dealt with the mail?" The agent looked at her this time, as expectant as a lawyer who asks a man if he still beats his wife.

"We both did. When I was home, I brought it in. But often he got home before I did. I work at a daycare center, or did until all this mess started. I'm off for a week right now. Why?"

"I want to know if you were aware of these?" Billings held up

"Bein' nice's no way to get along with men like those two. They set their hats on a thing and they'll roll over you just like so much pavement. You've had plenty enough of that so far in this mess."

"What are you doing here?" She looked at him like he was something on the shelf she had not noticed before.

"I thought I'd see if you need any lookin' after. That Gardner fellow thought I might keep an eye out for you every now and again. But I can keep on a goin'. My feet were movin' when I got here and I can keep right on walkin'."

"No. That's fine. Stay a while." She wrestled back what felt like a smile forming on her face. She waved a hand toward the inside, and reached to open the door for him.

The inside of the room was quiet, as still as death, though the faint, muffled sounds came up the stairs from the casino below—the wheel, the cranking slot machine sounds, the occasional tumble of coins in a rain on a tin tray, and the hum of people talking, some loud and brash, others more serious as they sought to change their fortunes in a house where they knew the odds were tilted against them. Mook Jackson stirred in his chair and looked around the room, an office, but not one much used. They had been waiting for three-quarters of an hour and still not a peep from his partner, Fred Redbear, but that was par. Fred had not spoken seven words in the past two years. He was part Cheyenne, but at least he didn't go on about it, how the white man had lied, treated them wrong. He didn't have the chronic problem with firewater, either. Mind you, every once in a while there was a morning he came around with red eyes and breath that smelled like the wrong end of a cistern, but never a drop while they worked.

The door snapped open, and the man outside finished speaking to someone with him and turned, came into the room by himself, and shut the door behind him. It was Tony Two Chins himself. He stood slender as a rail, dressed in a suit dark enough for an undertaker, and he had the distinctive cleft on the longish chin at the bottom of his narrow, otherwise handsome and well-groomed, face. His eyes glittered like steel that had not cooled all the way at the mill after being poured molten hot into a mold. Mook realized that the suit was a tuxedo, now that he got a good look at it. Two Chins eyed them both as he eased down into a chair facing them, his hands still half curled into fists.

Four years ago Mook had heard about Petralia as some nearly invisible "made" fellow on the fringe, one who had a knack for not getting caught or drawing much attention to himself. Yet he seemed to be successful at skimming off his share all the same. In a world fraught with risk, that ability had seemed attractive to Mook, who had done a dime the hard way and did not ever want to go back inside. Redbear, who had been his cell roomie for much of his stretch, and a near perfect one since he rarely ever spoke and was hard-knuckle loyal, had agreed with the odds; both knew they had little choice for the remainder of their careers about making anything in the world of everyday squares. A patron who drew little attention on law enforcement radar was just what they had wanted, so they had done an initial chore or two for gratis before getting more regular part-time work, enough to live on, but not enough to get fancy, which was okay with them. There was the odd rumor about Two Chins—a partner who had gone sour on him and had disappeared, what had happened to the man who gave him his defining scar, that sort of thing. That was the usual *lingua franca* of their world, the posturing and saber rattling that went with the bones of any leader among them.

"Tony, I didn't know you had a piece of this place," Mook said.

himself, and shut the door behind him. It was Tony Two Chins himself. He stood slender as a rail, dressed in a suit dark enough for an undertaker, and he had the distinctive cleft on the long-ish chin at the bottom of his narrow, otherwise handsome and well-groomed, face. His eyes glittered like steel that had not cooled all the way at the mill after being poured molten hot into a mold. Mook realized that the suit was a tuxedo, now that he got a good look at it. Two Chins eyed them both as he eased down into a chair facing them, his hands still half curled into fists.

Four years ago Mook had heard about Petralia as some nearly invisible "made" fellow on the fringe, one who had a knack for not getting caught or drawing much attention to himself. Yet he seemed to be successful at skimming off his share all the same. In a world fraught with risk, that ability had seemed attractive to Mook, who had done a dime the hard way and did not ever want to go back inside. Redbear, who had been his cell roomie for much of his stretch, and a near perfect one since he rarely ever spoke and was hard-knuckle loyal, had agreed with the odds; both knew they had little choice for the remainder of their careers about making anything in the world of everyday squares. A patron who drew little attention on law enforcement radar was just what they had wanted, so they had done an initial chore or two for gratis before getting more regular part-time work, enough to live on, but not enough to get fancy, which was okay with them. There was the odd rumor about Two Chins—a partner who had gone sour on him and had disappeared, what had happened to the man who gave him his defining scar, that sort of thing. That was the usual *lingua franca* of their world, the posturing and saber rattling that went with the bones of any leader among them.

"Tony, I didn't know you had a piece of this place," Mook said.

"Bein' nice's no way to get along with men like those two. They set their hats on a thing and they'll roll over you just like so much pavement. You've had plenty enough of that so far in this mess."

"What are you doing here?" She looked at him like he was something on the shelf she had not noticed before.

"I thought I'd see if you need any lookin' after. That Gardner fellow thought I might keep an eye out for you every now and again. But I can keep on a goin'. My feet were movin' when I got here and I can keep right on walkin'."

"No. That's fine. Stay a while." She wrestled back what felt like a smile forming on her face. She waved a hand toward the inside, and reached to open the door for him.

The inside of the room was quiet, as still as death, though the faint, muffled sounds came up the stairs from the casino below—the wheel, the cranking slot machine sounds, the occasional tumble of coins in a rain on a tin tray, and the hum of people talking, some loud and brash, others more serious as they sought to change their fortunes in a house where they knew the odds were tilted against them. Mook Jackson stirred in his chair and looked around the room, an office, but not one much used. They had been waiting for three-quarters of an hour and still not a peep from his partner, Fred Redbear, but that was par. Fred had not spoken seven words in the past two years. He was part Cheyenne, but at least he didn't go on about it, how the white man had lied, treated them wrong. He didn't have the chronic problem with firewater, either. Mind you, every once in a while there was a morning he came around with red eyes and breath that smelled like the wrong end of a cistern, but never a drop while they worked.

The door snapped open, and the man outside finished speaking to someone with him and turned, came into the room by

"Mook, I think you know the laws of the great state of Nevada. Of course, I don't have a piece of this or any other establishment you could call a casino, at least on paper. We're meeting here because it was convenient, and there was a way for you two to come in the back door." There was a subtle edge to the way he put it. No one connected to the mob could get past the screening of the gaming commission and Two Chins was letting them know they were not dealing with just him, which wasn't necessary since Mook had known for the while he had been doing the little chores here and there like a good soldier. He knew he was freelance at best, had little chance of ever becoming a made man himself, and that he was as expendable as you get. It wouldn't do to cross someone like Two Chins, who had been around longer than that Teflon Don without ever being taken down.

"To what do we owe the honor? Do you have another spot of work for us?"

"Do you know what happens when a contractor is building a house and the cement doesn't set right?"

"I suppose he has to go back and fix it," Mook said, no sense looking to Fred Redbear for a response. He sat there like some carved totem pole or cigar store Indian.

"Exactly right. Can you think back to what I last asked you to do?"

"That guy, down in Texas. We did like you asked, made it look like suicide, even put in the fix."

"Without going into a great deal of detail, how did you do that?"

"Cops start poking around, the trail leads back to a leather bar, Chains, where they get a little rough sometimes. We enrolled him in a bath house or two as well. Paper trail says he's queer, likes a bit of rough play. Cops just natural don't like that sort at all."

"And why all the bother?"

"We had to ax him a few questions, Tony, just like you said, see if we could get to his pile."

"But you didn't."

"Didn't what?"

"Get to his pile."

"No. No we didn't. But we worked him good, would have gotten it if anyone could. We did a slick job on him, Tony. That suicide rap was done good. It'll stick."

"Well, I'm sorry to inform you that it is threatening to become unstuck."

"What? No way."

"Way. Are you . . . ?"

"Tony, sorry to interrupt, but we wrapped this one tight. The ME and DA already came down with suicide. There's a good story, too. Seems the guy tangled with folks who just got rougher'n he expected."

"Mook, are you finished?"

"Yes."

"What I'm telling you is that your package has indeed come unwrapped, and to the extent that my name actually came up."

"No way."

"I hope you aren't going to continue to interrupt, or argue." The hands tightened all the way into fists, and his eyes glittered like the light coming from an open furnace door. "I very much want for you two to still be around and be the ones attending to the fix. Am I clear?" There was not any veil to the threat this time.

Mook nodded. A warning chill rippled through him. Redbear sat there as stoic as ever, though Mook could swear the eyes opened a fraction wider.

"Just so you know, this is all the way up to a federal level and needs very delicate and complete fixing."

"You know I've always been thorough, and careful, Tony."

Two Chins had been intense before, but now the furnace doors of those eyes opened all the way, and Mook realized the man had actually been holding himself back. His words got softer and more careful, as if he picked each step through a briar field. His unflinching glare had them pinned to their seats. "I don't really know that at all, which is why you two are here and are being given a chance to fix the situation. I will not be made a fool of by anyone . . . anyone."

Mook's mind whirred to keep up. Did Tony mean Roy Dean, or the two men seated in front of him right now? It was not a good time to raise a question, but Mook could not help himself. "Do you think . . . ?"

"I think you got unnecessarily fanciful," his stare shifted to Fred Redbear, "and that you didn't use the common sense God gave a ground squirrel." He shifted back to Mook. "Did it cross your feeble minds that the widow might have the money?"

Mook was afraid to speak.

"Well, did it?"

"Well, after we were back a while. . . ."

Tony held up the flat of a hand and cut him off. Each word got softer, more dangerous.

"I want things to wrap up and be done there. I want no mention of my name to be involved any more than it has. Is that much clear?"

"Yes."

"Then go. Do that."

Mook wanted to ask if they would get paid for the extra work. But the look Tony gave them didn't invite questions. He suspected that this one was going to have to come out of his own pocket. The price for failing, he knew, wasn't going to be a slap across the fingers, either.

Chapter Six

Esbeth listened to her deep inner voice and knew at this exact moment she still had a choice; she could sit in the car, or get out. We each one of us, she knew, must decide if we are to be a part of the world, whether we stir among others and share risks and sometimes the greater rewards—to vote, to contribute to charities, to participate in efforts that lead to the greater good of the community—or whether we heed the call of inertia and stay sheltered in our homes. You can stay home with a book or the television or you can get out on the streets and let the breeze rip through your hair. The dilemma is age-old, and the older you get the greater the tendency to want to close the doors and the devil with the world outside. The thought struck home all the harder for her with the sky black and people being long in their beds in the darkened houses they had passed on the way here. It was her car, but Gardner sat behind the steering wheel. He watched and waited. She glanced at the luminescent hands on her wristwatch—two a.m. She would have been asleep for hours by now.

Esbeth had the urge to pinch herself. Never in her life could she recall doing anything quite as stupid and daring as this. They sat parked in the vacant back lot of an abandoned grocery building that had a year or so back moved into larger quarters. No one had rented the old location yet. The large front parking lot was the scene of an occasional flea market, or casual farmer's market, or place to give away free puppies, but there was none of that going on at this hour. If she hadn't filled herself to the near rim with cups of stout coffee she wouldn't be here, either, but would be home in bed, where she belonged. Only the fiercest sense of injustice and awareness that they would get nowhere through any other means drew her out in October at an hour where ghosts and goblins had more right to be out in the coming Halloween moon.

"Don't let the perception of a thing become larger than what is," Gardner said.

She turned to look at him, could make out only angles and edges of his long face in the dim light.

"Whatever in the world do you mean?" she said.

"We have a moment or two. If you don't mind, let me tell you a story."

Oh, Lordy buckles, Esbeth thought. She didn't have a hurry-up notion to get out of the car, so she settled back into her seat.

"My friend Scotch's dad had a friend, a Mr. Gower, who owned a dairy farm, some sort of thirty-seventh degree Mason, or somesuch, who allowed us to come do some frog hunting late at night on his place. We ate frog legs, squirrel, all that sort of thing back then, as you probably did, too."

Esbeth nodded, though she doubted he could hear the rattle.

"The Gowers had a German shepherd dog that was the biggest one I'd ever seen before or since. It could stand with a paw on either of Scotch's father's shoulders and lick his face with a tongue like a washcloth. We were small then, eight or nine years old, and Major seemed as big as a horse. But one evening, at an hour when the night was every bit as black as this, when we got to the Gower farm Major was chained to a huge dog house with a logging chain. Mr. Gower had just finished the evening milking or some chore in the barn and came out to tell us to steer clear of Major. He'd gotten a taste for killing cows and had started ripping their throats out in the night. Gower didn't have the heart to put Major down, so he'd chained him. Down below, in the yard, I could see Major leap and pull, his shoulders pressed out hard where he pushed against the ground and his mouth open and red, snarling and snapping his white teeth at the air, and with each surge the dog house would lift up off the ground and lift a foot forward before banging back to earth again. We walked on out toward the pond, following the road the cows took each time they came in from the pastures for milking. Scotch's dad carried the lantern, Scotch the buckets and such for the frogs, and I brought up the rear carrying the frog gigs, three-tined points on the end of long bamboo poles tied together in a bundle with strips of rags. It was black around us. Thick cloud cover meant we couldn't even see any stars or the moon. In the distance I could hear the deep booming moos of the biggest frogs sounding very much like cattle themselves. Crickets chirped, and every step either rattled gravel or rustled grass. Then behind me, I heard footsteps coming at us, tentative at first, then running faster and faster. Scotch's dad had already crossed the three-strand, barbed-wire fence, had taken the buckets from Scotch and now held up the lantern. Scotch was just putting a leg over the top of the fence. The pounding footsteps were drumming the ground, louder, but no harder or faster than my heart was beating, at a pace that would have made a Marine Corps drummer embarrassed and sad. I shouted at the top of my lungs, 'MAJOR'S LOOSE!' Scotch's eyes were frozen open and wide as they could get as he stared back into the black behind me. I tossed the bundle of frog gigs over the fence, shoved Scotch as hard as I could—into a cow pie face first as I was to find out later—and dove myself completely in the air over the fence where I rolled and spun around. There, in the glow of the lantern, a pure black calf came galloping up to us on the other side of the fence, in the hopeful frenzy of thinking it had heard its mother."

Esbeth stared out into the black, ripples of electricity surged up and down her own arms like mice racing into the night.

"That's what I meant about not letting the perception of a thing become larger than what is. Now, do you feel better?" Gardner asked.

"Only if you happened to bring a change of underwear for me."

"Oh, come on. We might as well get going." He pulled on a thin pair of black gloves, much like the pair she wore, and opened the door on his side.

As she got out of the car into the dark of night, dogs barked in distant yards and the moon struggled to free itself from the grip of black clouds. She didn't need to pinch herself since a nip in the air this late took care of that for her. It helped keep her awake, though it didn't calm her. Gardner got out of his side of the car, having thought ahead to disable the overhead light before either door opened. He wore his dark suit, black socks and shoes. Instead of a white shirt and tie he wore a black lightweight turtleneck sweater. He looked the part of a cat burglar. She, on the other hand, wore a dark green pair of garden sneakers, dark blue slacks, and a dark gray sweatshirt. She felt as little like a smooth professional burglar as anyone can. Her insides rattled like maracas all the way to her gizzards.

"Are you ready?" he asked, quietly closing his door.

"As I'll ever be." No sense telling him she would as soon dance naked at a church social. She took a deep breath. There was no backing out now.

Gardner led the way down an alley behind houses and an occasional vacant lot. Esbeth saw at least one *BEWARE OF DOG* sign and it seemed odd they hadn't had at least a wiener dog or two throw itself at the fence as they passed until she saw a big black lab curled up by a dog house in one yard and a great

Dane snoozing in the next yard. As hard as it was to keep up with the lankier Gardner she shot ahead and grabbed him by an arm. "They're just sleeping, aren't they?" she whispered.

"Of course. You don't think I'm up to killing anyone's Lassie, do you?" he whispered back to her.

He gently pulled his arm away and started up the alley again, his long strides full of confidence. She had wondered where he had been earlier when out on a few errands while she was busy pouring enough coffee down herself to keep a factory night shift going. Had he done this sort of work before? He certainly knew how to lay down the groundwork for an adventure like this, although if she had her druthers she would have stayed at her house to keep the home fires burning. A scene passed through her head of them being caught, her in a cell, then a lineup. She doubted it would help her much socially. It would do little to endear her to the local law enforcement community that held her in low esteem.

Sounds around her magnified, each step like a tin bucket of gravel being emptied, the rustle of the leaves like someone playing at drums. Then there was the beat of her heart that made a racket of its own. The lights were widely spaced and dim, but she felt the two of them stuck out as visible as they would be at high noon, even though through the years she had learned that at night you are never as visible as you think. She tried to let the logic of her years of teaching comfort her, but she wouldn't want anyone to come up behind her just now and tap her on the shoulder with a bony finger.

Within a few minutes, which seemed more like hours, they approached the back receiving door of the Oakline Hills Rest Home, the place where trucks unloaded their goods that kept the kitchen going.

They both scanned the dimly lit area around the back door, bare except for two large green trash Dumpsters. Esbeth wished the lone bulb above the door was not there. Myrna Mae had supplied a key, from her days as a volunteer, and had assured them that the alarm was never on, that some folks were always trying to wander in and out. To cut down on alarms to the sheriff's department the staff kept the alarm system off whenever they could. Who wanted to steal a bunch of old people? At least that's the way some of the staff put it.

Gardner slid up to the door, leaned close and turned the key. Esbeth realized her eyes were shut tight and she had stopped breathing. When no alarm went off she took a relieved gulp of air. Gardner swung the door open and they shot inside. A dim light high on the far wall lit the inside of the loading area. It was quiet as it could get this late at night. Far off in a corner there was the slow drip of a leaking pipe or faucet, and a small gray mouse shot in a blur along the lower crease of one wall and rocketed out through a crack alongside the large metal door that rolled up when deliveries were made or ambulances or hearses had to back up close in the dark of night to keep from alarming the residents.

Above a panel of circuit breakers, Gardner reached high for the set of keys Myrna Mae had told them would be there. Only the cleaning staff was supposed to know about these, the back-up keys to the offices. But Myrna Mae had to lay low often enough when coming through the back way to bring cookies and make her clandestine visits that she had learned of the spot.

Esbeth didn't have time to contemplate whether Gardner's little pep talk yarn was having a positive effect on her or not. He slipped over to the other door, put an ear to it, and whipped it open. Those long legs of his hurried him down the hallway and it was all Esbeth could do to hang on and try to keep up.

At the office door, the one that led to the secretary's office where the files were kept, he had it open by the time Esbeth puffed up behind him. They whisked inside and she bent over with her hands on her knees and took deep gasping breaths.

"Are you okay?" Gardner turned on the small penlight he carried and bent down to peer sideways to take a good look at her face.

"Do you mean other than having a coronary?" She straightened up, took out her penlight, and looked around. She had never been in this room before, although Gardner had. Along one wall a row of four-drawer file cabinets stretched from one corner to the other.

Esbeth reached one of the file drawers. "Locked. I don't suppose Myrna Mae had keys for these, did she?"

"No. But I've an idea. Give me a hand." He went along the row until he found the cabinet he wanted, then took the papers off the top, reached behind it, and tilted it forward. They were able, together, to rock it out of its slot among the others. Once it stood out far enough, Gardner reached around behind and began to remove files out of the back side of the locked cabinet. He whispered, "I read about this in the biography of Richard Feynman. He was one of the geniuses at Los Alamos making the bomb back in the Second World War. He was always messing around and got wondering how secure all that top-classified paperwork was, so he came to the idea of looking to the rear of the file cabinets, and he found he could get at the supposedly top-secret stuff pretty easily. A lot of locking file cabinets have backs now, but not the older kind like these."

"Are these the files we need to see?" Esbeth whispered back.

Gardner snapped up straight, clicked off his penlight, and held a finger to his lips. Esbeth flicked off her light.

The only light that came into the room did so around the outside edges of the closed Venetian blinds, and from a bright bar of yellow white that ran along the bottom of the door that led to the lit hallway. At first Esbeth heard nothing. Then she heard the soft rasp of shoe soles on carpet. A black shadow started to move along the bottom edge of doorway light, then stopped, as if listening. Esbeth thought her pounding heart would climb right up inside her chest and try to get out. After a long pause the steps started again and the black line of shadow moved along and on down the hallway.

That would be the head night nurse, Helen Gurnes, a direct descendant of Attila the Hun, to hear Myrna Mae tell it. She was the only nurse to make Melba Jean Hurley, the day head nurse, seem like a ray of goodness and charitable spirit. Gardner had confirmed that sometimes she had awakened him just to be bothersome, or so he claimed. Esbeth had seen the woman in town a time or two at the grocery. She looked more like a defensive tackle for the Dallas Cowboys than anybody's idea of a night nurse. Her arms and legs were those of a blacksmith, that along with never smiling, with the jowls of a bulldog and looking ready to bite made her just the person you would not want to wake in the night to see hovering near your bed.

Esbeth and Gardner both waited for what seemed ten to twenty minutes before daring to turn on their small penlights again. Even Gardner still breathed in short restorative breaths when they lit their thin beams. Esbeth couldn't imagine what would happen if they were caught by the likes of Helen, but she began to wish in earnest that Gardner had kept that tale of the barking and snarling dog to himself earlier.

Gardner carried the files over and spread them across the secretary's desk and they began to look through them, an awkward enough enterprise while wearing gloves, but Esbeth didn't want to take hers off, and noticed that Gardner had not removed his.

They poured through the files together. Esbeth took notes, while Gardner put all the files back just as they had been. He had to reach far in and struggle to get the files back in the hanging sleeves, but they wanted it to look as if they had never been here. With each second Esbeth's nerves stretched tighter. She didn't know about Gardner, since he seemed on the surface to be cool under the pressure, but she suspected he was wound as tight as she was. Several of the files that remained were spread out across the desk when abruptly the door handle rattled. Someone was trying to come in.

They scurried to grab their penlights and snapped off the lights. It was all Esbeth could do to keep from climbing right outside of her skin. The door handle rattled again, harder.

Esbeth realized she hadn't taken a breath in too long; she began to get dizzy. The dark room around her swirled. She opened her mouth and forced out as quiet a gasp as she could manage and drew in air. Gardner's arm reached across and clamped hard on her forearm, but he need not have bothered. She couldn't move if she had to, even if the room burst into flames. She heard him take slow even breaths. So she mimicked that and waited, waited for disaster. A hard black shadow centered in the light coming in under the door.

Helen's voice boomed in the hallway. "What are you doing?"

What remaining portion of Esbeth's blood pressure that was not already up in the stratosphere shot up to join the rest. She was as close to hyperventilating as she had ever been. A rivulet of sweat trickled down along her spine and she felt clammy all over. Gardner's hand gripped her arm all the harder.

"Come on, then. You know you don't belong out here in the hallway at this hour."

Another line of shadow joined that in the light of the doorway. They both began to move slowly away.

"Forginna mazgot."

"None of that now. You're going back and you're going to be strapped in this time," Helen's voice snapped.

Gardner bent close to Esbeth. She felt the heat of his breath as he whispered in her ear, "Mrs. Foster. Alzheimer's."

It took what felt like twenty minutes for Esbeth's galloping heart to return to near normal. Gardner's light came on and she saw him shove the white sheets back into their folders as fast as he could. Her own fingers shook too much to help. But she did spring to assist him to shove the file case back into the slot where it belonged. They put the papers back on top as near like they had been as she could remember, and Gardner even bent to fluff the carpet, to erase the tracks of where they had slid the file cabinet out.

"We'd better go," he whispered, and she couldn't have agreed more.

They turned off their lights. Gardner slipped to the door and slowly opened it. The brilliance of light from the hallway seemed blinding. When he waved her forward, Esbeth shot through the door like a greased bar of soap. He locked it quietly behind them and they hurried down the hallway, ducked into the back receiving room just as the elevator came down from the upper floor and opened. He locked that door behind them as it had been. His actions seemed calm and methodical, but when he turned to her after he put the keys to the office back into place she could see his eyes were as wide open as hers. He gave a sudden wave and the two of them shot across the cement and ducked behind a pair of fifty-gallon drums in the far corner just as the door handle rattled. Not Mrs. Foster this time. The single bulb still lit the area. Esbeth and Gardner pressed down close, crammed into the small shadow behind the drums as keys rattled. The door swung open, seemed to stay that way for about a century and a half, before the door closed again with a bang that surely woke someone. They waited, and waited. Finally, Gardner pried her fingers off his arm and rose until he could peer over the barrel tops.

"The coast is clear," he whispered down to her. There was no humor in his voice, just the smallest bit of a quiver. It had been close, very close, closer than Esbeth ever wanted to experience again.

They waited another ten minutes until Esbeth felt she was going to cramp up from her continual crouch. Then Gardner led the way across to the metal door and they slipped outside into the cool of the night where Esbeth's breaths came out in small white clouds. He locked up and they went back down along the alleys until they climbed inside her car.

Without waiting, he started the engine and they pulled out, slipped along the still streets of the night on their way to her house.

In the dead of night, the whole city seemed to slumber. Far ahead she saw a lone patrol car pull into an all-night convenience store. The two policemen in it got out and went inside as the car slid past at about five miles an hour under the speed limit. She wanted to slink down low in the seat, but didn't have the remaining energy for that.

As soon as they were a block away from the store, Gardner took a long, slow breath. There were only a dozen blocks or so to go to her house. She wished her stupid body would relax.

Ahead a smashed orange pumpkin lay in the middle of the street. Someone's jack-o-lantern.

"Oh, the poor thing," Gardner said. "It tried to make a dash across the street but its little legs just couldn't make it and some car hit it."

"You needn't feel you have to amuse or humor me," Esbeth snapped.

"Are you okay?"

"Well, I'm not a drinker, but I wouldn't say no to a hearty dash of brandy in a glass just now," she gasped as the car turned the corner and she could see her small cottage half a block up ahead.

"But you don't keep any brandy."

"I suppose a cup of tea and a bite of chocolate will do."

"I didn't know you had any chocolate on hand."

"You caught me there. I do have a stash set aside for emergencies, ones just like this."

CHAPTER SEVEN

The sun, like an ember fanned to flame into a larger and brighter orange ball, eased toward the uneven horizon as Mook turned the small rental car off the main highway and headed the last few miles into Texas hill country toward the small town of Fearing. Heading west at this time of day had meant driving into the sun, but Mook didn't mind. At his first glimpse into the intense glare he slipped on his shades. Redbear, though, the deep lines of his darker skin showing in harsh detail, squinted ahead into the sun as if he enjoyed testing himself against its strength.

"You know, I was almost born in Texas," Mook said. "Dad was stationed in San Antonio, but he got shipped to Germany and my mom, who was pregnant, went along and had me there—don't make me a Kraut or anything. I never told Tony none of that. I doubt he'd care much one way or the other. He was sure bent outta shape this time, though, wasn't he?"

Mook didn't wait on a response, or even glance in Fred's direction. It was what made him a good travel mate. He rarely spoke and left room for Mook to cover that ground.

It was good to have someone like Redbear handy, as long as you kept a close eye on him. He was loyal, something Mook's mother said he was not—that for rolling over on his father, which is why he only got the dime and his father got life, which was not all that bad since he had died three years in. Irony, Mook figured, though his mom had never forgiven him, would not speak to him to this day. People sure put a lot in a word like loyalty. Dad had been the shooter and Mook had been along for the ride. What the hell. Life is a lot of fine distinctions for people with time enough to mull them over too much.

"So this is like coming home, back to Texas, though renting the cheapest car we could get at the farthest agency at the outside of the airport don't make for a snappy homecoming, but what the hey. We'll go to the Bluebonnet Café and get us some cornbread and deep-fried catfish and we'll be living large just the same."

Fred made a noise that could have been a hibernating bear turning in its sleep in a cave.

Mook didn't glance that way. They wouldn't be in this situation if he had kept a better watch on his partner. The thing about Fred Redbear is that you can't leave him alone with someone like that for however short of a time. He had only wanted to question Roy Dean at first, after it took the devil's own time tracking him down because of the name change. They had lured him to an out-of-the-way spot with the promise of easy money, the best kind of bait for someone like that, then had tied him up with duct tape back of an abandoned stone farmhouse that had been taken over by scorpions. Mook had gone to the car for a bare moment and when he had come back there was Fred with Roy Dean's shirt open, Fred holding up one nipple he had taken off with his broad knife as slick as you would remove a postage stamp. Mook had taken one look at the beads of sweat springing up on Roy Dean's handsome face, the look of terror in his eyes, and the mumbled screams from beneath the duct tape that covered his mouth and he had thought, well, maybe this *is* the way to get him talking. He had been pretty unsharing so far.

Man, the muffled screams that had come from that taped mouth. But when they pulled the tape back they got nothing but threats and pleading. Roy Dean was determined to say nothing about the money. None of this was Mook's sort of thing, so he had strolled off toward a stand of old pecan trees that were dotted with the wispy webs of tent caterpillars. He had just zipped back up when over comes Redbear holding something up like it's a trinket he found. It's the end off the guy's little finger. "What about the guy?" Mook asks. "Fainted," says Redbear, though Mook had given the guy a shot of his own prescription stuff for pain. Then they hear a car starting. Roy Dean somehow had gotten a start on the duct tape around his wrists and ankles, had torn himself loose, and had made it to his car.

They had scrambled back to their car and it was off to the races. Roy Dean had a good start, but he wove all over the road like some DWI. They were gaining on him when Roy Dean's car shoots off the road and flies down a hill and into a tree. Cars that witnessed the accident start to pull over, and Mook joins them just long enough to see that Roy Dean is as dead as their chances of ever getting that money back from him. It had never once occurred to him that the guy's wife might have the money. Leave Two Chins to come up with that angle. They had been told from the first to make Roy Dean's death look like a suicide, and for a while when Redbear was tinkering with him that looked like it was going to be hard to pull off, a real stretch. But Roy Dean running his car into a tree in front of witnesses had been a godsend. All Mook had to do was follow that up with a little fix here and there with those in positions to help and everything was smooth, except about the damn money, which was why they were down here again.

As they pulled into the little town of Fearing Mook felt the tiny town draw him down like some wet anchor. He liked Vegas for the lights, the fountains, all the silicon bouncing around on the stages. A town like this was all gray to him. Only one or two people walked the sidewalks of the dried up little downtown area, the rest drove in and out of strip malls along the outskirts of town, to get gas or groceries and then scurry home. Halloween, he could tell, was on its way soon. Some doors had a ghost, a witch, or a pumpkin, and one fellow had even taken the trouble to make a scarecrow bending over with the pants tugged down enough to show two smaller pumpkins. Almost cute. But the whole spirit of the town, or lack of it, made Mook tired. They would pick up some beer, soft drinks for Redbear, and a bucket of chicken and flip through the channels of the cable TV in the cheapest flop of a motel they could find. Well, the best thing to do is to make short work of the chore that brought them here and get headed back to Vegas as soon as they could.

He looked around. No strip clubs. Not even a pool hall. He didn't see any bars, either, and remembered from the last visit there had been only one or two. Plenty of churches, though. He tried not to let his spirits sink any lower. Across the street he saw a big sign that said: "SHRIMP RIBS." To Redbear he said, "Those can't be very big, can they? Hey, what d'ya say to some barbeque tonight? Beef ribs. Steak on a stick. Maybe some potato salad."

His partner just made a low grunting sound. A place like this small town didn't take Redbear's cork under. He didn't even make the most of things when they were in Vegas. The only thing that might make him enjoy himself is if he got to cut on someone. He'd had to stow his big knife in his checked bag, but as soon as they got to the rental he had gotten it out and strapped it on. The thing Fred liked most about Texas was you could go around with a damn Jim Bowie strapped to your leg for all anyone cared. Ol' Redbear there was born a hundred years too late is all.

Mook pulled the car into the restaurant lot and they got out. Place was designed like some big log cabin, smoke rolling out from the back where a row of big barbeque bins burned mesquite. Sign on this side said, *"PIE SOUP ETC."*

"Wonder what kind of mess that is?" Mook said. He would ask the waitress for some, see how that went over.

Redbear got out his side, patted the leather scabbard at his side, and looked ahead at the restaurant with the first eager look Mook had seen on his mug in a while. He hoped the brief flash of zeal was about food.

Silky's snug gray sweat suit had soaked through at the neck and waist by the time she finished her three-mile jog along the Town Lake running trail that went right past the shoreline behind the Four Seasons. On the elevator up to her room the woman of the couple sharing the ride nudged her husband in the short ribs. "That's what you should be doing, Roger."

Roger looked at Silky in a way that said he would like to be doing her all right. She was glad when she got off on an earlier floor than they did.

She opened the door to the suite and was barely inside the door when she knew there would be more trouble. The radio was on with classical music playing loud. A small clutter of crumpled candy wrappers lay in a pile on the glass coffee table that stretched in front of the poppy red leather couch. He had cleaned out the mini bar of sweets. That could not be good. Calloway wore a housecoat wrapped tight around his pudgy body and sat in one corner of the sofa with his head tilted to the music. He held up a finger to tell her to wait.

She went to her bathroom, got a hand towel, and came out rubbing her face and neck. As soon as the music stopped, he flicked a hand and she stepped over and turned off the radio.

"Franz Von Suppé," he said. "That was his 'Poet and Peasant.' A lot of people think liking his music speaks of a common background, and an earthiness in one's character. But I defy them to write as good or as stirring a piece themselves. Only the wide use of Suppé's work has made it anything like cliché, if it can even be called that."

"What is it? What are you on about this time?"

"I found this." He took a slip of paper out of his side pocket and tossed it onto the table next to the wrappers.

Silky picked it up and looked at it. It was the receipt for the car rental. Well, she could hardly have walked to Fearing and back. The receipt shared none of that, just that she had rented a car for a few hours and had turned it back in with a full tank. Why had she kept it? She should have pitched it like the receipt for the use of a computer and printer at the Kinko's store.

"You went through my purse?"

He stared back at her, the stern look had not wavered on his smug face. There were moments when she speculated that what he needed most in life was a good bitch slapping, but this was not the right moment for that.

"How dare you?" she snarled. She stepped closer and bent toward him.

"Working together the way we do requires trust," he said. He tried for the smug look he'd had, but it had slipped, which was a tell for someone who could be as good at that as he was.

"Trust. I see. That would account for those safety deposit boxes you keep in at least a dozen states?"

"Miss Barons. How could you?"

"Listen, my lumpy little dollop. I make money for the both of us, and you snatch your cut. I don't need to explain to you just how I make it, or even that I take expenses on my end that I don't make you share. Then you come around talking about trust like it's some four-letter word."

"But . . . but. . . ."

"Don't you even try to start. Trust, like respect, is a two-way street. I know that's all outside your particular expertise, since your work of a lifetime is geared to abuse it rather than use it. I expect you to stay out of my handbag and my business. As long as I'm helping you to the extent I am, and am giving up more of my share than I should, you stay clear of my things. Are we clear?"

She spun and left him seated there, his mouth opening and closing like a fish out of water. She had snatched the initiative away that time. She slammed her bedroom door behind her, but instead of leaning against it she took a deep breath and went over to the closet and got out her bags. Then she opened the dresser drawers, dumped the contents onto the bed, and began to pack.

Esbeth poured herself into the passenger seat of her own car like a bag of wet cement. If things kept perking along the lines they had in the past day or so she had better line up a room in a retirement home for herself. Between the unusual strain of having a houseguest and not enjoying the large doses of solitude she needed to recharge, coupled with late-night adventures that would leave the heartiest of cat burglars a faint shell of their former selves, she had not made any real progress on the two situations where she had promised to help and that was eating at her.

Gardner got into the driver's side, and Esbeth was glad enough to have him behind the wheel. Though she had slept until ten in the morning, a rare thing indeed for her, she still felt like the last chapter of "What's the Use." Two pots of tea and a lunch at the Bluebonnet had not even put her right. But she still had her wits about her, if needed, although she would hate to be called on to sprint a hundred-yard dash just at the moment. Gardner, in contrast, had been chipper enough all day. The night of thrills and crime seemed to do him good, rejuvenate him. Perhaps the fountains of youth for some people are pure poison for others.

"Where are we going?" she asked.

"That call a while back was from Boose. He's over seeing after Adele and says there's company, not inside, but parked and waiting outside."

The sun had slipped over the horizon like a runny egg off a plate an hour ago, and the growing dark did not make Esbeth feel any better about another outing. She sat and watched the houses go by, an occasional light flicked on here and there as they rode into the growing dark.

Near Adele's house Gardner pulled over half a block early. They sat in the car and listened to the engine tick for a couple of minutes as it cooled.

She watched Gardner scan the area around them until he fixed on another car, parked a bit closer to the house. "What is it?"

"Over there. Your tax dollars at work. I was hoping to run into him."

"Who?"

Gardner opened his door and got out of the car. "Come on," he whispered in to her.

She got out her side and wondered what laws they would break tonight.

He led the way down the sidewalk, crossed the street, and eased up beside a dark car that she recognized now that they were closer. Gardner had bent forward and tapped on the passenger window by the time she caught up.

The electric window whined open. "What do you want?" Inside sat Carson Billings, the FBI Special Agent.

"Just a chat," Gardner said, "a chance to compare notes."

Without waiting for an answer he reached and unlocked the door and swung it open for Esbeth to slide into the front passenger seat. The locks clicked as Gardner toggled the switch before he closed the door. He got into the backseat.

"Are you trying to compromise the work I'm doing?" Billings said. He stared at Gardner and ignored Esbeth for the moment.

Esbeth let a snort of air escape. "When you come to a town this small you never had any cover. From the time you got here people knew who you were and everything about you, down to your shoe size and underwear color."

"White," the agent said. He was a lot calmer than Esbeth expected. "Does that settle any bets?"

"Esbeth and I have another bet going we thought you might settle. She says there were no fingerprints or DNA on those letters you found the other day at Adele's place. What do you say?"

"He has experience as a forensic pathologist," Esbeth said, "and he is familiar with the case. As a courtesy, the sheriff shared a set of copies of the letters. Do you think Adele made those letters and planted them so she could collect a larger insurance amount?"

The agent looked back and forth between them. "I'm not used to being asked questions about investigations, other than from impertinent journalists, and then, too, I share nothing."

"Let me take a guess here, Agent Billings," Gardner said. "You did your Quantico and early years with the Bu a long time back, then you left to make more money in the real world. But you always had a taste for it. One day you just told yourself you were going back and complete the kind of work you'd found to be the most fulfilling in your life, which is how we come to have an agent out here who is a good twenty to twenty-five years older than the usual Special Agent. Is that close?"

"For my money," Esbeth said, "I'd rather have a dozen like you than any one of the overzealous career types I've met in the past."

Something like a grin flickered across the agent's face. "You

I've heard about," he said to Esbeth. "That Texas Ranger Mac-rory says you actually know things, though you rarely ever share them, at least until it's almost too late. He says you're a retired school teacher and you kept saying, 'If I tell you everything you won't ever learn anything.' "

"Well, I might have said some such silliness," she confessed.

"And you," he spoke to Gardner, "have been part of law enforcement long enough to know about how much informa-tion I'm free to share. So you can both spare us some embar-rassment by not pushing for information I probably don't even have."

"How about the other insurance policy? You mentioned only the one about Adele. There's another policy, too, isn't there?"

"What do you know about that?"

"I didn't even know for sure there was one until now," Es-beth admitted. "But the sheriff will have to tell us anyhow since we're representing Mrs. Kilgore in this. I just put that together from the logic. You clearly don't have enough on Adele to mat-ter, and I doubt if it's her you're after. Her surprise about the letters being found seemed too genuine to me, and I imagine you thought the same. She cares too little about her own insur-ance claim and is after justice. My hunch says the late Vance, or Roy Dean, whatever, was involved in something that you are interested in, or rather the Bureau is. One agent, out here work-ing on his own. Could be you're part of a group working on something bigger altogether, and this is just a thread you were sent to chase down. Is it this Two Chins fellow? Sounds like a mob handle to me. What do you think, Gardner?"

The agent looked at her in an annoyed yet amused way. He was prepared to share as much as the stone faces on Mount Rushmore.

"I think it's time we got out of the agent's hair, Esbeth, back to your place, and hope he passes along all he needs to on what concerns us through the sheriff. We've got other fish to fry, and I imagine, somehow, he does, too."

Gardner's eyes snapped open at the sound of a metal clink coming from the kitchen. The living room of the cottage was still as dark as the inside of a cow. He lifted up his watch hand and held the dial almost to his face. It was after four-thirty a.m. He heard the sound of water being poured into a kettle slowly. He sighed and pushed himself up from the air mattress on the floor, never an easy task when you are long and lanky and too old to be camped out each night, or tend to wake and think you are on a lounge chair of the tilting deck of the *Titanic* and at any moment the cold, briny waves would lap at the spot where you rested and sharks were about to have a go at you for breakfast. Once he was upright, he wrapped the blanket around his bony shoulders and felt his way to the kitchen.

His hand slid along the wall until he found the switch and he flipped it on. There, like a raccoon caught prying open the hen-house was Esbeth. She wore a housecoat and slippers and was putting a pot of water onto one of the burners on top of the stove and was having a difficult time of it in the dark. She blinked at him.

"What's the matter, couldn't you sleep?" she said.

"Well . . . um . . . no."

"Me neither." She reached up into the cabinet and got out a box of tea bags. "Thought I'd have a cup of Chai with a dab of honey in it. Sound good to you?"

Sleep sounded good to him just then, but he said, "Sure. Let me slip into my clothes."

Back in the living area he scrambled into his clothes and folded the bedclothes and leaned the air mattress over against the wall. He couldn't recall being up this early since his time in the Army back a lifetime or so ago.

When he came back into the kitchen she poured cups of tea. The honey had gone waxy and white so she heated up the jar in a small pan of water. He watched the honey inside turn a golden brown as he eased down into one of the chairs.

"What has you up and stirring?" he asked. "Couldn't sleep?"

She put half a teaspoon of honey in her cup of tea, stirred it, then used the same spoon to put more into his cup of tea. "I've been going over everything again and again in my head until it's a whirling mess, the way your head gets when you get half an idea buzzing around like a bee in a basin all night. The trouble is, after teaching math all those years I have the logic of a bear trap, and I just can't see how I'm ever going to pull off what I committed to do this time."

"Don't all the little tangles you help with have a stage like this, where you doubt the possibility of an outcome?"

"No. Usually I have a toe or two touching bottom. But I'm adrift right now, and not very comfortable about it. I've even thought of that modern fuzzy math that the kids think is such a delight, where one puddle and one puddle equals one puddle, and eating a Snickers bar and a Diet Coke cancels each other out so the calories come out zero."

He sipped his tea. It was quite good. There was some cinnamon in there, and perhaps nutmeg, too, with the black and green tea leaves. The honey gave it all a boost.

"Perhaps it's too soon to panic."

"I'll confess that the reason I never buy a lottery ticket is because of knowing probability calculus. The odds don't make sense. And right now, seeing my way to the end of either case is as cloudy or more. Did you ever have days like that when you worked, I mean, everyday in a professional way?" She looked as awkward as that had been put.

"Don't worry about it. I'll tell you, what I did was different than you think. I didn't have many conjectures or hypotheses. I worked with hard, and often cold data and evidence—the way blood settles in a body once it's a corpse, the bruises that show or don't postmortem, the condition of a body after it's been in warm or cold water for three days. All of that I just observe and comment upon, and perhaps, though not as often as everyone thinks, even establish time of death. What a detective does is more complex, piecing together a whole story backwards. That's the kind of thing asked of you."

"I just feel about as useless right now as a bucket under a bull."

"Your problem is that you care."

"Knowing that doesn't help much."

"You should take your mind off it."

"How?" What she didn't have to add was that she didn't have children or grandchildren to fix on, or anyone else all that close and personal in her life, either, for all that.

"I used to play chess." He knew when he said it he had made a mistake. Her eyes lit up—not like a kid on Christmas morning, but more like a shark near an injured fish.

"There's a board around here somewhere, and a set of wooden pieces."

"Staunton?"

"Of course."

The sun had just come up to light up the eastern windows a good while later when Esbeth moved her knight and looked up from the board. "Checkmate."

Gardner shook his head, though he had seen it coming seven moves ago, but he was trapped in the endgame by then. "Did you play much back in your day?"

"Oh, some," she admitted.

"You know," he said, "I was a tournament player once, ranked eighteen-five back when Bobby Fischer was twenty-three-hundred. That's by way of saying I was more than a fair player."

"I guess I just got lucky," she said, and almost suppressed a smile.

"You're a lot of things, but I wouldn't say lucky is one of them." He wouldn't have said that if he had had the least idea he was being prophetic.

CHAPTER EIGHT

Esbeth stood beside Gardner in a shady overhang of the metal barn-like feed store next to the Bluebonnet Café and listened to cars crunch into parking spots in the gravel. She had the metallic, edgy, and woozy feel of having not gotten enough sleep. Normally she would cop a nap later during the day, but didn't know how she was going to manage that with Gardner staying at her cottage. The flush of victory from her win at chess had since faded. Some psychologists say that people who play games do so because it gives them the feel of winning, often in a life where they are otherwise losers. Esbeth had come full circle by now until she felt less than successful, which is about as much fun as a hangover from a three-day binge, or so she imagined since she had not had a drink in a couple of decades, unless she counted a splash of hard cider about eleven years ago.

The beige truck with the antenna and spotlight pulled into the lot and Tillis Macrory got out of the driver's side and waved over to her. The offer to buy the Texas Ranger breakfast had been too good for him to pass up, even though he had to know she would want some small thing in return.

Seated in a booth with mugs of steaming coffee in front of them and their orders placed with the waitress, his white hat upside down on the seat next to him, Macrory leaned closer and said, "Okay. What is it?"

Esbeth glanced toward Gardner, and he nodded for her to go ahead and make the pitch. She leaned closer. "It's the rest home.

There's a pattern in the paperwork there worth looking into."

Tillis took a sip of his coffee and frowned over the rim at her. He lowered the cup and reached for one of the containers of cream. "Like what?"

"In at least seven cases, people have died within two weeks of when their Medicare ran out. I know something about numbers, and that's heavy for a coincidence."

"And you found this out how?" His look was not from the coffee being bitter.

Gardner nodded for her to do the talking.

"Let's just say a search warrant would bear us out. The paperwork's all there. And here's another bone for you. In all but one case, that of a Gilbert Hayes, the bodies were cremated, something the rest home encouraged."

"That's not really a plus, is it?" He looked at Gardner when he said it.

"If the paper trail's good and the Hayes family agrees to exhume the body, or you get a warrant for that too, then you'd have something, wouldn't you?" Esbeth said.

Macrory shook his head. He switched his stare to Esbeth. "You should know better. Let's say I was able to get the sheriff to act; he'd have to be involved, and on the basis of what I can only imagine was information gained by illegal means; I'd need complaints from at least a majority of the families before I would act. If what you say is correct about the cremations, these people probably don't care all that much, at least enough to make the kind of fuss and accusations you're talking about."

"Then you won't do it?"

"Won't do it? I can't do it. You get me a majority petition of concerned next of kin and then, maybe. But, even then I'm going to regret it."

The Bluebonnet Café has more than once been voted the best breakfast in Texas by magazines and other media sources.

The omelets are made from the eggs of contented chickens and the biscuits are flaky and rich with milk and butter. But for Esbeth, the food was ashes in her mouth, which is why she only asked for one extra dish of biscuits this time, and just a bit more gravy.

Before he headed toward his truck, Tillis put on his white hat in the parking lot and turned to Esbeth. "Now, don't you go and get yourself into any kind of trouble. You hear?"

From a booth across the room, Mook Jackson and Fred Redbear stood up and Mook headed toward the cash register to pay while Redbear went outside to wait by the car. I always end up with the tab, Mook thought. That wasn't so bad when they were on expenses. But it was a crank when they were on their own nickel, or at least on Mook's. He'd keep an eye open and see if any way to turn up some money came by.

Outside, he used the little electric gadget on the key chain to snap open the car's locks, and Fred slid in his side with a toothpick stuck out of the corner of his mouth. He held out an extra toothpick to Mook, who shook his head. Fred shrugged and took out the small sharpening stone from its little leather pocket on the outside of the knife sheath. He took out the long knife and began to run its edge over the stone, again and again in a rasping noise that drove Mook nuts, though he didn't complain out loud, just headed the car in the direction of the widow's place.

Traffic was the stop-and-go variety that comes of a small town being near enough the string of lakes that head at an angle through hill country toward Austin for some older people to have retired in the town where the cost of living was lower than in the city, while young people with jet skis and water-ski boats who also liked the prices came out for the resort qualities. The combination resulted in a traffic pattern somewhere between a geriatric ward and the *Dukes of Hazard* television series—some people shot out of intersections like they were in a chase scene while others puttered and poked.

Mook was fit to bang on the steering wheel by the time they turned onto the street where this Adele Kilgore lived. Redbear saw the parked stakeout car at the same time Mook did and slunk lower in his seat, held up a hand to cover his face. Mook never slowed or took his eyes off the street; he kept it steady until they pulled around the corner. Then he sped up and spoke for the first time. "Federal. Only one of them, though." His jaw tightened and he kept his foot on the accelerator as much as the traffic allowed until they were back at the motel. Redbear, his knife held tight along his thigh slid it into its sheath and got out of the car. Mook watched him walk toward the motel room; for all he showed they could have been rained out of a morning of golf. Damn, Mook thought, I wish sometimes I had whatever keeps him calm as the center seed of a cucumber on ice.

Gardner didn't say a word all the way back to the cottage. Esbeth still boiled like a teapot left on the range too long. As soon as they were back to her place she got out her address book and headed to the phone. It took two tries until she got through. "Zick Robin," she said, and waited for the receptionist to put her through. There is a rule about grocery shopping, which is never do it when you are hungry. The same goes for making phone calls, Gardner knew—don't call when angry— and right now Esbeth looked mad enough to crush a grape. He had seen his own dear wife, who usually had a smile for everyone, slip to the dark side now and again and he was hoping Esbeth was not headed for anything like the hissy fits his former wife could throw, but he was experienced enough to keep his thoughts to himself.

"Zick? It's Esbeth Walters here . . . No, I didn't find another arm in my flowerbed . . . No body in a lake, either . . . Look, why don't I talk a minute and save you all the guesswork . . . Fine. I'm calling because your byline was on a story about a guy from out here who was ruled a suicide even though he had tape on his limbs and had his nipples cut off . . . Yeah, I thought it rang funny, too . . . No, I can't tell you anything about that just yet, though I am tinkering with it . . . That's right, if there's a scoop I'll owe you, but I . . . Yes, the widow is offering a fifty-thousand-dollar reward . . . Listen, this other thing is about a rest home where patients are dying just before their Medicare runs out . . . Seven of them we know about. I'll give you their names . . . All but one were cremated . . . I know. Here's the thing. If you can get the family of Gilbert Hayes, the only one of them who was buried, to order an exhumation . . . I know, huge pain, but if you're ever to land a Pulitzer, Zick. . . ."

Gardner listened as she fed him the details from her notes, as well as which rest home and who he might talk to and who he should avoid. When she hung up, she looked tired, but wrestled her way to a near smile. "Back in the logging days the way they cleared a log jam was to dynamite it. These two messes were never going to clear themselves up. I had to light a fuse."

She waited, but he felt tired and let it show. He doubted if he could rise from the couch.

"And the reporter," she said, "do you think he'll be what we need?"

"That's hard to say," Gardner said. "But I couldn't have done better myself. You played him like a trout."

Esbeth hesitated, the way someone will when weighing words that it might be better not to say, then blurted, "I hope you can understand why, when chasing a con artist, your comment isn't as flattering as you may think it is."

"I'm only saying that you may well be better at their game

than they are."

"That's still not a good thing," she said.

Gardner knew when it was best to stay mum, so he fluffed up a pillow and settled out on the couch letting her grump off to her bedroom.

Esbeth woke and sat up in bed blinking. It was getting dark outside. Lordy buckles, she had gone and gotten her days and nights turned around. She got up and climbed back into her clothes, then took a look in the mirror at her hair. Well, this close to Halloween maybe she could pull off the look.

She opened the bedroom door and there was Gardner, asleep on the couch. It made her feel better that she wasn't the only one who had been pooped from burning her candle at both ends. Rest was good; she didn't even feel on edge about him being in the house just now. He looked peaceful, lying there asleep, and she was glad to have him here. How long would he be around? For some reason she thought of an old tidbit she had shared once with someone else who was asking for advice— *without change, something in us sleeps.* She went into the kitchen and poured water into the pot.

After a while she heard him stir, then water ran in the bathroom, and when he came to the breakfast nook he was neatly dressed and so clean he sparkled like a new penny. He sat down in one of her chairs, still uncertain about how he moved about in her home. "Sleep certainly does knit the unraveled sleeve of care," he said.

"Oh, don't lean on Shakespeare," she said as she popped bread into the toaster. "There was a man in one of my digging around situations once who did that all the time."

"What happened to him?"

"He died."

"Well, we all do, sooner or later. Some just sooner."

111

It was quiet in the nook for a few ticks while she removed the toast, buttered it, and slid a slice on a saucer in front of him. She poured the tea before she got to what she had to say. "I thought when I woke I'd feel better about everything, but I don't."

"You started things rolling with that reporter. You could have gone to the Hayes family yourself, see if they'd go for the exhumation. Why did you sic a reporter on them?"

Esbeth repressed a frown. "That whole aspect of the rest home was off target, and was just to stir things up until something else might be found about whether there was any connection between that Mr. Furlong and anyone ripping off residents, which I begin to doubt. From the beginning I've known that catching a con artist is a pretty hopeless enterprise."

"But you took it on anyway."

"I had to. Boose asked and the whole thing touched a chord. We all have innermost deeps where we're vulnerable, and mine is never wanting to live in a place like that at all, although I suppose I may have no choice someday."

He looked down at his toast, but didn't reach for it.

"I'm sorry if I've stung you just then."

"No." He looked up. She feared the rested sparkle might have gone from his eyes, but it had not. "I realize that the reason I was in that rest home had more to do with mourning than anything. I'd just given up for a spell when I didn't need to. Things hadn't gone like I'd expected, or hoped, and I had given up. I'd planned to travel and be with my wife, then things took a turn or two. Well, hell. There's a fellow in that place who bought books all his life, planning to read every moment of his retirement, but he went blind—macular degeneration. Life doesn't seem fair sometimes, but there's no reason to roll over just because it sends a test our way." He picked up his toast and took a bite out of it.

Esbeth's spirits lifted. When she poured the tea, she said, "You're the expert of these things. If and when they do exhume the late Mr. Hayes, what do you think they could find?"

"It could be a number of things. He could have been given a barely traceable drug, which would mean a battery of tests. Or, it could have been as simple as the time-tested method of smothering with a pillow, which leaves bruises beneath the lips and a few other traces. But in hindsight, from a body that's been prepared and buried, there's really not much chance of finding anything that's going to prove anything, especially in the instance of an individual case. If there were several other matching situations, there might be hope. Since the others were all cremated, that's out."

Any elation Esbeth had felt earlier hit rock bottom. "Why didn't you stop me, then, when I was talking with Zick Robin?"

"You said it yourself. It did represent something to do. Maybe he'll find nothing, at least nothing he can prove enough to print. But he could stir things up. Something very wrong is going on there. You and I know that, even if no one else does."

"But what will Zick think of me if this blows up in his face? He certainly won't want to help with Adele's case, where I need him."

"Of course, he will. You played your cards in the right order. Any reporter worth his salt will drool after a story with all the macabre details that one has. There's still enough spice there to keep him on the hook, even if the other does go phut."

"The only thing likely to go phut around here is my foot on your hindquarters. How could you let me . . . ?"

"Come now, Esbeth. When you played chess you on three occasions offered up a sacrifice, which if I'd taken would have led to a much quicker end to the game. Your only weakness is the human goodness that doesn't make you prone to treat humans like chess pieces. That lack of Machiavellian proclivity is to your credit. It makes you virtually the opposite of a con person, the perfect person to foil one."

"Hmmm." Esbeth took a moment to sort through and see if there was any flimsy flattery going on here, but decided in the end that Gardner had a point and had made it well. She said, "I should think that another con artist would be more ideal."

"And I'm sure if anyone can become one for the few ticks that it's needed, you will be capable of that if and when that time comes."

Esbeth let that sink in for a few sips of tea. It felt good, really, though modesty forbid that she admit to that. "What about Adele's situation?"

"You don't think there's something there that won't turn up? The FBI showing an interest changed all that. That Carson Billings doesn't seem anyone's fool."

"But there's only one of him."

"True enough, and we're refreshed. Do you feel like taking a spin over to Adele's place? After a quick check maybe we can grab an ice cream or a true bit of dinner on the way back."

There was something in the way he said that which sent a ripple through Esbeth, though not an altogether unpleasant one. "Let me rid up the dishes real quick and we'll be off like a herd of turtles."

James Calloway opened the door to his suite that evening with the contented feeling that only a couple or three of the very driest Bombay Sapphire martinis can produce—the driest being when the word "vermouth" is uttered in an adjacent room, is never added, and even the quick shake with ice is not overdone. That Samuel, the bartender, could follow directions. James recalled being off his game earlier, but his good spirits were restored to the extent he broke into a whistle as he crossed the room. The tune was the opening to Tchaikovsky's Concerto number one in B-flat minor, the way Van Cliburn had played it in all the vigor of his youth.

What had turned the evening was an argument with a red wine drinker beside him about music. Beethoven and Mozart were all the man could say—a musical lemming. "Beethoven may have heart and brains," James had said, "but Tchaikovsky has soul." When the man persisted, James said, "Being louder about it doesn't make you more right." In the man's fury he had agreed to flip for bar tabs, which one should never attempt against a con artist, so James' dinner and drinks had been free. It put him in a right proper state of mind.

Then he thought to check on Silky, who had said she was a bit under and would stay in instead of dine out. Funny. He had seen no room service tray out in the hall by the doorway.

He eased over to the door of her bedroom and tapped lightly with one knuckle. "Silky? Are you feeling better?"

No answer.

He tapped again. Waited. Finally, the quiet penetrated, the utter quiet of the suite. He grabbed the handle and swung the door to her room open. Empty. The bed was made, rumpled only where she had put her bags on it to pack. He rushed to her closet. Empty. Dresser drawers, the same. Inside her bathroom, he screeched to a halt. Everything was gone, except a rumpled towel on the floor. On the mirror, in large red lipstick letters, he read, "Goodbye, sucker."

He blinked, rocked back a step, then felt warm fire shoot up through him in flames that raced across his chest into his temples. The nearest object was a half-empty body lotion bottle and an empty shampoo one. He grabbed them and hurled them through the open glass shower doors into the tub. Nothing. They did not break, just bounced. He needed to break something. By the time he got back in the living area he had throttled back. Think, he commanded himself, but the inside of his brain was still white with rage.

He crossed the room and turned on the radio. The rich sounds of a cello filled the suite. He knew this piece, one featuring Yo-Yo Ma doing the works of Ennio Morricone. Normally, he would have paused and let it sweep him away. Well, it might as damn well been "Yo Mama" for all it soothed the savage beast beating in Calloway's chest at the moment. He snapped the radio off and began to pace and try to think. *Think, damn it.*

His head snapped up again. *Oh, no.* He ran this time, no easy feat for someone of his girth, spun through the door to his room and rushed to his suitcase. He slipped a hand inside, felt down along the side, lifted the flap that concealed the small compartment. *Nothing.* He ran his hand from one end to the other. *Still nothing.* He heaved the suitcase onto the bed, emptied it, and yanked open the flap to where the small leather bag containing his safe deposit keys should have been. It was not there. The whole slot was empty, even of the small stash of bills he had slipped there after taking his cut from Silky.

This time his internal gaskets could not take it. He saw stark red as he grabbed the suitcase and hurled it against the wall. He reached for the lamp beside the bed, stopped himself just in time. There was already a ding on the wall. *Calm down. Stop. Think.*

He straightened and walked out into the living room with the stiff inner control of a drunk trying to drive home late and avoid a DWI. It was all he could do to keep himself in check. Think. He began to pace back and forth across the living room, ignoring the view of city lights of the south end of Austin across the river. He retraced his steps, played back every moment of his last few chats with Silky. He had been so busy working Mrs. Rasmussen that he had not paid attention to Silky. But that was not it. Something else, far bigger was in her craw. He played the recent moments back until he came to when she had grabbed away part of his morning paper; it was the Metro & State section. He had long ago thrown out the rest of the paper, and that section of the paper had not been in her room. There was no place he could think of to see a copy at this hour. In the morning he would go check at the library, see what she was on about. There was nothing he could do until then. He glanced toward the mini bar, but told himself no. He began to pace back and forth across the living area carpet.

When Gardner and Esbeth pulled up in front of Adele's house an hour after dark there was no sign of the FBI agent's car. Either he was well hid or he had taken a much needed break, since there was, in fact, only one of him.

Esbeth glanced up and down the block while Gardner parked.

She rang the doorbell. It took a few minutes before Adele answered, and when she did, Boose stood behind her and he gave Esbeth the eye while he tucked in his shirttail.

"It being this close to Halloween I was all set to get out some goodies if you two hadn't scared us so bad without even wearing masks," Boose said.

"What are you doing here?" Esbeth asked Boose as Adele ushered them into the living room.

"He told me to keep an eye on her." Boose nodded toward Gardner.

"I said a casual eye, not one focused on every anatomical detail!"

Adele could have, should have reason to take offense at that. Instead she suppressed a giggle.

"Lord love a duck," Esbeth muttered. Don't you dare try and wink at me, Boose Hargate, she thought, but she had known well enough of his animal magnetism when she had allowed the two to meet, so she had to take some of the blame.

When they were seated in the living room, Esbeth and Adele

on the couch, Gardner in an easy chair, and Boose in a straight-backed chair turned the other way with him straddling it, Adele said, "Where are my manners? Does anyone want a beverage?"

Esbeth and Gardner declined, but Boose bustled into the kitchen and came back with a can of Budweiser in one hand and a wine cooler in the other for Adele.

Esbeth figured it would not be long before she would have to check at the nearest Wal-Mart to see what flatware they had registered for the wedding. But she said nothing.

"What have you found out so far?" Adele asked, after she took a sip.

"Honey, I wish I could tell you we're making great strides. But, truth be told, we're not," Esbeth said. "If anything, we seem to take a step back now and then. Do you have anything to add to the soup we're in?"

Adele gave Boose a look that asked what happened to that great detective you were bragging about? She turned to Esbeth and said, "We learned from that FBI guy that Vance, or Roy Dean if you buy into the agent's version, had an insurance policy on him. I mean beside the one I had. Two of them, in fact. Some woman named Sylvia Baron had two five-hundred-thousand-dollar policies on him, and they were paid to date. That's a million dollars, only she'd only get two hundred and fifty thousand if the suicide ruling holds. The agent asked if I'd heard from this Sylvia woman, but I don't know her from Adam's house cat."

"Why do you suppose she had the policies?" Esbeth asked.

"That agent fellow says it's because they were partners once, in some sort of con racket or other. Can you imagine Vance be-ing a con man? Sure, he could be a smooth talker when he wanted, but he pretty well jumped when I snapped my fingers."

"I imagine he did," Esbeth said. "Quite unlike Boose, eh?"

"Boose here is a fresh breeze. I'll give you that."

For the first time, some color began to show in Boose's cheeks. "Everything's not always the way it seems," Boose said.

"I'll have to have Gardner here give you his story about how a person's perception can sometimes be a deception," Esbeth said.

"I have time now, if you two don't mind," Gardner said.

Before Esbeth could sigh, Gardner said to her, "I could give a slightly different version, so you don't get bored."

"Just a minute," Boose said. "Let me round up a fresh dose of aluminum poisoning." He dashed into the kitchen and in a minute was back astraddle in his chair with another beaded can of beer in one hand.

Esbeth caught the way Adele's eyes followed Boose out of the room and back in again, as if reluctant to let go of the awareness of his presence. From a nonphysical relationship, and one in which she had probably dominated the man, she seemed to have taken a whole new tack with Boose, who could be as visceral as it gets in Esbeth's experience. Lord love a duck.

"Fire away," Boose said, as he settled in his chair. "There wasn't time to do up no popcorn."

Esbeth thought the two younger ones might mind. She and Gardner both came from a pre–television era where people regularly traded stories; it was how they entertained, connected, and informed each other back then. But Adele and Boose both seemed glued to Gardner as he started to speak.

"My friend Scotch and I were at the same college, only I was pre-med then and he had taken a zoological turn. He always did like animals. I didn't take my twist in the road toward forensic pathology until later. But I was always eager to help him do his work on his thesis, which involved recording the rectal temperature of bats while they slept."

"Do you mean . . . ?" Boose started to say.

"Save any questions for the end," Esbeth said, "or we'll never get through this."

"I had a cuss of an old mustered-out Army jeep back then with a rebuilt transmission and a cranky attitude in general. To get to the cave where he did most of his work, hauling a low trailer with all the gear on it, meant winding up steep switchbacks on this hill all the way to the top. We took turns going in first to make sure the coast was clear, that no bear or mountain lion had decided to visit, and it was my turn, so I went all the way back in past the hanging bats to check on the back holes and crevasses of the cave. It was dark back in there, and spooky, and I had just a carbide lamp on my head. Well, I got all the way back in there and for some reason Scotch took it into his head on this occasion to start making the sound of a mountain lion up at the front of the cave. I was pretty nervous anyway, but I could tell it was him and not anything like some puma. It kind of ticked me off, though, him trying to rattle me that way, and far back along the shaft I was in I could see a flicker of light. The notion crossed my mind to go along that way and see if I could get to the outside and come around to the front of the cave and scare him back. He deserved as much, I thought. So I started back toward the light, though the ceiling of the cave got lower and lower as I went. Then the upper third was covered with spider webs. I was ducking so low that I got onto my back and was sliding along, inch by inch beneath the thick white mass of those webs. Scotch, meanwhile, was keeping up his mountain lion imitation. I don't know why, but somewhere along in the middle I began to wonder about that thick mass of webs. I'd been looking back and ahead while I scooted. So I stopped and looked straight up, and do you know what I saw?"

"I'm betting it wasn't Sandy Claws," Boose said. Adele slid forward to the edge of the couch, and Esbeth realized she had done the same.

"No. It was spiders, clear ones, the kind you find in a cave where they've never had to develop pigment. On the belly of each one was a little, shiny red hourglass."

"Black widows?" Boose said. He leaned forward.

"Yes. Hundred of them. Thousands. All hanging right over my head like so many Christmas ornaments, thick as stars. I could have reached out and picked them."

"What'd you do?" The beer in Boose's hand hung there, forgotten.

"I started to slide slowly back, inch by inch, back the way I'd come. It seemed to take forever. But as soon as I was clear of the mass of webs I jumped up and brushed myself off all over and scurried back toward the front of the cave. Scotch was there, but I buzzed past him and said, 'Let's go.' We got into the jeep and I guess he felt foolish enough not to say anything. I was in a quiet smolder myself as I started down the even more tricky way through the switchbacks, changing gears, and with the trailer swaying back and forth behind us. That's when I felt it. Something was crawling up my leg inside my jeans. I felt each step of those insect legs and I mean to say a chill went up and down me, but I never said a word to Scotch. I was still that miffed at him. But I did reach a hand down and grab that spot on my jeans. I crushed it in my hands and lifted out hard, hoping on hope I didn't get bit in the process. My fist stayed in a clenched knot gripping that patch of my jeans. That meant driving the rest of the way down slow through all those switchbacks, shifting and steering with one hand. Scotch never said a word. After a glance or two my way he just stared straight ahead. As soon as we got to the bottom of the hill I got the jeep to a stop, pulled on the brake and hopped out. I yanked off those jeans and shook them out, with Scotch giving me a deadpan puzzled look as I did. And do you know what rolled out of one of those pants legs?"

"No, what?" Boose couldn't help himself.

Gardner took a long breath, then said, "A squashed cricket."

Esbeth felt herself relax and ease back onto the couch, but she wasn't so relaxed the tale was going to help her sleep any. Her glance to Adele and Boose registered that the story seemed to have had the same effect on them.

While they all sat close, in that nerve-rattled sort of state, Esbeth heard the smallest bit of rattle at the house's back doorknob.

Adele's eyes popped open wide. Boose shot up out of his chair and opened the door of a closet across the room. He took out an aluminum softball bat with one hand and held up a finger to his lips with the other.

Gardner started to rise, and Boose held up the flat of a hand for him to stay put. Then he rushed off by himself toward the back of the house through the darkened kitchen.

CHAPTER NINE

A small town like this, Mook figured, has in the course of time sent its share of otherwise sane people to the booby hatch. If the monotony of going by the exact same strip-mall stores didn't drive you bonkers, then the traffic lights that sometimes seemed to work in synchronized rhythm and most other times didn't, along with vehicles either going too fast or too slow, would sooner or later make you look for the fire ax and run amuck.

It had just begun to get dark, and the town's lights flickered on, most white or yellow, and cheap in general—nothing like the glitter and false reality Vegas had to offer. All afternoon he had sat in the motel room watching old reruns of *Andy Griffith* and *I Love Lucy* to the sound of Fred Redbear, who without pause sharpened his knife. Mook was strung tight as fishnet stockings on a street-corner hooker in a bad part of the south side of Chicago.

He changed lanes in an abrupt swerve to avoid a pickup truck that lunged into traffic from a side street, and such was the funk he was in that he didn't even yell at this particular redneck doofus. Redbear sat in the passenger seat in the glazed-over state he slipped into just before there might be a chance for knife work, which Mook hoped wasn't going to be the case. All he wanted to do was get next to the Kilgore widow and rattle a bit of information or money from her. If she wasn't home, getting her bank account numbers would do. Two Chins would know how to empty those.

Mook knew what still bugged him most—that it was his time and his dime. That's no way to get ahead. Back in his cell-sitting days he had pictured a flurry of profitable activity with as little risk as possible, the kind that would allow him in time to head for Bora Bora and sit on the shore with a tall, cold one while he watched the waves climb onto the shore in regular rhythm. He didn't see Redbear in that scenario, though there was a Polynesian woman on the lounge next to him who wore little and drank a rum-spiked beverage from a coconut.

When he turned the corner onto the street where the Kilgore widow lived he saw the same federal car still sitting there. Damn. He pulled into a drive, backed out and headed the other way in a controlled smolder. They didn't have six weeks to take care of this. Two Chins probably sat up there in grand style, while down here they burned time and expenses. Well, might as well put the time to good use.

He cruised the edges of the town, the back industrial streets and the repair garages and body shops, rows of storage sheds, and empty lots that would soon become more of the same. He didn't tell Redbear what he looked for. The man had his knife out again and worked at the edge with his stone.

Years of experience made this shift of activities as easy for him as the decision to stop by the bakery on the way home would be for someone from the normal world, where laws were things to be venerated and obeyed.

Less than twenty minutes later he saw what he sought—a small house with body shop attached, a towering pile of junk out back, and a pickup truck that pulled out of the drive with a round red NRA sticker in the back window. Perfect. The lights in the house were out. Mook drove by, gave the truck time to get down to the corner, turn, and soon pass out of sight. Then he looped back around and drove up to the garage bold as brass. He parked on the shadow side of the house where the bluish cast of the mercury vapor light did not light up the gravel. "Be right back," he said. Redbear didn't even grunt this time.

The back door had a white wooden frame with small squares of glass. No Fort Knox this place. He picked up a scrap of a wooden two-by-four that lay flush along the back of the building's concrete slab and tapped out a pane. The glass crumpled and fell inside. He reached in through the hole and undid the lock.

Logic eliminated a lot of possible spots, and the fact that this was not some nicer three-bedroom, ranch-style home in the suburbs eliminated the probability of a locked gun safe. A single drawer in the bedside end table yielded what he had come for, a .357 magnum Smith & Wesson revolver. There was no spare box of shells beside it, though all six cylinders were loaded. Mook popped the cylinder open, eyed the rounds, gave it a spin and whipped the cylinder back into place, then shoved the gun barrel down inside his belt at the small of his back. There were probably a few rifles and shotguns in the house if that NRA symbol meant anything, and in this part of Texas any self-respecting member might even have an assault weapon. He had what he had come for, and even though he hadn't found any spare ammo for the gun it was wise to make this back-door shopping trip short in case the guy had just run to the corner for beer or smokes.

He slipped outside and into the car in a couple more ticks. Fred Redbear didn't look up from where he still whetted the edge of his pig sticker.

By this time it had gotten darker out. Mook drove their car around the corner toward the widow's place. There was no staked-out fed this time, at least one you could see. There was no telling for sure. Mook went around the block twice before he eased up the alleyway behind the house. He counted houses until he was sure he was in back of the right one. He turned off the lights, engine, and nodded at Redbear, who climbed out of the car and moved brisk enough Mook had to scramble to catch up.

They had been through this at the motel. No knife play, he had said. But Redbear's blade flickered silver in the dim light from the back windows. Mook stepped lively to catch up while his partner reached for the back door. Normally, he would case the place better, make sure the lady didn't have company, or an economy-sized dog in there. But they had been in that stinking motel too long. Redbear twisted the knob. The back door wasn't even locked. It began to open. Then all hell broke loose.

Boose shot through the kitchen at near the speed of light, or at least an armadillo on fire. It wasn't his house, but his basic primal defense urges had raw adrenalin and testosterone shooting to all points inside him. The back doorknob twisted all the way and the door began to open. The first thing through the growing gap was the glittering blade of a knife—a huge Jim Bowie of a knife. Boose never hesitated. The bat was a good one, about thirty-two inches long, aluminum softball shaped with white zinc oxide tape wrapped in cross-hatches up and down the handle. He snapped it high around in a loop and smashed down on the hand that held the knife.

The hand snapped down and then back out the crack of the door. The knife rattled to the brown Spanish tiles of the kitchen floor. It was sure a big one, all right. Its chrome blade glittered and the rawhide handle was wrapped in silver braided threads. Boose didn't linger to inspect it. He swung the door all the way open and charged out into the dark of the night. His eyes were still adjusting, but he could make out two of them. Then one spun to look back. A flash burst from his hand that Boose knew only too well—gunfire. Two or three frames of the glass door behind him shattered and bullets slammed into the wall inside.

He rolled to one side in the backyard into a low bramble of stickery berry bushes. The flash of gunshots blinded the shooter as much as Boose, because the shooter fired the next two shots back at the dim light from the open door.

The two men turned and ran. Car doors slammed as Boose got to his feet. The car peeled out and threw gravel as it turned the corner by the time Boose got out into the alley.

When he came back into the house Adele had turned on every light. The kitchen was lit up brighter than the Superbowl and Esbeth, Gardner, and Adele looked him over as he came back inside. He still gripped the softball bat.

"Are you okay?" Esbeth asked.

"Yeah," Boose breathed hard, "but if I get near those two guys again I'd hate to be the one responsible for their dental bills."

Adele looked too rattled to speak. Her eyes shifted from checking Boose to the holes that were in the wall, and then down to the knife that lay on the floor. "Am I supposed to say, 'Now that's a knife'?"

"Don't anyone touch it." Gardner moved closer. Esbeth peered down at it, too, though she did not reach for it.

"One of them is sure enough a knife man," Esbeth said. "Look at that. When you sharpen a knife enough you wear away the original shape and you get that kind of worn sway-backed look. I'll bet you could shave with that, Boose."

"That's good," Gardner said. "A man who spends time with any tool, as much time as has been spent with this knife, leaves part of himself behind. There's lots to learn from this. I don't have the lab for it, but our FBI friend does. Adele, do you have one of those big freezer Ziploc bags—one big enough to hold this?"

She nodded and was back in a couple of ticks with one big enough for him to use tongs and slip the knife in, butt first.

"You think sharing that will put us in good with that FBI guy?" Esbeth asked.

"I'm not sure. But I have a sneaking hunch that our stock might be going to slip on the local law enforcement stock exchange within a short while, so it won't hurt to do anything that might soften the crash a bit."

Silky Baron drove into greater metropolitan Fearing, population somewhere around seven or eight thousand, that same day, just as evening set in. Her car was a rented Dodge, the kind you get at a Rent-A-Wreck agency, a 1995 Intrepid—a damn good car, the agent had said enough times for Silky to doubt his word. She had hesitated to go to any mainstream car rental agency since ol' Jimbo knew she had traveled that way before, and these folks were willing to grab a cash deposit and accept a fake ID, the kind she was rarely without. She felt untraceable and quite detached from her days of work with James Calloway. No doubt he was back at his swank hotel room throwing his chest out as usual—more like the spinnaker of a racing yacht turning a corner outside the Great Barrier Reef off Australia if you asked Silky. She had stayed long enough with the man, too long.

Perhaps my only mistake, she figured as she wove through the more sporadic traffic of the town at this hour, was in taking those damn safe deposit keys. But she had wanted to sting. Still, it was "gratuitous," as Calloway would say. She wouldn't be able to open the drawers herself. So it was just a gesture, one that might well put him into "a right tizzy."

In the two times she had been to Fearing before she had not given the town a full reconnoiter. She and Calloway had stayed at a pretty ritzy motel, to hear the locals speak of it, a Hampton Inn nestled along the shore of what was a series of lakes. The motel had no room service and they had to go out for meals, which is how they discovered the Bluebonnet Café for breakfast and a surprisingly elegant dining establishment within walking distance of the motel called The Flamingo's Smile, established by two gay men who came out to these hinterlands with the express intent of sharing their advanced level of sophistication with the locals while they shook the pockets of the affluent of the area, most of whom were retired. Their mission was so in tune with James Calloway, III, that Jimbo had gravitated toward the spot each of the few evenings they had been in town to work their scams until the moment came to move on.

Now she scouted the area with a different eye. She wanted someplace low-profile to stay, and the same went for spots where she could dine, though she might even resort to buying food at a local grocery to eat in her room, something she had not done for enough years she had to think about the process and what foods worked for that scenario. God, what a little primp I've become, she thought. If her parents could see her now. Raised on macaroni and cheese, fried chicken on the odd Sunday now and again, she had blossomed in Cedar City, Utah, to the extent boys came after her in swarms. At first she had been flattered, then she had calculated how it could take her out of her home and into a better life. Somewhere in the whirlwind of the heady male–female attractions of her late teens it had penetrated that the sort of men to whom she was attracted didn't want a better life; they didn't want the small house with white picket fence. They had wanted one thing, and until then she had made the classic mistake of being too free with that.

With that epiphany in mind, she had left the outskirts of Cedar City for the glitter of the outskirts of Las Vegas, where her education about men in general was borne out by the many whose pathetic drools or mock smugness she had to endure each night as they shoved dollar bills into her garter and believed, many of them, that a mere glimpse of themselves in the audience, in a setting like this, made her eager to spend more personal time with them. Pathetic.

The appeal of someone like Roy Dean Vanderhael was that, for the first time in quite a while, a man was interested in her not for the flesh that had grown on her with very little help from gyms or planning, but had just happened on its own in a normal and healthy way. He didn't drool, nor did he even push for sex once they spent most of their free time together. Van had a confident breeze of cool wind about him that was very hard to resist. It was difficult to believe now that he had come to this, the messy end that smacked more of pathos than tragedy, more of grizzly detail than heartfelt intrigue. Yet, here she was in the town he had moved to and settled down in—all to ensure that she get her fair share, the million that would be hers if the notion of suicide could just be overturned. She had given the thing a nudge when she planted those threat letters, but it was hard to tell if there had been any effect from that. There had been nothing in the papers or other media. That meant coming out here herself to see what she could learn about what was going on. It also was not a bad place to lay low from Calloway, whose shorts had to be in a right proper knot by this point. Maybe she should have left those keys where they were, tucked away in his suitcase. Though it was sure fun to imagine his reaction when he found them missing.

The faint smile slipped off her face as she looped back through town and came to the motel she had settled on, the Hill Country Rustic Inn, an unlikely place for her to be found. Rustic was one of those euphemistic words meant to put a positive spin on a negative thing. The place was a dump. Face it.

When she had her room key and crossed the parking lot to get her bags and lug them to her room she heard two guys having an argument in the parking lot. Well, only one of them was talking—shouting really. He shut up when he saw her. The two of them spun and sulked off to one of the rooms on the lower level. It was in the opposite direction from her room. Good. She had enough on her hands right now without a couple of dinkhead men tangled in her life.

Redbear sat on an uncomfortable chair in the corner of the room and muttered to himself. When Mook could catch a word here and there, ones that weren't strings of profanity, it was about that damned knife. If that damned Injun hadn't been so hopped and ready to use it, they might have gone in slower, or not at all. He popped the top of another can of warm beer and took a long drink. It promised to be a long night. Ol' Fred there never says a word for years and now he's the Tower of Babble.

Finally, to shut him up, Mook said, "Look, we'll get you a new knife tomorrow. Okay? Plus, I might as well get some more shells. Used up most of what I had laying down a cover for us to scat."

Redbear gave him a sullen look; one hand stroked the empty sheath at his side.

Damn fool. You'd think he had lost a kid tonight instead of some hunk of metal and leather. That petulant scowl could belong to an eleven-year-old kid.

There had been times back in the prison yard that Redbear had pulled Mook's bacon from the fire. But he needed to be watched. There was that time when, just out of stir, they had been on a job and a dog was barking. He had told Redbear to do something about it. Five minutes later the damned Injun had climbed back over the fence with a pair of Cocker Spaniel ears in one hand. A Cocker Spaniel, for Pete's sake, the same kind of dog Mook had grown up with.

Another time, they had stopped out by a fence in what they supposed was a forgotten back piece of Texas to use nature as a bathroom, when some stupid emu had come running up to

131

them, stuck its head through the fence and had damn near done ol' Redbear some serious and permanent harm. Leave it to the Injun to climb the fence and go after that big bird, but it wasn't sound judgment. The emu had gotten the best of him and he was lucky to get out of there with his knife and only the scratches that came from leaping the fence to roll out into the gravel along the road. That was Redbear for you—steady as they get most of the time, but as loose a cannon as can be when he goes full moon on you.

Mook finished the beer, crumpled the can, and tossed it into the corner. Yeah, things would be different enough tomorrow. Maybe this time Fred would listen to a plan, and do a sensible scout first, the way Injuns are supposed to instead of flying off the handle and damn near compromising the whole deal. There was a federal agent in the mix too that bore watching. Next time things will be more steady, better planned, and more careful. He would see to that if he had to scalp ol' Redbear there himself.

The phone rang the next morning and Esbeth picked it up.

"You'd better get over here," Tillis Macrory said.

"Where's here?"

"The Oakline Hills Rest Home. I trust you don't need directions."

She hung up and looked over to Gardner, who sat on his side of the breakfast nook.

"Bad?" he asked.

"Pretty bad," she admitted, though she only had the Texas Ranger's tone on which to go.

She drove this time, because she needed something to do on the way over. Still, she fretted all the way, and beside her Gardner was silent.

The skies were overcast, forbidding, and traffic was the usual snarl of people headed places they probably did not need to be going to so fast.

Esbeth and Gardner pulled up half a block away from the rest home. Cars and a media van crowded the way to the place. They walked along a row of vehicles until they saw the small crowd of people on the front lawn of the place. Oh, dear. This did not look good at all—the stern, disappointed look she got from Zick Robin, the Austin reporter, the forced neutral expressions of Sheriff Johnny Gonzalez and the Texas Ranger, Tillis Macrory, the not entirely suppressed gloat of Deputy Chunk Philips, the stern piercing look from Karl Williams, director of the Kendall-Williams Funeral Home, and the businesslike menace that emanated from Torrence Furlong and Melba Jean Hurley. Esbeth heard someone mutter, "Here she comes now."

"Ah," Furlong said. "Glad you could join us since you seem to be the impetus behind this little gathering. I was just telling these men of law, as well as this . . . um . . . journalist, that we have nothing to hide here. We're willing to open our arms, hearts, and our files to one and all who are here today. It's just that, in case it matters, we never, ever keep files on residents who have passed on. That's our practice, as it has been for years. Isn't that right, Melba Jean?"

She nodded, but she stared right at Esbeth as she did so.

All eyes turned to Esbeth, but what could she say? That they were lying? Chances were that there were no files now, though there certainly had been the other night.

Well, Gardner had hinted that their stock might soon fall, and she would have hated to try and buy a share now on the open market. With about everyone in this crowd right now her stock was lower than whale residue.

With all eyes on her, Furlong took a step closer himself and looked at her as he said, "I have just one thing I want to hear from you, Miss Walters."

Esbeth was reminded of the time she had watched a blacksmith putting shoes on a mule. The mule had given a sudden surge and had rammed a hoof into the man's stomach. He had made a loud "oof" and his eyes had crossed. That was how her insides felt at this moment, except for the wind whistling in an eerie note through her sense of being alone and unwanted in the world.

"Well, goodbye, then. Guess I'll get out of your hair, for now," she croaked.

"And good riddance," Chunk Philips added, though it got him a frown from the sheriff.

"Oh, and Mr. Burke," Furlong said. He turned to Gardner. "Those are your things in that pile beside the door. Feel free to take them with you when the two of you go. You are no longer welcome at The Oakline Hills Rest Home."

This time, when Esbeth glanced Gardner's way, she felt that he too now numbered among those who wouldn't throw her a rope if she was drowning, unless it was to throw her both ends.

Tillis Macrory pulled into the gravel lot in front of the local coffee shop, The Daily Grind. Fearing was still too small to have its own Starbucks, but in keeping with the times you could get a decaf mocha cappuccino in town if you were of a mind to.

When he entered the shop he could see Carson Billings sunk deep in an overstuffed cowhide leather chair that had the fur on the outside, a Holstein if Tillis knew his cattle, and he did. The FBI agent had one of the large ceramic grande mugs in front of him—must be planning another all-night stakeout of the Kilgore place. Too bad he had been away when the only event worth watching had occurred.

Tillis carried his regular black coffee over to the corner table and sat in a chair that matched the one in which the agent sat. He took off his white hat and put it upside down on the table between them, the way you are supposed to treat a Stetson.

Billings allowed the beginning of a grin to slip loose. "That old gal you were bragging about sure got her comeuppance today, I hear. Sorry I wasn't there to see it."

"Esbeth?"

"Yeah. I hear her cannon is spiked for quite a while now. I saw her myself today, and she didn't look too proud of herself. She and that old gaffer brought by the knife from the Kilgore house I was telling you about. Maybe she'll stay out of all this now."

"You get anything from the knife?"

"Too soon. I FedExed it to Virginia. I'll let you know. Now, come on. Admit you were wrong about that old gal."

Tillis grinned. "Maybe something in the line of a wager would teach you something."

"Make it a beer?"

"Make it a case, and winner picks the brand. I'm already leaning toward Shiner Bock."

"You're damned confident. You really think she's going to still meddle at all after today?" One of Carson's eyebrows lifted a quarter of an inch.

"I think you don't know very much about that ol' gal at all. Now is when things just start to get lively and interesting. She'll roll up her sleeves, spit in your eye, and before you know it you'll be the one wondering what happened."

"If she has a plan," the agent said, "I wish I knew what it was. This is the least proactive case I've ever been on. Everything is sit and wait."

"And hope you don't miss the action, the way it went the other night?"

Carson frowned.

"Don't you worry," Tillis said. "She may not even know what

she's going to do next, but when she gets in gear she sure enough works in mysterious ways her wonders to perform."

CHAPTER TEN

Gardner woke and saw that Esbeth stared out the kitchen window at the bird feeder but hadn't put on a pot of water to start making coffee. He almost spoke, then stopped himself and tried to think of some famous statue or other of which she reminded him. It wasn't *The Thinker.* He puzzled over it for another minute while she still didn't move. Then he had it. She was a vision of immortal sadness.

He rose and slunk off to shower, shaved and dressed before coming back to the kitchen. She still stood there, in her housecoat, and no coffee was made. Not good.

Yesterday had been a long afternoon after Esbeth's embarrassment, stonewalled by Furlong and having failed to deliver a story to the reporter she had lured all the way out here—all this in front of the core of the local law enforcement. She hadn't just lost a battle; it had darn near been a Waterloo.

He sat down at the breakfast nook, but didn't speak. He thought through what he might say, or should say.

"You know what," he finally spoke, "when my wife died I went back to our house and it seemed about as big as a football stadium, and empty. Being alone is an awful thing—that is, for someone used to being with someone."

Esbeth turned to look at him, her brow wrinkled into furrows.

"You find out how strong you are then," Gardner went on, as if he hadn't noticed her disapproval. "I moped around and didn't go out much. You find out who your friends are then, or that you sure don't have many. At our age the support group we had, family, neighbors, classmates has all dwindled down considerably. I admit I was down for a spell, and I can be a pretty up kind of guy. I got to a place where I doubted myself, where I considered taking my own life, and I don't want to get to that place again. It's what allowed me to let myself move into a place like that Oakline. Hell, I'm glad they kicked me out. I might not have had the mustard to do it myself these days."

He paused. Esbeth did not speak, just turned to watch the birds feeding, which seemed to fascinate her at the moment.

"All that's by way of saying how much I admire you, Esbeth. I mean, you've lived alone your whole adult life and from what I can tell don't have so many close friends that you can't count them on the fingers of one hand. Yet you're tough as shoe leather and bounce back better than the best rodeo clown. Anger is a passion. That's good. Use it. I'll bet even as I speak your wheels are turning and you have a new plan of action. Am I right?"

Esbeth glanced his way again, her mouth pressed into a tight grumpy line, but the sparkle had returned to her eyes.

"You're just out of those wacky things to yell out there at the rest home is all," she finally said.

"Oh, yeah. What about this one? Don't think of it as a bully of a star; think of it as a bossy nova."

"Oh, Lord love a duck. I got you out of there just in time. Now, don't you start in on one of those yarns, either, about perception. You hear?"

Whatever had just transpired shook Esbeth back to normal enough she turned and bustled around getting the coffee and some toast going.

"Watch things while I get into battle gear," she told Gardner, which suited him just fine.

When she came back to the kitchen she wore everyday

clothes—jeans, white blouse, comfortable shoes. Gardner looked up from where he spread marmalade on toast for both of them. "What did you have in mind?"

"That knife," she said. "That's the first solid bit we've had."

"The FBI lab is good, but if it's been cleaned real good I doubt they can establish any clear link to Adele's late husband, though they might well get DNA on the knife's owner, probably no prints, though, since it's the kind of handle designed against that."

"What I mean is how it was honed. That's a knife someone loved too much. It's been sharpened a lot. I had a neighbor once who wore the paint off his 1949 Mercury because he washed it every single night. That's too much love, just like that knife. Whoever owned it is one knife-wielding person, and likely as not right now he's feeling as naked as a streaker."

She's gotten herself all the way back to a smile, Gardner thought, and a pretty determined and evil one at that. "He's going to want to get a replacement, and soon. Where's the best place around here?"

Esbeth crammed the rest of the piece of toast she held into her mouth and wiped away an orange trickle of marmalade from the corner of her mouth. She washed the bite she chewed down with coffee and stood up.

"The rattlesnake store," she said. "That's where we're going."

Traffic bunched up at the light just past the bridge into Fearing. Poised halfway up a hill that overlooked the town, in his rental Lincoln Town Car, James Calloway could see the cozy little burg nestled like an oyster on the half shell, waiting for him to happen to it, again. He had done well here before, but he could say that of many such hapless towns where hope springs eternal and the hayseeds practically line up to hand him their life savings. In all the time he had rolled from city to city, he had never once gone back to a place where he had scored well. There was no need for it, and it went against every rule of his grand plan, and for that reason it rankled him now. He seethed. He had read somewhere that Texas gets hit by more than a hundred and twenty tornadoes per year, and right now he was mad enough to be one of them. Inside he felt the burning razor edge of a motivation, the like of which he had not felt in some time. It was fueled by the newspaper clippings he had torn from the public library copies of the *Austin American Statesman*. Silky had told him of her past with Roy Dean Vanderhael, and it had taken him but a second to make the mental leap to Vance Kilgore from this town in the articles once he had played back her response to the back page of that section of the paper. He had been slack to miss that before.

Connection drives the lives of normal people—family, friends, lovers. His kind of work demanded that others extend that kind of trust so he could exploit it. But he did not function that way himself, nor did Silky. He had forgotten that fundamental truth. Working together had lulled him into trusting her, and now he felt the chump, something that was only supposed to happen to his victims. Unlike those he ripped off, he was not going to take it. Did not *have* to take it. He was all cold steel and cunning now, along with the rippling fires of anger.

The light changed and cars began to stir all the way back to his. He took his foot off the brake and rolled down the hill in the flow of vehicles. He felt a keen elation, one he had not expected to feel. It was the thrill of the hunt. For a while there he had been swept up in the white heat of the moment. Now that he was taking clear, deliberate steps to catch up to her he felt the resolve of a man of action, honed to the point he could and would hurt someone—Silky.

The car slid through the halting stop-and-go of traffic as he steered toward the Hampton Inn. It was the best place to stay around here, though nothing at all like the Four Seasons where he had been; but it had a tolerable view of Lake Kiowa and tonight he would slip over to The Flamingo's Smile for some of their *Châteaubriand*. Remember, he told himself, you are not here to recreate. This was a matter of extreme urgency. She had taken everything. Everything. Someone viewing his life might find irony in betrayal being tops on his list of things that rattled him to his core, but he himself found nothing amusing in the concept, nothing amusing at all.

In the soft, kid leather briefcase on the passenger seat beside him, along with the clippings, was a 9mm Glock, with its serial number filed off, one he had bought for a ridiculous two thousand from a fellow who ran an auto detailing shop—a chop shop, if truth be told—in an alley off the far east side of Seventh Avenue. His short-term close friend Samuel, the bartender, had been reluctant to send him there until Calloway had sworn he was no cop or even some FBI agent. Fact was, though cops did drink, few had his build and consumed as much gin, so he got the lead to a brother-in-law of Samuel, who, if push came to shove, Samuel would not mind seeing get locked up.

Calloway spent part of the time on the ride out to Fearing imagining what he would do to Silky with the gun, and where, when not doing countless permutations over the little amount of cash he had to his name. He was as close to broke as he had ever been, barring that long-ago painful time at the damn Indian casino.

The woman behind the registration desk—Dorene, according to the metal name tag she wore—took in his dark suit, red tie, and crisply ironed shirt, something she saw little enough of out here unless it was from business travelers, along with his request for the best room she could manage. The question was in her eyes, though she was well-trained enough not to ask. Telling Samuel he was not an agent had given him the idea to mock up a set of FBI credentials. He had seen a set once, and only needed a leather case and enough verisimilitude to the details to look good in a quick flash.

He slipped the slim black wallet out now, gave Dorene a very fast peek. Had she been more worldly and less influenced by the mystique Hollywood had invested upon anyone who flashes a badge or credentials when not wearing a uniform, she might have looked more closely at Calloway's pudgy physique and wondered if the training program at Quantico had gone to hell in a handbasket. As it was, she paid rapt attention when he asked if there was a woman staying there who fit Silky's description.

Dorene went secret agent on him herself and leaned closer. "No. But d'you have anything to do with that other agent staying here?"

Well, that was a tidbit of information he had not expected. *Other agent?* Calloway was too smooth to show being ruffled. He bowed close, "Do you mean . . . ?"

"Mr. Billings," she said. "He didn't let me know, but I can tell. Besides, he gets faxes through my machine."

She touched a finger to the side of her nose, as if she was handy with detective work herself.

Calloway carried his bags up to his room. There was much to think over, and about which to be all the more careful.

"Why do folks call it the 'rattlesnake store'?"

Esbeth glanced toward Gardner, then shifted her attention back to the street, where a trailer full of mowers behind a lawn care business pickup truck swayed back and forth through two lanes and made anyone behind think twice about going by in the second lane. "You'll see."

In her quick look she noticed he had missed a patch of white and gray stubble on the underside of his left cheek. She said,

"You know, according to Arthur Conan Doyle, Sherlock Holmes was able to tell from which direction the sun shone into a man's bathroom by the way he shaved, though how that helped him solve any crimes eludes me some."

Gardner's hand moved up and rubbed his face until he found the spot he had missed. "Sherlock's thinking never allowed for simple mistakes, serendipity, or stark coincidence. Sometimes what seem to be clues are mere scraps of clutter littering a case. It's good to free the mind of any of that, when you have the luxury of time."

They could have hashed over the topic, but Esbeth pulled into the asphalt and gravel parking lot of a sporting goods store on the corner of one of the main streets in Fearing. A sign with moveable letters on the outside proclaimed the end of the Texas dove season, the approaching end of bow season, and it offered a special on Ruger handguns—all this in breathless urgency. The corner picture window drew Gardner closer after they were out of the car and neared the store's front door. Inside were five adult diamondback rattlesnakes. Rocks were arranged to look like a natural habitat, with the snakes curled up on top of some as well as in the shadowy crevices beneath.

"That," said Esbeth, "is why they call this the rattlesnake store."

"Do they sell them?"

"No. Who'd want them? They're for local color. You probably know about the annual Sweetwater round-up, don't you?"

"The one where every year men get to show off their macho sides by tromping through the wilds to gather up rattlesnakes with just a stick and a sack, only to follow that with events in an arena in front of a crowd with the snakes? Guys get bitten every year, and there have been some deaths. Oh, and I can tell by that slight curl to your lip that you find the whole enterprise as enchanting as I do. Don't think I'm one of those sorts of men,

143

though I have done a snake-bite autopsy or two."

Before Esbeth could respond, a woman Esbeth's age stuck her head out the front door of the store. "Hi. I'm May Bell. Stay where you are, and I'll rile 'em up a touch for you." Her gray head popped back inside.

In a minute a small door opened near the top of the enclosed snake pit and a stick poked through. It banged against a rock and all the snakes sprang to the defensive with lifted heads, jaws open while their tails rattled the rows of their buttons. One had a head that was black. The snakes looked around, seeking what had disturbed them from their naps. The stick withdrew, so they fixed on the faces that looked in at them from outside, mouths open, tails rattling, poised to strike. The black-headed snake made a lunge at the glass that made both Gardner and Esbeth take an abrupt step back, nearly bumping into each other as they did. Gardner looked at her, then chuckled.

"Come on, let's get inside." Esbeth waved a hand and led the way, but she had to fight back a grin. Her heart was going like a racehorse.

Inside, May Bell was behind the counter putting away her stick. "That black-headed one sure has an attitude. Don't he now?"

"They're . . . interesting," Esbeth said.

"Feedin' them is a crank, though. I've got to use little baby chickies, fresh out of their eggs. I got softhearted once and took the little chickens home, but it was a mistake."

The rest of the store stretched out with a section for fishing tackle, another for bow equipment next to camping gear. Upstairs was the gun area. The glass, waist-high counter that ran along the inside front of the store, behind which the sales clerk stood, was filled with knives—pocket knives, hunting knives, and even a few gift boxes that contained presentation collector knives. As soon as Esbeth spotted the glittering blades and velvet-lined wooden cases of the better knives she leaned closer with rapt attention. As she did she heard a harsh urgent rattle. Her head pivoted right to look right into the red maw and dripping fangs of a rattlesnake mouth inches from her eyes.

She shot backward in a reverse long jump that might well have raised eyebrows on an Olympic committee. As she did, she banged into Gardner, who was doing some rapid backpedaling himself.

"Great bobs of gibbering grits," Esbeth snapped. "What the . . . ?"

"Oh, sorry." May Bell rushed over to that end of the counter and reached behind a coiled rattlesnake on a flat rock on the counter. She flipped a switch and the rattling stopped, the mouth closed, and the head lowered back into a sleeping repose. "That's the boss's idea. There are three of these things scattered here and there in the store. He thinks it's cute, though I've had to learn CPR, and half a dozen times I've nearly scared the giblets out of my own self. It's got a motion detector and runs on batteries. Cute? He won't think so someday when EMS is hauling a corpse outta here. If you wanna buy any, though, we sell them. Now, what can I do for you folks?"

Esbeth pressed a hand to her chest and could still feel her heart galloping for the high hills.

Gardner stepped back closer to the counter and kept his voice low. "These are some beautiful knives. But does anyone ever buy them?"

May Bell seemed eager for a subject change that did not involve customers frightened to death. "Yeah. Sold one of the best of them just this mornin'. Two or three locals make the knives from scratch. It's an art. The one this mornin' was one whopper of a Bowie knife with a nice elk horn handle. Man knew his steel, too. Didn't want enough carbon content to make the blade brittle, but wanted one that would hold an edge like dammit. Pardon that slip, ma'am. I'm still a touch jangled my own self."

Esbeth pulled herself back together enough to slip closer, and together they steered the conversation so that by the time they climbed back into the car outside, Gardner was able to say, "I don't like the idea of those two men buying a box of three-fifty-seven ammo, too."

"The part I did like, though, was one of them saying the sound of a train jolted them out of his bed in the middle of the night. That eliminates almost all but one motel, the Hill Country Rustic Inn."

Ten minutes later they pulled into the parking lot of the motel. As they climbed out of the car, a woman came down the stairs from the second tier of rooms and slid into an older model Dodge Intrepid with a Rent-A-Wreck car sticker on its back bumper. Something out-of-tune clanged in Esbeth's head; the woman was young, attractive, and looked like money. Nothing about her fit with either the car or the motel. But there was a lot about what went on at small country motels that Esbeth probably did not want or need to know.

Inside the office a mousy-looking clerk who was losing his hair, and his patience as well, banged on the side of a computer monitor. The clerk wore no name tag, but on the wall there was a small chalk *ON DUTY* slate on which someone had chalked in *Eustace,* which had to be real; no one would fake that. He looked up with a look of mixed guilt and anger, which faded the minute Gardner spoke.

"Young man, I'm Burke and this is Walters. I'm going to ask you to help me with something that is so urgent and discreet that a person's life may very well hang on this."

Esbeth watched the young man's face. She admired how Gardner had not once said they were police detectives, but had used the authoritative tone that had suggested they were. If the desk clerk had thought about it he might question the city having two detectives their age. The handful of city cops in Fearing often got maligned as able to handle parking and speeding tickets, but little else. They farmed out any real detective work to the Texas Rangers or the Sheriff's department, but the clerk didn't seem to know that. The young fellow was having a frustrating day and being called on for a kind of help that seemed serious was plasma to him; his was a life that needed some adventure right now, however small. One minute he begrudged the quotidian drag of his life in general and this day in particular, and the next he pictured himself as some kind of personal assistant to James Bond. She noticed how he didn't ask to see credentials.

"Yes, sir," he said, glued in rapt attention to Gardner's face.

"Two men are staying here. I just need their names and the make and model of the vehicle they're driving."

"Sure thing."

A few minutes later Esbeth and Gardner got into her car after a quick look around the parking lot.

"Looks like they've already gone," Esbeth said. "The names they gave were probably fake anyway, though we know what make of car to watch for. Maybe I'd best drive over to Adele's place."

"You're way ahead of me. I was just going to suggest that."

When they got there, no one was home. The house looked empty and the lights were out. No cars were parked outside, neither the FBI agent nor the car of the two men who had stocked up on a new knife and ammo. For a while they sat in the car as evening settled over the town like a damp rag. They watched traffic until Esbeth said, "You see that car there?"

"The one that's gone by twice before?"

"Yeah. If that isn't the same one we saw a woman get into back at the motel I'll be dipped in wet cornbread dough."

"What do you suppose she's up to?"

"Your guess is as good as mine. Maybe Detective Burke ought to have another chat with that forthcoming clerk back there at the motel." Esbeth watched the street for quite a little while, but the car didn't come by again.

CHAPTER ELEVEN

The rolling hills got steeper and rockier as Gardner looked out his window while Esbeth drove. Though it was late October, the leaves had still not fallen from most trees and there was a fair amount of green where the brownish-red of soil didn't show through in places. Even the steepest cliffs were dotted here and there with green, though it was often cactus or yucca—almost all of the vegetation out here had prickles, poison, or thorns of some kind.

"How many siblings did you say Boose has?" he said after a couple of miles of quiet from Esbeth.

"What?" She had been deep in thought, far, far away on another galaxy for the effort it took her to shake the mist away.

He repeated the question.

"Twelve. That makes thirteen kids, counting him."

"Folks sure had real families back in the day, didn't they?"

"You'll note, too, that of all those kids, he's the one who responds to his momma's need the most and sees that she's taken care of, even though he tries hard to be known as the world's crustiest curmudgeon."

"I thought you held that title."

Esbeth glanced his way, to see if he wore a smile when he said it. He passed, but conversation died again until they got out to Boose's place.

By the time they got there Gardner felt more turned around and befuddled about directions than he liked to admit. He had looked around all the way out. The woods, houses, and even the view down into dry creek or riverbeds from the bridges all looked darker, mysterious. Perhaps it was the mood, but sinister forces seemed to reside out in these parts, far from the comforts of Austin or the small-town charm of Fearing.

Esbeth slowed at a mailbox she recognized and pulled over near it. Boose had parked his truck somewhere else for now, back by the barn he had said. He could see no sign of a house, only a trail that started through the thicker patch of woods and meandered out of sight. Gardner knew they were near the lake, which was down a cliff at what would be the back of the property. He had been about to write off his apprehension to a stressed imagination until he saw what looked like a gun barrel pointing from behind a thick clump of sage.

"Esbeth?" he said, not sure they should be here.

"Yeah, yeah." She got out of her side of the car. "I've got one bit of sound advice for you. Touch nothing. Hear me?"

He heard the rustle of leaves in the wind as he got out of the car. Then there was the baying and yap of dogs—about a million of them, from the sound of it. Three of them came tearing around from the back of the house—a big black lab, a hound, sort of, and another dog of indescribable muttness. They were all bark and snarl until they caught a whiff of Esbeth. They veered and circled around her, nearly knocking her down. The hound stayed to lick at Esbeth's hand while the other dogs surged on to have a sniff of Gardner.

"That big lab there is Whitey; the hound here is Spook Daddy; and the other one, whatever junkyard breed it is, is Bitch Dog."

While she talked, Whitey shoved his muzzle into Gardner's crotch hard enough to double him over in pain like a jackknife.

"Don't encourage them," Esbeth said.

If Gardner could have said anything, it would have been in a high squeak. He straightened, his face a mask of pain, while he pushed Whitey away.

"Yo, Boose," Esbeth called out. "Come out and call off your dogs."

A loud whistle sounded from a thick part of the woods and the dogs all whirled and shot off in so many furry blurs headed that direction.

Gardner bent over and clung to a corner wooden fence post with one hand while the color came back to his face.

"You going to be all right?" Esbeth asked. "You aren't going to slow me down here, are you?"

"Heaven forbid," he gasped, and reached up to rub at one watering eye.

Boose walked toward them from what looked like the thickest part of the woods. "I dint know you were comin' or I'd have fetched out the good silver." He winked at Esbeth, at least that's what the convulsion on that side of his face looked like to Gardner. He wore a white T-shirt, jeans, and boots, all of which made him look lean as a rail and hard as rawhide, an impression that was not softened by the Colt .45 automatic shoved down into the front of his jeans behind the belt buckle where if it was to go off he would be singing with the Vienna Boys Choir, though Boose didn't look the sort to have accidents with guns.

He winked at Gardner and he said, "I wouldn't go up that trail to the house if I was you."

"What have you done, Boose? Is the place a maze of booby traps?" Esbeth tried to peer ahead up the trail.

"Let's just say this is a safer place for Adele than her house back in Fearing, though it meant Momma has to move into Pearl's place for a spell. How 'bout yourself? Talk's all over town 'bout how that Furlong fellow put plenty of egg on your face. How're you rolling with all that? You're usually the sort to get your hindquarters up over your back 'bout a thing like that."

"Just fine," she said, each word a crisp bite. To Gardner her tone said otherwise.

Boose shrugged and turned to lead the way, and it was a circuitous path that wove through unlikely thick patches of woods and avoided the open spaces. They even went all the way out by a low barn and started back toward the house past a sty, of which the centerpieces were two of the largest pigs Gardner had ever seen. These were covered in black fur and had sharp, white curved tusks that looked able to disembowel an armored knight. Their feisty attitudes as they rushed toward the fence didn't ease Gardner's mind. Nor did he gain comfort from the fine, but sturdy, braided wire he spotted later that led up to a tree.

Boose reached out and stopped him with a hand on Gardner's chest. "You'd best step over the trip wire." He pointed to a dark thread of the wire that stretched across the path they were on.

"Trip wire?" Gardner looked up. A huge metal cage hung overhead from a stout limb of a live oak tree. "What's that thing?"

"It's a cage I use for trapping wild boars when they're young. Pretty heavy, too—has to be to keep a wild boar from making off with it. Those two back in the pen were caught that way, though they've growed up some since. Don't go too far to the other side, either. I've dug a tolerable deep pit over there."

By stretching high, Gardner could see over a bush down into the yawning mouth of quite a dandy hole. It was well over ten feet deep and looked like a person could drop a car down into it.

"I've an idea," Esbeth said. She motioned Boose closer and leaned to whisper into his ear.

His sudden grin was as demonic as anything Gardner had ever seen on a civilized man. Boose stepped back to take a look

152

at Esbeth. "Why you're just plain evil's what you are. Wish I'd of thought of that."

"What?" Gardner asked.

"Best you don't know," Boose said, "in case it ever comes to you having to give testimony."

Gardner didn't like the sound of that. He had no idea what Boose meant, but he stayed closer as they made their way along the rest of the path to the back door of the house.

Boose paused near the house, sniffed the air, and glanced up at the sky and said, "We'd best get inside. A bad piece of weather's headed this way. It's fixin' to rain like a cow pissin' on a flat rock."

Gardner looked up but didn't see or smell whatever Boose had. Then he had his hands full stepping lively to keep up with Boose and Esbeth as they wove through a few more snares and traps Boose had set out in wild abandon all over the place. Ahead, he could see a squat, sprawling, bluish-white building through the brush.

Adele stood in the doorway of Boose's small house. She held the door open for them and looked around while she waited.

So far, there had not been a single calming thing about the visit out here, and Gardner was not reassured by the woman's wariness, though it was probably a good idea.

"Better kennel up the dogs," Boose muttered. He grabbed at a couple of their collars and started to haul them toward the barn.

"I'd have thought if there was ever a time to leave them loose, this was it," Gardner said.

"You're right." Adele waved them in the door. "But a pack of wild dogs pulled a seven-year-old girl off her bike in the county just a few weeks back and tried to eat her. The parents and relatives kicked up an awful fuss, and the poor kid is going to need a dozen operations the family can't afford. There's a big crackdown on loose dogs now, and as much as Boose would like them loose now as part of whatever he's been dithering with all day he'll kennel them. The law scooped in two of his friend Brady Stuart's dogs and euthanized them before Brady could get to the pound. It was a knee-jerk reaction, but that's no stranger out in these parts."

Gardner was impressed she had used a word like "euthanized" when most folks out here would have said "put to sleep."

Inside, the place was neat and as tidy as Esbeth's house, which probably meant Adele had been filling some of her time by cleaning and straightening. Boose was fair game for a lot of things, but being anal retentive didn't seem to number among them, though his Navy years on a submarine may have attributed to a tendency to keep few possessions and to stow those. Gardner had been in the homes of other bachelors where he'd had to wade through the residue of earlier civilizations. Here there was a halfway comfortable-looking couch, a wing chair, a rocker, and a wooden gun case that held rifles and shotguns. An overhead lamp at the center of a ceiling fan lit the living room. There were no other lamps or bookcases—quite a contrast from Esbeth's bookish place. Everything looked Spartan, the furniture clean and the walls and crown molding recently painted. There was no separate dining room from the kitchen, but a small table with four wooden captain's chairs centered in the kitchen, as is the case in many small homes. Adele excused herself to clear away the dishes, and Esbeth volunteered Gardner and herself to help.

A white linen tablecloth covered the small table, and black linen napkins were beside each of the two place settings. The silverware all matched and a candle in a holder stood in the center of the table. Well, Boose seemed to have another side after all.

"Smoked salmon and pickled beets," Adele said when she

caught Esbeth's eyebrows raise as she helped gather up the plates. "I wouldn't have thought it would work, but it did, especially with a glass of merlot. Boose put together the meal, all cold items, but tasty."

It appeared they had shared an endive salad with slivers of purple onion and sliced almonds tossed in what looked to Gardner like a home-made red wine vinaigrette dressing. Well, well, well. Maybe there was more than animal magnetism to the five wives Esbeth had told Gardner had come and gone before in Boose's life like so many spins of a revolving door.

Gardner heard Boose's boots stomp as he shook any mud at the door. He had taken them off and was down to a pair of worn white socks by the time he joined them in the kitchen.

"What's on your so-called mind?" Boose asked Esbeth, after they were all settled into the chairs around the cleared off kitchen table, and the guests had turned down the offer of a refreshment, though Boose had used the opportunity to snag himself a can of beer.

Esbeth turned to the woman who Gardner had a hard time thinking of as Mrs. Kilgore. A remarkable woman. Gardner might have been a lab rat most of his life, but he fancied he knew some types of people, and he wondered what a woman who looked so independent was doing with a domineering sort like Boose, who could hardly be called uxorious. "I had some questions for Adele, really. If that's okay?"

"Fine with me," Adele said. Her face, with its upturned nose and pixie-like short hair showed none of the impishness of which she was capable. She gave Esbeth her full serious attention. "Fire away."

"I hope this isn't too personal, but I was wondering about you and Vance," Esbeth said, "why you ended up marrying him. If that's too nosy, just say so."

Adele let her amusement show. "That's okay." She gave Boose

a quick glance before panning back to Esbeth. "I'll put it in a simple way. He understood me . . . in the way I wished to be understood, then."

"Does the same go for Boose?"

"Of course." The impish smile showed again on Adele's face.

Gardner glanced to Boose, who he figured was being strung along as a bodyguard, but Boose didn't seem to mind as much as he should.

Adele caught the look. She seemed to miss nothing. "You think I'm a taker, don't you?" she said to Gardner.

"Well, I . . ." Gardner didn't know what he thought, except to wonder if sometimes women couldn't read minds, something he had thought his late wife capable of a time or two.

"Oh, it's all right," Adele said. "Boose doesn't mind what I'm taking. Do you, Boose?"

He didn't respond other than to wink her way over the tilted top of his beer can.

"That's not what I really wanted to ask you about," Esbeth admitted.

"I didn't think so." A dimple showed in Adele's cheek for the first time.

"I want to know about the questions that FBI agent asked you."

"Like what?" The smile was replaced by a thoughtful frown.

"Did he say anything about who or what he was after?"

"No."

Esbeth glanced at Gardner. He said, "That's consistent with FBI procedure."

She turned back to Adele. "All this business about Vance Kilgore being Roy Dean Vanderhael was new to you, wasn't it?"

"Yes."

"Did he ask you about whether Vance ever mentioned this other woman, the one who holds a million dollars' worth of insurance on Vanderhael?"

"He asked, but I didn't know anything about her."

"Did he say anything about these other two guys, the ones who left a knife behind the other evening?"

"He didn't mention them the first time we talked, but he did ask me about them after you two turned over the knife to him. He sent it off somewhere, but I haven't heard back on that yet, either."

"I doubt you will," Gardner said. "Those FBI fellows play their cards close to the vest."

"What are you after?" Adele asked Esbeth.

Esbeth stood and brushed a couple of dog hairs off the side of her blouse. "I was just nosing around, poking at an idea that isn't all the way baked yet. I'm not dead sure yet what the glue is here. This could be just a dog chasing its own tail for all I know. But I will admit that those two fellows worry me. I'd keep your eyes open."

Boose tilted back the beer he held until it was empty and crushed the can into a small lump as he lowered it. "I look forward to meeting those two again, speaking only for myself." His eyes narrowed to slits that reminded Gardner more of the attitude of the boars out back than anything else. There was no reason to feel any sympathy for such men, but the look on Boose's face made Gardner glad he wasn't either of those men. The look softened, though, when Boose turned to Adele. "I got a little errand to run first, though, since speaking with Esbeth. You gonna be okay?"

"I'll be just fine until you get back." She looked her assertive and confident self again, as well she might with the maze of traps Boose had set around the house.

"We've got to be going, too," Esbeth said. "I have a little chore of my own, something that's been in my craw for a spell that needs looking into."

"I better show you the way again," Boose volunteered.

"Please do," Gardner said.

A pickup truck buzzed by, a black Ford 150 with a blue heeler in the bed barking its fool head off—a favorite dog to own in this part of Texas, a breed that originally came from Australia, part dingo and part sheep dog, just right for cruising around in the back of pickups. The dog continued to bark frantically at nothing. Then the rain began to pour.

First the drops were tentative. As suddenly, the downpour was so relentless Mook couldn't see three feet in front of their vehicle. They sat still in the motel parking lot, Redbear in the shotgun seat, and watched the rain hammer down like it was some primeval raw form of anger.

Mook had been ready to turn the key when it started. Redbear didn't say a word. Big surprise. He just slid the Carborundum from its slot in the sheath and then took out the new knife. The persistent rasp of steel on rock was at least nearly drowned out by the pounding raindrops.

No use getting out of the car now and making a run for the motel room. Might as well head over to the woman's place. Rain would be good cover. He started the car and pulled away from the motel. The rain didn't keep a lot of other Tom Fools from driving around in the erratic style that marked the small town, but Mook was calm and his resolution steel as he drove methodically while he rehearsed what he was going to say. As soon as they pulled into the alley, he switched off the lights and engine, and turned to Redbear. "You let me take point this time, and we go slow. Got it?"

The Injun just nodded, didn't look at Mook.

He turned off the car's dome light and eased out, holding the .357 down at his side, ready for anything. He was instantly soaked by the pouring rain, but it was good cover. All he heard

from the other side of the car was the quiet snick of the door closing. That Redbear could tread as light as a butterfly—a wet one tonight, though.

A couple yards away a dog barked, but no one paid it any mind, or at least no one wanted to poke a head into the rain to hush it.

Mook took slow, careful steps as he eased through the gate and across the backyard toward the darkened house. He thought about that fellow who had swung at Redbear with the bat. It would take more than a bat this time. All he had seen over Redbear's shoulder, as he fired shots to cover their retreat, was a lean fellow, about five-eleven or so, buzz hair cut, and the kind of face and eyes you would find in the yard. He doubted the fellow had been to prison, but the actions and the brief glance he had gotten of that determined mug made him cautious.

This time Mook tested the back doorknob, found it locked, not open like the last time, and he reached for his lock-pick kit, a soft leather flap that held a small assortment of slender bits of wire. The door didn't need much. The lock was old-fashioned, the kind a skeleton key could open. In his day he had picked some of the most unpickable locks made. He had spent about as much time practicing the skill as Redbear spent sharpening his knives. This lock might as well have been made of cheese. The ease of entry only made him more suspicious.

The door opened at his touch and he stood back with gun leveled. A low, metal clang sounded. He waited. Nothing. His first step inside crunched. He clicked on the small flashlight he held in his left hand and swept it across the floor. Some fool had scattered native paper-shell pecan nuts across the floor. His foot started forward and stopped. He lowered it again, careful not to step on one of the crunching nuts as he did so. With one toe he swept the nuts nearest him to one side while he swept the light beam to every corner of the darkened back porch and kitchen. He pushed the door all the way open until it made another clang. With the gun held back so no one could knock it out of his hand, he slid out into the room until he could peer behind the door. Someone had tied the handles of a couple pots and a skillet there, the same person who had spread the nuts on the floor probably.

Though he sought to keep his mind open and alert, Mook couldn't help thinking of that aluminum bat sweeping down on Redbear's knife hand. The house was silent except for the sound of the rain that hammered on the roof and the creak of a wooden beam nudged by the wind. Still, that wiry little bastard could be anywhere. The man was a menace. Without knowing he was doing it he eased the hammer back all the way, glanced down at it in surprise when it clicked.

Redbear eased out around, sliding his feet to keep from crunching any nuts. He didn't have a light, didn't need any. The dim light in the darkened house was enough for his night eyes. Mook almost called to him to stay back, then thought what the hell, let him lead if he wants. He knew what had happened last time.

Each corner they went around showed only empty rooms until Mook took a paper towel and went around turning on the lights. Then he took out a packet of plastic surgical gloves, tossed a set to Redbear, pulled on a pair himself, and they started through the place in earnest. At first they were methodical. Then Mook felt the warm flush of anger creep up his neck and spread across his face, and Redbear caught the mood. Soon they were kicking open closet doors and dumping out drawers onto the floor. They tossed each room, the anger and disappointment grew, but there wasn't so much as a checkbook or bank book, only clothes and the usual clutter of a married couple's years together.

Mook stood in the kitchen. Why all the bother with the pans

and the nuts? Maybe it was for when they were still at the house and he had just left it that way, or maybe it was to screw with their heads. Mook started to hope he did run into that feisty fellow again.

When Redbear appeared beside him, without making a sound, Mook waved him toward the door. They left all the lights on in the place and the door open. See whose head gets messed with now.

In the car he paused a moment before he turned the key. When he started the car he knew where they needed to go. Back on the main thoroughfare that passed through the center of the town he had seen the red, green, and blue neon lights of a bar's sign. It was a dive, but that was even better. Perfect, in fact.

Twenty minutes later, with a sulking Redbear who was ticked because Mook had made him take the sheath off his belt and leave the knife in the car, they entered the layered smoke of one of the dingiest bars Mook had ever been in. He knew this town was no Vegas, but he had seen livelier bathrooms back there compared to this dump.

The bar ran along the back wall until it got to the men's room that had a dart board on its door. A pay phone stall pressed next to that. A corner was broken off the big mirror behind the bottles in back of the bar, and a fake moose head on an opposing wall was missing an antler, but someone had supplied it with a John Deere green hat that was now as dusty as the rest of the plastic trophy.

There were only half a dozen other customers in the place, along with a disinterested bartender; three men sat at the bar and one pushed pool balls around on a three-quarter-size table with the felt worn almost off the rails. Two women, who could be truck drivers or arm wrestling champions, sat off to themselves at a booth with heads bent low together talking. The whole scene was as depressing as a painting Mook had seen of James Dean, Marilyn Monroe, and some other folks sitting at a diner over cups of coffee.

You come to a town like this as strangers and people are wary until they get a clear story in their head. Mook decided they would be workers off an oil rig trying to look up an old comrade who owed them money. That was a tale the locals could hang their hats on and would save some of the speculative gossip that went with small towns like this.

It took him three beers along with two club sodas for Redbear until he knew the bartender well enough to call him by his name, Raffert, to endure his sudden booming "hawr hawr" laughing at his own stories, to learn the intimate details of the man's year-long quest for a divorce that doesn't leave him penniless, and to ask him about a fellow of the description of the one with the bat. He spun his yarn about how he had worked with the scrappy fellow, had dinged his car back then and wanted to make it right. When he got to the feisty part, the bartender's eyes lit up and he straightened up behind the bar. "Sounds to me like you're describing Boose Hargate. Hawr hawr hawr hawr. Didn't know he worked on them oil rigs. If it's him I wouldn't go near him if I was you, even with the both of you. Your chances in a tangle with him are as good as with those two over there." He nodded toward the women who had ignored everyone else in the bar the whole time.

"Screw women," Mook said, with sudden heartfelt vehemence. "They're all bitches. You live where I do you rent 'em for the night, don't ax them no questions 'cause they'll just lie, and you leave never lookin' back." He intended the outburst to bond with the bartender, but it stung. His own ex, Melanie, hadn't paid a single conjugal visit and had sold everything he owned by the time he got out. Then she had filed for divorce, slam-dunking the whole three years they had lived together before his fall with less concern than she would give throwing away a used Kleenex tissue. He glanced to Redbear, who only nodded, though he had his own stories he could share if he chose to speak.

"You sure got that right," Raffert agreed, though one eyebrow lifted. "Hawr hawr hawr hawr."

"This Boose guy, is he dangerous?" Mook said, back to the subject. He took a sip of his long neck Shiner Bock and looked at the bartender, then glanced across the room to where a small phone book hung beside the pay phone just outside the men's room door.

"Dangerous? Why I'd flat out say he is. You know how some fellas go into a scrap with a hundred and ten percent and never let up 'til the other fella's laid out on the gravel. Well, that's Boose, only with some bobcat and badger thrown in. Hawr hawr. Don't you mess with him, if he's the fella. Steer clear is my advice. That Boose is one plum damn crazy sonbitch."

"What was it bugging you back there you couldn't talk about?" Gardner asked.

Esbeth leaned forward as she drove, a habit of hers when it was raining this hard.

"I got to thinking and wondering," she said. She would have glanced his way, but it took all of her attention to drive in a monsoon. Severe weather was not her friend, and she was never comfortable when operating her heavy machine through the midst of a sample like this. Silver lines slanted across in front of the windshield yet managed to land in bursts on it as if hurled directly at the vehicle.

"About what?"

"Of all those people who were gathered there to get a chuckle out of my coming up a cropper when Torrence Furlong buried the paper trail there, one person was out of place, shouldn't have been there."

"Who?"

"Karl Williams."

"The funeral director? He's a pal of Torrence Furlong from what I hear, and like him he's as tight as the bark on a tree."

"That's what I'm counting on, his looking for ways to save a buck here and there. Did you notice his shoes? He must've had them twenty years and has polished them until the polish is what holds them together, and takes them to get fixed instead of buying new shoes. Same goes for his suit. It's been touched up and mended, though nicely, a number of times. This is a man who values a penny."

"What about it?"

"It just rubs the wrong way with something else I heard about him. With two peas from the same pod like Torrence Furlong and Karl Williams it most often comes down to money."

"Oh. I guess that explains why we're headed the direction we are." Gardner glanced around at the town's landmarks they could dimly make out through the storm.

"Yeah, his hearse has low mileage according to my mechanic friend Shiner, and I don't see him paying to make special shipments, not cheap as he is, and a small funeral home like his isn't likely to have its own crematorium."

Esbeth turned and headed out a different road until the large brick funeral home loomed ahead through the storm.

"You know," a nervous edge had worked its way into Gardner's voice, "I'd kind of been putting off coming to this place too soon."

Esbeth chuckled, then snapped a glance in his direction. He did seem to have gone pale on her. She recalled how she had felt when she first faced that long walk up the sidewalk to the rest home, a place that gave her the willies. Stood to reason that Gardner might have the wobblies about a place, too, and what better one than a funeral home. It seemed kind of ironic, though, that a man who had dealt with as much death as he had would have this particular squeamishness, but she understood and kept silent.

The good thing was that in the downpour there had been very little traffic, and there was even less out here. There were places out in this part of Texas where land could still be bought for a thousand dollars an acre, though at the edge of a town it ran higher. Still, a lot of businesses bought ahead against the future, and the funeral home had been one of them. The building snugged up against one of the chief secondary streets in town. Behind the building as much as ten acres of land sprawled in a field, eased into a small copse of woods, and sprawled up a hill to a table of land up on a higher level of hills. A road ran along beside the property, and a chain-link fence with "No Trespassing" signs every few sections ran along beside the road.

Esbeth turned down the road and halfway back the length of the property she slowed and pulled over beside the funeral parlor's land. A patch of thorny chaparral ran close to the fence, then the land opened into the trees that looked to be a mix of live oak, scrub elm, mesquite, chinaberry, sumac, and a sycamore or two along the creek.

"You're sure about this, are you?"

Her lips pressed tight and she felt her eyes narrow. Truth be told, she wasn't sure about most things. But she did subscribe to the notion that intellectualism outweighed intelligence any day of the week, and that intellectualism is just raw curiosity when you get right down to it. Maybe that was just a polite way of justifying her being nosy, but it worked for her. She was going to have a look, and it didn't matter it was raining hard enough to fill a wire basket.

"There're a couple of flashlights in the glove box if you don't mind getting them out for me," she said. "You don't have to come along on what promises to be my most foolhardy jaunt yet if you don't want." She gave him a close look, expecting to see the pale still there, but he had got his color back and a spark of irritation at her patronizing him, too.

"I'll be just fine," he said, each word on the crisp side. "We're far enough away from that place here it won't get up my sleeve so much."

She grinned to herself, but didn't let him see. Then she was out the door into the rain and it was all she could do to find her way to the fence. She was mulling over a way to get her roundish self over the chain-link fence when Gardner leaned close and shouted over the sound of the downpour. "There's a gate down this way a piece."

His hair was matted down in a gray gull's wing over his forehead and water streamed down his face like so many tears. But his face looked set and determined for all that.

Blinking to be able to see at all, Esbeth followed his taller, gaunt form as he slogged through the thick grass along the fence until they came to a gate, which fortunately could be opened by lifting a U-shaped flap and swinging the gate open. There was no need for the flashlights yet. She didn't want to alert anyone back at the funeral home that they were back here tromping about, although she doubted if anyone was looking this way during a storm like this. Rivulets of water parted the grass in small streams heading down the slight slope in the direction of the creek. They splashed through them, not getting any wetter, though not getting any less wet. That hardly mattered. They had been soaked to the skin as soon as they had gotten out of the car.

As they entered the copse of trees Esbeth slowed and turned on her light. By now she was sure that Gardner knew as well as she what they looked for.

"Over here," he called out. He had strayed, so she headed

that way. He stood with his light fixed on a wet rectangular mound of mud.

She swung her light around. "There's another one, and one over there, too," she said. She stood and thought for a moment. "Let's see how close we can get to the creek without falling in."

She had her light on the path and didn't get to see any expression on his face, which was just as well.

The sound of water high on the banks as it rushed through the normally trickling stream was louder by the time Gardner called out to her. "Over here. I think this is what you were looking for."

She slipped a half step, slowed down, and took her time getting to where he stood. At least she made it without nose-diving into a mud bath.

This time the erosion of water coursing its way down to the creek had cut a groove through one of the rectangular squares. Gardner bent close, though even from where she stood Esbeth could make out a shoulder and part of an arm. This body had not been buried deep, barely a foot and a half under ground.

Gardner brushed tenderly at the face until the rain rinsed off the rest of the dirt covering it.

"Gladys Cravetts," Gardner said. Esbeth had to bend close to hear him at all.

This body had not been prepared for a funeral, which meant little had been done to it at all—another savings for the funeral home. Esbeth's flashlight beam spotlighted the wet, dead face. Gardner lifted her lips open with a finger. Dark bruises showed inside the upper and lower lips.

"Well?" Esbeth asked.

"We've got enough lividity. If the other patients are like this it's enough to generate a complete round of autopsies."

"So it's not just guesswork now," Esbeth said.

"We'd best get out of here," Gardner said, barely loud enough to be heard. He stood and stepped away from the eroding grave. "Anything we do here would just mess up what comes next. The wonderful new gadgets the crews have these days can make far more from this than I could have back in the day, or even now without a lab."

"Yeah, you're right."

They slogged across the wet field in the rain back to the road.

In the car, Esbeth sat for a few seconds, let what they had seen soak in. "Do you think this will help?"

"It might. How did you ever get your head ticking in this direction?"

"Everyone has a vice or a weakness," she said, "and the lust for money over doing right by people isn't all that new."

"It just proves that greed, like stupidity, has no limits. How about you?"

"How about me what?"

"Do you have a weakness or vice?"

"Got them? I spend ninety percent of my time and energy compensating for them. But we're not talking about me here."

Gardner nodded, and a bead of water dripped from his wet hair onto his lap. "I guess I expected Torrence Furlong to be too clever to ever let his slip show. But sometimes it is the people you associate with who do you in if the right person stumbles onto a thing like this."

"There isn't really anything about this after all that feels all that easy and convenient. I feel like I haven't slept since 1967 and we've only started to pick at the scab of this whole mess and haven't really fixed a ding-dong thing. Now, let's get out of here. Quick." She turned the key and the engine, fortunately, cooperated.

A slight shiver set in on the way back to her house, and she wasn't altogether sure it was from the cold and the rain. She glanced at Gardner and his face was gray and his lips blue. He stared ahead, deep in thought.

At the house they piled out and rushed inside. Esbeth grabbed a pile of towels she carried out into the living room when the phone began to ring. She tossed a couple of the towels to Gardner and rubbed her own face and hair as she picked up the phone. It was Tillis Macrory, the Texas Ranger.

"We got a fix on those men who were at Adele's place. I've been trying to reach her, but she's not home."

"She's at Boose's place, where he thought he could keep her safe," Esbeth said. "Why? Who are they?"

"Some pretty bad characters. One's Fred Redbear. The knife was his. That makes the guy with him probably his other half, a guy named Mook Jackson, who's his keeper and is usually around when Redbear is. They both do chores in Las Vegas for Tony Two Chins."

"There's that name again," she said.

"I want to warn you to stay away from these men. They're not to be fooled with. Boose might've got lucky once, but these are very bad men."

"No other DNA on the knife?"

"Do you mean of Vance Kilgore, aka Roy Dean Vanderhael? No. No there wasn't. The knife had been cleaned good, though there was enough to tie Redbear to it now. We still have some homework to do, but you stay clear and let us do it. You hear?"

"One other thing," she said.

"What's that?"

"It costs a lot of money to cremate people, doesn't it?"

There was silence on the other end for a moment. "Esbeth. What have you been up to?"

"If you look behind the Kendall-Williams Funeral Home, way back in those trees near that creek, I believe you'll find some fresh handmade graves where someone has been saving a few bucks by not shipping or delivering bodies to the cremato-rium. Chances are, there are even a few of those bodies from the Oakline Hills Rest Home that could benefit from a careful second look. That *is* against the law, isn't it, burying people on the cheap? Is that ranger business, or will the sheriff be wanting in on this?"

"Esbeth. Dammit. Leave it to you to see that the shit hits the fan just when everything else is taking off like the cowboy who hopped on his horse and rode off in all directions."

The phone banged onto its receiver on the other end, and Esbeth smiled as she continued to rub herself dry.

Gardner came out of the bathroom. He wore a robe and his hair shone wet but neatly combed and parted. "Did what you shared make that ranger happy?"

Esbeth poured water into the pot so they could have tea once she wrestled into a dry change of clothes herself. She looked at Gardner, and if she had not been so chilled and exhausted she would have managed a wink. "It made him a lot of things," she said, "but happy wasn't one of them."

CHAPTER TWELVE

The damn roof leaked. Special Agent Carson Billings reached up to wipe a dribble of water from his forehead. What could you expect? Bill Morrison had made it from scrap lumber for his grandkids, who all had better sense than to be in the damn thing when it rained. Bill and his wife Helen were off in the RV to a spot near Brownsville, though Carson had been able to reach them by their cell phone to ask if he could use the tree house. He could tell from the back noise as Bill said yes that Helen itched to drive back so as not to miss a thing. But he had cautioned them to keep clear a few more days. It was obvious that Bill was a home repair wannabe at best, and that while the structure would hold the grandkids in the tree to play that it hadn't been built to withstand the weather. The spot was perfect for observation, though, and also meant his own car wasn't in the area to be spotted. He could see cars pass along in front of the Kilgore home and he had a clear view of the backyard as well. When the rain had first started he had wrestled on a London Fog trench coat over his suit, and for a while he felt like a private detective on a domestic case as he scanned the backyard with night-vision goggles and watched the street in front through the telescope lens of a camera mounted on a short tripod. It had been a damp bust for a long stretch, then business had picked up in earnest around the house.

The first moth to the flame was an older rental car that cruised up and then back down the street, which allowed Carson to catch the sticker on the back bumper before it settled to roost across the street and about half a block down. A woman was behind the wheel and when Carson zoomed in on her he smiled to himself. "Well, Silky Baron. I wonder just what you're doing in a small town like this? Could it be about those policies you held on the late Roy Dean Vanderhael?"

With no one in the darkened house, he spent the next hour watching Silky watch the house. She seemed to be mulling over possibilities. Suddenly, she ducked. That gave Carson a stir. He zoomed in on the Lincoln Town Car that rolled slowly by. The driver looked for house numbers and settled on the Kilgore home. The street was otherwise empty in the pouring rain, so the car came to a near stop before it rolled forward again. It went back and forth a couple more times and gave Carson plenty of opportunities to catch a head shot of the driver in the telescopic lens of his digital camera, even through the rain. Then the car zoomed away. After a while, Silky's head lifted to show behind the steering wheel, and she turned on her car and eased down the street in the rain. It was quiet around the house for about an hour, except for when an occasional distant dog barked. Then business picked up at the back door of the house.

Carson heard the car ease to a stop and the two men get out. While they sneaked across the backyard in the rain he snapped a few shots with his camera. It was Jackson and Redbear, all right. Carson had not seen the Kilgore woman all day, and the house was dark, so he let things run their course, the lock picked, the crashing around that went on inside. After twenty-seven minutes of frustrated noise, he watched through the night-vision goggles as the two men came back outside and slipped to their car and pulled away. At the very least he had them for B & E, if he wanted. But they were small fry, not who he was after.

He figured that would be it for the night, unless the Kilgore woman would add to the circus by coming home to find her place trashed and all the lights left on. Might as well get out of here. He packed up and was easing toward the rickety wooden steps designed for smaller bodies than his when the cell phone in his breast pocket began to vibrate. He had switched it to vibrate from ring before climbing up into the tree house earlier. Carson eased it out and glanced at the number on the lit screen. He punched a button and lifted it to his ear. "Yeah, Tillis, what is it?"

"You better get over here and have a look. I thought it might be so much air at first, but one corpse was just about dug up and I dug up another of them myself. I've got the sheriff and K-9 crew over here now and we've got eight more bodies so far."

"Just what in the pluperfect devil are you talking about?"

"We're behind the funeral home, back in the woods. You can't miss us. Light crews are set up and we have backhoes and diggers going full blast. Come have a look before the media gets wind of this."

"That's all fine, real tickety-boo. But what I'd really like to know is where in the devil that Kilgore woman's gotten to."

"Oh, she's out at Boose Hargate's place. You can thank Esbeth Walters for that tidbit."

"And where exactly is that?"

"When you're heading south on Main Street you see a fork in the road where Bell Mountain Road heads off from behind the Shell station there."

"I know, when I come to the fork in the road, take it."

"You go out about three or four miles and look for the mailbox. You can't see the house from the road. But it's back there. The lake isn't too much beyond that. Why?"

"Oh, I've just got an itch I'd like to scratch is all." Carson closed the phone and slipped it back into his pocket. He glanced up at the pouring rain. It would be nice to dry off before going anywhere, and send off a photo by E-mail. He doubted anything would happen so fast he wouldn't have time to slip into a clean and dry set of clothes first, so he headed back toward the Hampton Inn.

They knew where the bastard lived now, and not all the rain in the world—all it would take to float Noah's ark—could stop them now. In fact, it might lay down a nice cover. It was sure enough one frog-walloper of a rain storm. Mook grinned to himself and even Redbear was content enough to leave his knife in its sheath for the moment, though he had been quick enough to strap it back on as soon as they got in the car after their visit to that bar.

He wasn't sure if they had gotten the directions right after a quick glance at the phone book map until they slowed and he leaned out to look close at a mailbox. Yep. Hargate. This was the place. All he could see from here was an impenetrable looking stretch of woods being sluiced out by streams of pouring rain water. Swell. He reached and got the S&W out of the glove box, switched off the dome light, and nodded for Redbear to lead the way this time. The Injun's obsidian eyes glittered as he slid out the passenger door and eased into the edge of the woods.

Mook held the pistol tight and rushed to catch up. But Redbear had slowed, was bent close to look at every detail of the path. Something bothered him. Mook took out his flashlight and coned the end with his fingers so only the barest sliver of light showed on the muddy ground. He started to go around Redbear, who held up the flat of a hand to him. He stopped, let the Indian have his scouting moment. In the distance, through the woods and rain, he could hear dogs barking. It was the frustrated barking of dogs in a cage, and that gave him some relief, since he wouldn't have to see Redbear and his knife have a go at them. The damn Injun would be wearing their ears for a necklace if it was up to him. They didn't need that just now.

The rain hammered down, but they took their time. The trail meandered all over the place. Visibility was almost nonexistent. Mook did risk letting his flashlight beam show all the way now while they sneaked forward. A couple of times he tried to peer around to see that Redbear followed, but if there was a trail it was all soup to him. He pressed closer when they circled wide around a low stand of prickly bushes. Mook itched to go faster, but a sudden rattle at their feet froze them both in place. It sounded very close. Mook flipped the light that way and saw a rattlesnake curled into a strike position, its long, white fangs bared and red mouth open as it lunged. He took a sudden step back just as Redbear slashed at the head and took it off at the neck, let wires show through the center of rubber.

"What the hell?" He wasn't talking about the snake being fake, probably run by a motion detector. He was responding to what his leg had hit. He swung the light down. A trip wire. He looked up just in time to see Redbear give him a sudden surprised and disappointed look before his own head panned straight up above them. A cage of steel shot down at them faster than an elevator. Mook shuffled as fast as he could back the way they had come just as the huge frame of steel bars landed on Redbear.

The crash shook the woods. Mook froze in place, breathing hard. He couldn't believe it. "Fred? You okay?" He heard a low moan. He had lost his light, though he had hung onto the gun. It took him a few moments of groping in the mud to find the flashlight, even though it was still on. Mud covered the bulb end. He wiped it off and lit the way over to where Redbear lay half under the steel cage. It rested across his twisted two legs, pinning him to the ground. Mook went closer, tried to lift the cage. It was way too heavy for that. He swept the light across Redbear, who covered his eyes to save his night vision and reached for his knife.

"No," Mook said, thinking Redbear was going to cut off his own legs to free himself. But Redbear only used the knife to dig at the mud around his legs. Then Mook heard another sound, the soft rustle of leaves filtered through the rain as someone headed in their direction through the thick growth. That would be that crazy sonbitch with the bat, that Boose fellow they had heard about, only he probably had more than a bat this time.

Mook turned to run back up the trail and he had only taken a few steps when another rattlesnake popped up ready to strike. It was just like the other one, and part of his mind screamed at him that it was probably fake, too. But he had already taken a sideways hop and one foot hovered over nothing, just air. He felt himself fall, then the squelch of mud covered him as he hit at the deep bottom of a pit. For a second or two he struggled to slip and slide to his feet, then rubbed at his eyes to clear them as he blinked them open. He still held the gun, though he had lost that damned flashlight again. The Smith & Wesson was a good gun to have in a situation like this, far better than an automatic, in his opinion. He could count on a revolver. If he needed it, it would work.

He felt around at the walls of the hole on all sides. Too steep for him to climb. He tried to take a step up, but the dirt wall crumbled away beneath his foot. So he stopped and stood still.

Above the hammer of rain he heard the rustle of bushes again. He raised the gun, aimed it up, and waited. Up at the edge of the pit, which seemed to be a good ten feet deep, he saw a figure appear silhouetted dark against the sky. It had to be that Boose fellow. Mook squeezed the trigger and for a second the flash and roar of the big gun blinded and deafened him. He caught just enough to see the figure half spin and drop back. Got him.

It was quiet in the rain then, and Mook had a chance to

think. That was damned smart now, wasn't it? The one fellow who could lower a rope and get Mook out of here and he had shot him. Real smooth going there. He lowered himself to sit at the bottom of the pit, squatting on his legs with the mud coming up to mid thigh. He sat and waited, though at that precise second he didn't know for what.

"Are you tired?"

Esbeth gave Gardner a quick glance. It was going on one in the morning and outside the car windows it was dark, and, oh yes, it still rained hard. Her hands tightened on the steering wheel as she looked back at the hard-to-see road ahead.

"Yeah, I'm tired," she said. "I'm tired of a lot of things. I'm tired of childproof containers on bottles I can't get open myself when I really have a headache. I'm tired of being called senior. That was okay when I was in high school, but hasn't been that much fun ever since. I'm tired of thinking like a sixteen year old but when I tell my body to do things only to have it react at its real age. Yeah, I'm tired. But I'm also doing something about life, maybe even making a difference, and if you don't think that matters to an old piece of shoe leather like me then you have another think coming. Why?"

"Do you ever get tired of being alone?"

That stopped her. Her head rocked back half an inch. "Why, Gardner Burke, you old hound dog you. Are you making a pass at me?"

"Why . . . no . . . I . . . um . . . just wondered."

Esbeth grinned to herself without showing it and kept her concentration on the slippery when wet road.

It was quiet in the car the rest of the way to the motel.

As they pulled into the parking lot, Esbeth thought of making a case for going right to the woman's room. The decision was settled for her by a Lincoln Town Car parked outside the carport beside the motel office. Another car, a late-model Ford Escort, was parked underneath the cover from the rain, and that had kept the Town Car out in the rain. The Lincoln looked as out of place as smiles on the faces of people who headed into an IRS office. The parking lot was otherwise half filled with pickup trucks and older model cars.

"What do you think?" Esbeth nodded toward the car.

"Doesn't fit, does it?" Gardner took in the motel. "This place sure isn't the Ritz Carlton."

"It isn't even a Ritz cracker," Esbeth said, as she pulled the car into a slot where they could keep an eye on the office door.

"I think we just got lucky," Gardner said. He pulled down the sun flap and used the tiny mirror there to comb his hair. Then he pulled his collar up until he looked like an older B-movie cop again. "Let's hope our luck holds."

He got out and bent forward as he scurried in the rain toward the motel office door.

As soon as Gardner swung the door open and rushed inside, the clerk looked up at him. Gardner knew their luck was holding; it was Eustace, the easily impressed, bored, and mousy-looking clerk. Not much usually happened in a small town like this, and his face lit up when he spotted Gardner. The kid was like a crime scene waiting to happen.

A younger couple stood in front of the counter, the man filled the card and paused long enough to make up fake names for the two of them. Eustace closed the drawer after putting away their cash payment. The woman looked around with nervous irritation, and no doubt wished she had stayed in the car. She wore a diamond ring and wedding band, but Gardner was willing to bet even money that the man with her wasn't the one who had given them to her.

Along the wall, looking at a metal rack of tourist brochures as if interested, stood a man in a dripping coat that alone had to cost more than Gardner's complete ensemble. A red silk tie on white shirt showed at the neck, and the man's figure said he had not often enough said no to the dessert cart. His hair, though wet, was impeccably combed, his face had the insolence of someone having a hard time being in a place like this at all, much less having to be patient. His nails were manicured, and a darned expensive job of it if Gardner knew his business.

Eustace's face still beamed with expectation at Gardner's arrival. As he took the couple's card he called over to him in his most obsequious tone, "Be right with you, detective." His self-esteem was the type that needed to let everyone be aware he was in the know and that he was involved in something far more important than anything in their mundane existence.

The comment had a profound effect on the couple. The woman grabbed the man's elbow and tried to yank him toward the door. He, as vigorously, tried to keep his cool and make the exit an amble. He was the more experienced of the two at such motel liaisons, and her guilt was by far higher and more tightly strung.

In the subtle confusion and tension of the moment, the smooth-looking, stout fellow in the expensive coat slipped quietly to the door and went out into the night.

Eustace called something to Gardner, but he didn't hear just what since he eased out the door himself as the Town Car backed away and eased around the carport. Gardner doubted if Eustace would have given out a room number, so the man must have been on a fishing trip hoping to trick the boy out of information, which wouldn't have been all that hard if Gardner's experience with the clerk was any indication. The man's fine clothing and manners, though, didn't click at all with the motel's rustic style; he had sure looked as out of place here as the fish on the bicycle.

The Town Car gave an abrupt spray of gravel as the driver gassed it in irritation when he left the lot. Gardner glanced up at the woman's room, saw the curtain part ever so briefly then close. He slid into the passenger seat and closed his door. Without a pause Esbeth backed out, left the lot, and pulled out into traffic far enough behind the Town Car not to be spotted as they followed it.

The driver of the Town Car knew what to expect, though, and began a series of diverting quick turns without signals into streets and alleys that had Esbeth gripping the wheel and alternately gassing and braking until they pulled back out onto the main thoroughfare and couldn't see the Town Car in any direction.

"Well, now. Doesn't that just scald my preserves," Esbeth muttered.

"What's the best motel or hotel around here?" Gardner said.

"Oh, shoot a bug. I should've thought of that. My brain's gone rusty on me in all this rain."

Not to mention being on the go with little rest, Gardner thought.

Within minutes they pulled into the Hampton Inn parking lot all the way across town. Esbeth eased over and turned out the lights. After a few minutes a dome light flickered on across the lot where a stout driver got out of his parked Town Car. He had parked on the far side of the lot even though it still poured hard and there were one or two open spaces closer to the motel. He ducked low against the pouring rain and headed for the lobby.

Silky tossed the last of her clothes into her open bag on the bed, her nerves as jittery as they had ever been. A knock sounded on the door. She froze, wished for about the two hundredth time that she had gotten a gun somewhere. Since she had spotted James Calloway earlier outside the Kilgore home and then again outside at the motel, she had ramped up to being as jumpy as a cocaine-using jackrabbit. If she could have just mailed those safe deposit keys back to the chubby creep she would have done so. Now it was too late. He had gotten as close to her as this, though she had been congratulating herself that he had not gotten all the way to her yet when the knock came. She looked around the room for something she could use as a weapon. The television was bolted to the dresser, always the sign of a quality place. There was a cheap black plastic coffeemaker with plastic cups, a chair in front of the desk, and a lamp fixed to the wall over the bed.

For the first time in a while Silky felt some missing aspects of not having a partner. Independence is nice, but it would be nice to have the security and support at the same time. Perhaps, she thought, this is the dilemma of female-to-male relationships all around. It had been why she had worked with Van and from there had ended up with the likes of Calloway. When you are by yourself you turn and find no one there and it's a hollow, empty sense of not being entirely whole, of having no complete defense against the world.

"Hey, open up," an older woman's voice shouted. "I need to speak to you. You're in trouble unless you listen."

"What reason might I have to want to speak with you?" Silky's mind raced. If it was a cop, not likely from the voice, there would be talk of a warrant, probable cause, or some reason to bother her. Her thoughts hadn't come easily away from James Calloway, so she wasn't sure what to think.

"Oh, I'm betting there are lots of reasons—about a million of them."

Silky eased over to the door and peeked out the keyhole. At first all she could see was a white bump of hair. She panned down and could make out the face of a roundish older woman standing there. Silky looked all around, then made a decision. She unlocked the deadbolt and opened the door until it was open just as far as the chain would let it. The woman seemed to be all by herself until Silky spotted the tall man standing back out of the rain under the overhang that covered the walks to each motel room. The little round woman sure didn't look like a cop, but she was going to have to say something awfully clever for Silky to trust her enough to open the door all the way.

"I'm Esbeth Walters," the woman said. "Let me ask you about that roly-poly fellow who's trying to track you down. Do you have something of his?"

"What makes you say that?" It was the one thing, Silky thought, that might make her listen.

"It's the only reason I can think of why he'd follow you all the way out here."

"I think you're just guessing."

"Oh, I guess about all sorts of things. I guess you know this town too well for someone who's visiting for the first time. I'll bet if the law ever matches your voice with the one backing up that bank examiner you'd be facing some serious time."

"Keep talking." Silky didn't care much for the look in the older woman's eyes. Sure the lady was tired, and perhaps a touch cranky, but behind all that she saw the glimmer of raw intelligence, the sort she had long ago learned to steer clear of when trying to shake down anyone. There wasn't any slack in the expression of the man next to her, either. Though he hadn't said a word yet, he looked sharp as a hawk. They sure don't make old geezers the way they used to. These weren't the sort of people she would normally tamper with.

"I'd guess that Vance Kilgore, call him Roy Dean Vanderhael if you like, was your partner earlier. . . ."

"Van," Silky interrupted.

"What?"

"His name was Van. I called him that. You can, too."

"Okay." The Walters lady faltered for a beat, but was soon back up to speed. "Anyway, the two of you tried to put the con on Tony Two Chins, only it didn't take. I'm guessing Roy Dean . . . sorry, Van made off with your share of that, but that you took a policy on him, one you're hoping to collect on. But I don't guess that's going to happen if his death stays ruled a suicide. So you came out to Fearing and tried to nudge the finding from suicide with those phony letters you left at the Kilgore house. I'll go farther and guess that the chubby fellow in the Town Car was your latest partner, and that you've skinned him, and almost got away with it."

"That's all some pretty tall guessing."

"Don't think it's just me who's onto you," the little round lady said. "There's an FBI agent around here, too, on the loose, and just because no one's seen him for a spell doesn't mean he's not still a factor. You figure an FBI agent's here one moment and gone the next, I figure he's just done something a leopard can't do and that is changed his spots. Man like that's got to have a nose that could fit on Mount Rushmore. He isn't going to drift far on a spicy mess like this. And he's not even the last card I need to play. There are the other two fellows, the ones who work for Tony Two Chins. Pretty nasty fellows, I hear. You're smack in the middle of all this, and if you have any hope of getting out of this at all it's me."

"Why should I trust you?"

"Because you're in a business where information is valuable, and you're in a town where you don't have near enough, but I do. I know the law in this county, and whether they like me or not doesn't matter so much as that I know which way they'll jump and why, given sufficient opportunity. Unless you have a helicopter in your hip pocket, young lady, there's no direction you can take out of this town that you can't get headed off at the pass—that's the dickens of being out in a small spot like this. The law isn't even the worst of your troubles. I know where those two thugs of Tony Two Chins are staying—right here in this very same motel where you've been staying. And I know where your chubby pal is staying, and where you can hide where he can't find you. I may be the only one who is motivated to, and can and will help you. I'm your brand-new close and personal best friend."

CHAPTER THIRTEEN

Adele sat alone listening to the rain drumming on the tin roofing of Boose's small, creaking wooden house when she heard the shot above the sound of the rain, and then the dogs began to bark even more hysterically from their kennel. She thought for a second of going to turn them loose. But they weren't her dogs, and she would feel awful if something happened to one of them, the way she worried about Boose. It had only been a few moments, but seemed like an hour since he had charged out there alone.

When she had brief moments to herself she reflected on what she had become, how men fit in her life. She hadn't meant to be dependent on them, and it made her upset with herself when she was even close to being so. All her life she had viewed herself as independent, above needing anyone to take care of her. At first with Vance—she still couldn't bring herself to think of him as Roy Dean Vanderhael—it had been the companionship. He had been a "best friend" and there wasn't much else besides that, except for living together and sharing a home, one with separate bedrooms. Boose was a whole other plate of beans. At first she had thought it was that he was such a rough-and-ready contrast to Vance that had drawn her to him. Still, had she just been wanting his protection? She hoped that wasn't all there was to it. When something as gruesome as what happened to Vance occurs in a small town like Fearing you begin to doubt your security in general. Protection can be a pretty attractive thing. Well, there wasn't all that much of it at the moment. He had shot out the door quickly enough, and now she was by herself with no one between her and the door.

It suddenly seemed a very small house, and a vulnerable one. There was the gun rack of rifles along one corner of the living room. But, responsible person that Boose was, he had put locks in the trigger guards of each, so they were useless to her. She did have the map he had drawn for her that showed the way to the road if she needed it. She hadn't thought she would. After five more minutes of waiting, she heard only the distant rumble of thunder and even more frantic barking from Boose's dogs. She slipped into Boose's rain jacket, the one he had been in too much of a rush to slip on, tucked her purse inside under one arm, grabbed a flashlight, and slipped out the door into the hammering rain.

It was almost impossible to see, and she couldn't know the way well through the maze of snares and traps even on a clear day. The "pencil on lined paper" map was soaked the second she sought to check it with her flashlight. She followed along, checked the damp paper from time to time and occasionally got startled half to death by one of the half dozen fake snakes Boose had put along the way. Even though she had seen him take them out of the boxes and put in the batteries, they still about made her jump out of her gizzards every time one rattled. That and the rain kept her mind occupied until she looked ahead on the trail and there in the middle of the path lay Boose. Next to him a man slid along through the mud. He pulled himself with his arms, one of which held a glittering stretch of steel. She stopped in the rain and stood still, hoping he hadn't seen her. His large head twisted until he looked up at her. His eyes weren't full of pain, though he dragged his legs, but those narrowed black eyes did show the glitter of determination even as he pulled himself the final few inches toward Boose. He laid the shining blade of the knife along the side of Boose's neck, and said to her, "Get a rope."

She stood still. Inside her head a short frantic list of options formed. She could maybe dodge around this fellow, though she wasn't sure she would miss any of the traps Boose had set, and didn't know the way out to the road and didn't trust the soggy map she clutched in one hand. She could dive for the gun that lay loose in Boose's unconscious hand. She could dash back to the house and lock the doors and hope the man couldn't follow, although it was almost certain he would kill Boose. She wasn't sure she would like having that hang over her head during any future days. Or, she could buy some time and get the man his damned rope.

Sensing her hesitation, the man lifted the knife tip and flicked it, taking off the lower tip of the lobe off Boose's nearest ear. Blood began to ooze out of the wound, and she stared at it as if she had been slapped. It was at that exact moment that she knew for absolute sure that these were the same men who had tortured Vance, the ones who had driven him to his death. The white heat of awareness rippled through her like lightning.

"Go. Now." The man's words were harsh whispers, but sounded like the crack of a whip.

Adele spun and started back toward the house.

After a frantic search of the house she thought to check the barn. Boose had a workshop bench along one wall, with a secretary's chair on wheels pulled up to its edge, which she nearly tripped over as she frantically searched for a rope hanging among the tools on a pegboard behind the bench. She was ready to give up, but knew she couldn't. Boose depended on her. She spun and cast the beam of her light into every corner and across every wall of the barn. There it was—a coil of fairly new, thick nylon rope hung on a peg beside the big sliding door, a rope Boose must have thought too new to use when he set his traps. She grabbed it and rushed back out into the rain, carrying the rope as she came back up the trail again.

At first she saw one man sprawled across the other. Then the man with the knife lifted his head and looked at her. The knife still rested against Boose's neck, though Boose's eyes were open now. The man had taken the gun Boose had held and had it in his other hand.

"Are you okay?" Adele ignored the man, bent closer and talked instead to Boose.

One of Boose's arms lifted slowly until his fingers touched the bleeding tip of his ear. "Well, damn. Now that's going to leave a mark. I guess this shoots my chance of ever wearing earrings."

"Shut up, the two of you," the man with the knife snapped.

Adele stood up and backed up a step.

"Tie it there." The man pointed with the gun to the trunk of a mid-sized scrub elm.

She did.

"Throw the other end there." He pointed.

Adele fed the line out until she came to the edge of the pit. She swept the light down into it and saw the man pointing a gun at her. She held the rest of the coil of rope over the edge and let it drop down the side. The man there shoved the gun into his belt and started to pull himself up the side of the muddy pit. He slipped a few times, his feet had a hard time gaining purchase, but he panted and cursed his way to the top, where he pulled the gun from his waist and aimed it at her.

Adele realized that she held her breath, expecting the worst. She waited for the blast of the gun and the shock of the pain. But the man just stood, breathed deeply and let the rain wash mud off him for a moment, then said, "Give me a hand getting him to the house."

"We take Boose, too," she said. She couldn't just leave him

out here to die. Everything he had done had been for her.

"No."

She straightened up. "Yes, or I don't help."

"You're in no position to bargain."

"Yes. Yes, I am."

He glared at her. Rain poured off his face while he thought. For the next whole minute Adele stood, wet and cold, and listened to the rain pour relentlessly. Her head lowered, her hair stringy and plastered to her forehead, and she watched the water collect on a single broad leaf until it bent and the rain poured off the pointed end, then the leaf sprang back up and began to collect again. "Okay," he finally said, "but we take Redbear here first."

The cell phone vibrated in his pocket again and Carson realized he hadn't switched it back to ring. Just as well.

"Where are you?" It was Tillis Macrory, the Texas Ranger.

"I'll be along. You've started fine without me. That's still a local matter and you're good to go with it."

"You sure? You're missing all the fun. Karl Williams, the funeral director, just tried to get a restraining order against us even though we have him locked up, same lawyer Torrence Furlong uses, too. If it wasn't for digging up all these bodies back here there would be some moments of high comedy. When that guy over in Georgia got nabbed for burying people instead of cremating them, most mortuaries took that as a message to clean up their acts. This Williams, apparently, took it as a suggestion on how he might trim expenses, probably figured no one would ever check up on an out-of-the-way place like this town. Then you know what this Williams says?"

"Not the foggiest."

"He says, 'It was only those folks from the rest home,' like that makes it all okay."

"That's all very interesting, Tillis. You stick to the trail."

"That's not like you. The sheriff stopped by to question that Melba Jean from the rest home to see what light she could shed. She acted too squirrely and gave him the silent treatment at first, but he took her in until he could get a warrant and search her place as well as the rest home. Then she starts singing like the whole Mormon Tabernacle Choir. Turns out she has all kinds of duplicate records at home. We just need a little time to straighten everything out, but it doesn't look like we're gonna get that. The media crews got wind of all this and they're on the way. It's going to be one helluva circus."

"I'm sure you can handle it all just fine," the agent said.

"What the hell are you up to on your end? Are you up to something else, something even bigger than this?"

"I'm just taking a short rest. I'll catch up with you in due time."

Carson clicked the cell phone off and slipped it into his pocket, listened to the rain pound on the car's top, then slipped the night-vision goggles back on and leaned forward so he could see past the thick brush he had backed his car into off the road. From here he could just make out the car parked by the road near Boose's mailbox. If he had had backup or if there had been more than one agent here he would have gone back in for a closer look. For now he sat and watched while the rain streaked the windshield and beat hard on the roof of the car.

"You broke the big rule of the con game, didn't you?" Esbeth said.

"Not for the first time," Silky muttered. She had been sulky and unsure since they had gotten her into the passenger seat.

"What's the big rule?" Gardner asked from the backseat.

"She didn't blow off the mark and forgot to put in the fix." Esbeth glanced over at Silky. "Did you?"

"I was never that good at this. I was going to get the insurance money and go clean."

"I'm sure you were," Esbeth said, but there was no conviction in her tone. "So all you needed was to ensure that Two Chins' couple of goons got fingered, or at least murder was the cause of Vanderhael's death?"

"Van. I said to call him Van," Silky said.

"Okay. Van. Is that the way it stands with his death?"

"Something like that. Look, do you two know what you're doing? I've told you what you haven't already figured out, so you know you're dealing with some serious characters here. None of us wants to wake up missing our nipples or a finger. I can't believe the cops ruled suicide."

"You poison someone and they jump off a bridge their death is still from the fall and drowning, and it's suicide," Gardner said from the backseat. His voice was low and rumbled in tune to the rain hammering the car as Esbeth drove. They passed a convenience store landmark and turned onto the road that led out to Boose's place. "I mean, technically everyone's death is caused by blood not getting to the brain, but there are numerous other causes that lead to that."

"But we can try to pitch Silky's case favorably, can't we, Gardner?" Esbeth said.

Gardner got her nudge. "Oh, yeah. Sure, if we can show enough to the right people, we might get those in official places to rule suspicious circumstances in the death."

Esbeth watched the road through the slanting lines of hard rain. All she needed was for a deer to dart out in front of them just now, though most of them were probably hunkered down against the storm.

"Why don't you sell me on this plan of yours again," Silky said.

Esbeth let out an exasperated sigh. She said, "We need

someone who knows the con to finish the job you bungled on your recent partner. If we can pull it off, he'll do as the fall guy. Someone has to be expendable in all this, you know, for it to work. I promised Boose I'd find whoever ripped off his momma. If you don't want your pal for it, we could use you just the same. The law out in these parts isn't all that fussy when it comes right down to it."

"I heard you clearly on that part earlier. That's why I'm here when I could, should be elsewhere."

"On the other front, if we can get the law looking hard at the two goons who roughed up Adele's Vance, I mean your Van, then you have a better chance of collecting that insurance."

"Not a perfect chance."

"But a better one, and you hopefully have contributed to getting them off the streets. They're a menace, and from what you say they'd as soon go for you since you still owe Two Chins. Right? What do you think?"

"I think I should have kept my mouth shut and just lit out for the border or something. That's what I think."

"Look. It's simple. You get rid of what your partner is after, and you get rid of him. You maybe collect the insurance, and we look the other way while you scat."

"But you're not speaking for the law, are you?"

"The law doesn't know everything I know at this point, and they don't have to. You show the right reluctance, and help reel in your partner and you're clear. What could go wrong?"

"Yeah, what?"

The Sheriff, the Texas Ranger, and a couple of the deputies were huddled together out in the open under a couple of oversized umbrellas, away from the trees that still dripped as hard as the rain fell. Zick Robin stumbled on a wet pile of dirt that was turning into mud and almost fell. He staggered back into a jog as he neared the men.

"Macrory. Sheriff Gonzalez. Can I get a statement from either of you?"

All the men looked up and stared at the reporter. "What are you doing out here? This is a roped-off crime scene," Chunk Philips, the deputy, snapped at him. Sheriff Johnny Gonzalez stared past his deputy's shoulder at Zick with that obsidian-eyed look of his that was neither hostile nor friendly.

"You fellows are out here, and I only stepped where you went."

"That don't give you no special right." Chunk moved out away from the others and had to stand in the rain to be between the reporter and his boss.

The scene around them was a circus. Halogen light stands had been set up and two backhoes dug away at the loose soil between the trees. Several of the exhumed coarsely buried bodies had been hauled away by EMS vehicles, which were in such shortage that three more body bags still waited in a row. State troopers and men in black "Crime Scene" jackets were thick in the scurry of men still finding new spots to dig.

Tillis Macrory stepped around Chunk and let the rain pour off his plastic-covered white hat while he faced the reporter. "Look, Zick. We've got every media crew within a drive of here already waiting over there to talk. We'll work up a press conference in the morning, but right now we have our hands full. Your paper's already been put to bed for the morning, so don't play that 'public needs to know' tune."

"It's just like that Esbeth Walters said, though, isn't it?" Zick said. "Are you going to be doing fresh autopsies on these bodies?"

"That'll be part of the morning press conference. You'll get it in the morning with everyone else. My suggestion to you is to try and find a motel room that isn't taken and bed down until then, where it's dry. Okay?"

"But you've locked up that rest home director, too. Tell me that has nothing to do with what Miss Walters was saying."

"That old coot. . . ." Chunk stopped himself, realized he had spoken out loud, and took on a more official tone. "This has been an ongoing investigation instigated by the Sheriff's department and any credit. . . ."

The sheriff stirred at last and stepped forward. He held out the flat of a hand toward his deputy, stopped whatever Chunk was going to say. He turned back to Zick, and kept his voice Texas friendly, "You just get some rest and let us sort all this out. Right now our heads aren't clear on all the details and no one's guilty of anything yet until we have more proof. You'll get what everyone else does at the press conference. Now, go on."

The reporter glanced around the circle of men nearest him, caught the stone face on the Texas Ranger and the sudden non-communicative look on Deputy Chunk Philips. He knew he had pushed this as far as he could, and had gotten more than he should have.

There was nothing for Zick to do but turn back and head toward the edge of the property. He spun and started off in that direction, already writing the opening sentence in his head. There were at least a dozen bodies so far, he knew from the count of the other media tracking the ambulance flow. Maybe he could put together something he might string to AP. He had an intern back at the paper digging up all she could on the Georgia crematorium case. If they could get some names of the bodies here they could start to check to see if there was a pattern to those from the rest home for systematically being just about to run out of Medicare. He suspected there would be. This was sure enough going to be a story to remember. That Esbeth had been spot-on after all. For just a second he wondered where she was right now. He jogged through the mud, careful not to slip and get even wetter than he already was.

CHAPTER FOURTEEN

Esbeth eased her car up to the roadside front of Boose's property as the rain trickled and drizzled to a stop. Her headlight beams swept over a car parked by the mailbox. Boose's truck would still be out back tucked away behind the barn. She turned off the wipers and the three of them stared at the car, at the rental sticker on the back bumper. "What do you think?" she asked Gardner.

"We could take off, but I doubt if we could stand ourselves later," he said. "I think we have to go back there. See if everyone's okay. You can't dial 911, either, just because a car you don't know is parked somewhere. Besides, I have more than half an idea where that Texas Ranger and most of the sheriff's men are anyway."

"Yeah, that's what I was afraid of. This is the car we saw two guys get into at the motel, isn't it?"

"I've seen it there, too," Silky said. "Is that the one Two Chins' two goons are using? If it is, I say we cut out, and right now. To hell with your damn noble instincts. What you ought to do, the common sense thing to do, is to get away, far away from here, and call the law, anonymously."

"I'd like to," Esbeth said. "But we can't just leave Adele and Boose back there with them, if it is. Remember what we talked about, Gardner."

"I hope this isn't about the sacrifice play we were discussing after chess."

"We don't have any choice," Esbeth said. "Besides, chances are if it is the two men they are in one or another of those traps Boose set."

"What traps?" Silky peered into the thick woods where in the dark water dripped down from the trees. "I wish this was up north where at least in October in Utah the leaves have the sense to fall off the trees so we could see anything."

"I doubt that would help, dark as it still is. Come on," Esbeth said. She reached to the glove box, got out her flashlight, then pushed open her door and got out.

Silky hesitated, while Gardner climbed out from the backseat. She looked up at Esbeth who had come around to the passenger side of her car. "Can't I just stay here?"

"I doubt that would do you much good. Now get your princess butt out of that car."

"You're either the bravest little old lady I ever met, or the most foolish."

"You can have your pick," Gardner said. "Depending on the day your odds are good in either direction."

"Well, depending on today for a sample I know how I'd bet," Silky said. She got out of the car and let Esbeth lock up behind them. "I have a bad feeling about this."

"I'd worry more about you if you had a good feeling," Gardner said.

Esbeth led the way with her flashlight beam. Silky pushed closer than she needed to as she came along behind her, and Gardner muttered low curses as wet limbs snatched at him with their stickers as he came along behind.

It was cold, and dark. As they got closer she could hear the dogs barking frantically, all from one place, so they were still in their kennel. Esbeth didn't know whether to take that for good or bad news.

The first time a motion detector sensed their presence and

one of the fake rattlesnakes popped up into a strike position Esbeth nearly had Silky climb right up her back.

"I guess I should have mentioned those. Don't worry. They're fake." But Esbeth could feel her own heart hammering away like the late great drummer Gene Krupa showing off. If she ever got out of this in one piece she made up her mind she was going to take about forty-seven naps in a row. Just see if she ever came out at night after ten p.m. again.

Her light swept back and forth along the same trail they had followed the first time. Muddy tracks had all but been obliterated by the rain and puddles that had formed. She saw signs that others had passed this way—the broken edges of bushes, a half a shoe print here and there, and even a small snatch of cloth on one low, thorny mesquite.

They came around a stand of the thickest of the chaparral and she saw the steel cage that lay across most of the path. She froze, swept the light around, but found no one pinned underneath it. Beneath the corner on one side of the huge trap a small ditch had been dug, but no one was stuck there. She let out a low sigh of relief.

"Stay right where you are," a man's low voice snapped. It sounded harsh and deep, and far closer to them than she liked. "I've got a gun pointed on the three of you. If you move, I won't hesitate to shoot."

"I hope you don't count shaking in place as moving," Gardner said.

"Shut up, the three of you, and stay shut." The man stepped out from behind the tree where he had waited. A rattlesnake rattled, but he ignored it. "If you're looking for a victim here you won't find it."

Esbeth could barely make the man out in the dark. She started to swing her flashlight up toward his face, and she saw enough to know he was a big man whose clothes were wet and still partially covered with mud before he snatched the light out of her hand. "Give me that. Now, come on. Start down this way and go where I tell you. I'll be right behind you."

They stumbled along with the only lights coming from the ones the man held, which made the going slow in the dark. Sometimes they had to stop until the man showed the way with one of the beams. All the while Esbeth worried about Boose and Adele. Were they already dead? The man pushed them on and didn't seem to have anything to lose at this point. The fact he didn't just shoot them where they stood gave her a ray of hope. She stumbled over a root that stretched across the path and muttered, "I don't think I'm getting shorter as the years go on, but the ground does seem like its getting higher all the time."

"I said shut up." No sympathy there.

They got to the house after what seemed like a half hour of careful weaving through the wet brush, and more than once Esbeth had opportunity to rue her sad comic suggestion to Boose to buy a few of the fake rattlesnakes.

At the door, the man said, "Go ahead and open it. Go on inside."

Esbeth was the first to the door, so she opened it, and blinked at the brighter lights inside. At first she thought she might be seeing things. They were led into the kitchen where the small dinette table had been returned. Boose sat in one of the captain's chairs, his hands behind him, and from here Esbeth could see silver duct tape around his ankles binding him to the chair. His shirt was off and white gauze covered his upper torso from the neck to the shoulder and dipped down to cover part of his wiry but firm hairy chest. The man who sat on a rolling chair that had once been an office typing chair Boose had used out at this workshop bench where he tinkered with fixing things had a leg wrapped in the same kind of tape. The shape of a couple of boards showed through the tape where a home-made splint had been applied to the leg. He was a thick-bodied, square-shaped man with a face that could have crawled off the flip side of a buffalo nickel, and he looked about as happy as you would expect from someone who had a recently broken leg when there were no pain killers handy.

"Glad you're back," Adele said to the man who had brought Esbeth and the others to the house. "I've had the devil's own time keeping your friend Redbear here away from Boose with that knife. If he hadn't been slowed down by that game leg and I hadn't had to play Florence Nightingale, Boose would have had a hot time of it."

The man with the gun trained on the others shrugged. "Do up these others," he said.

Adele sighed and waved the way over to the three remaining captain's chairs at the kitchen's small dining area. "This way folks."

As she bent over Esbeth and she fastened her wrists to the chair with the spool of duct tape, she whispered fast and low, "He threw all Boose's other guns in the pit when Boose wouldn't tell him where the keys were. Hang in there."

Esbeth looked at Boose, who had a couple of bruises on his face, cheekbone on one side and forehead on the other. She imagined the man with the gun had done that. The other looked too eager to get out his knife, which explained the white tape on one of Boose's ears that seemed smaller now. He looked her way and winked, but she didn't feel so chipper herself. Gardner was giving her the "What have you gotten us into?" look, and Silky wouldn't look her way at all as Adele taped them each to their chairs.

The man who had brought them to the house was going through Silky's purse. Why she had even brought it along, Esbeth didn't know until the man pulled out a thick wad of bills.

There had to be a couple or three thousand there.

"Well, that's more like. First time this whole mess has started to pay for itself." Then he paused, pulled out a soft leather pouch and looked inside. "What do we have here? Security deposit box keys?" He looked at Silky.

"They won't do you any good. They're not mine. I couldn't open the boxes, either."

Redbear spoke for the first time, and Esbeth wished he hadn't. He sounded like a large cat coughing up a hairball. "Unicorn place, Mook?"

Esbeth didn't like it at all that they felt no reluctance to use each other's names. That was a bad sign.

"No. Not right now."

Redbear tried to push himself across the floor with his good leg to where Silky was bound to her chair. One hand reached down toward his knife sheath and had it out of its sheath so fast Esbeth could barely blink.

"I said no," Adele snapped. She reached to the table and picked up an eight-inch iron skillet blackened by much use she apparently had used to keep Redbear away from Boose earlier. She stood between Redbear and Silky. The Indian stopped, and frowned, and spun to the chair where Boose was tied. He gave a quick flick of his hand to the ear not already wearing white tape that was turning pink. The lobe flew off so fast Esbeth couldn't believe what she had just witnessed. Blood began to well and drip from the shortened ear.

Adele's action was almost as fast. She swung the frying pan and hit Redbear's hand, sending his knife skittering across the floor. She slipped to stand between Boose and the Indian, who pushed with one foot to roll toward where the knife had landed.

"No means no," Adele said, her face as close to a snarl as Esbeth had ever seen.

"I do like the cut of your jib," Mook said. One eyebrow had

lifted a bit. "All the years I been around him I haven't been able to control him half so good."

Redbear shifted his frown to Mook while he leaned down to pick up the knife. But he didn't try to get past Adele, and instead checked the edge on his blade, then slid the knife back into its sheath.

"You okay?" Adele asked Boose over her shoulder, not taking her eyes off Redbear.

"Yeah, I was gonna have to even up that ear anyhow to match the other one. This just saves me the bother."

Silky glared at Esbeth. "Gosh, I'm glad I listened to you. You're right on top of this situation."

Mook's free hand swung in a loud slap across Silky's cheek, which blushed bright pink as soon as her head had swayed back to stare hard at Mook.

Esbeth had a picture of these men in her head she didn't like, them working over the late Van, one with a knife, the other with the rough stuff as they sought information. These weren't the sort of men you fool around with.

Adele took a few seconds to pinch a piece of silver duct tape on Boose's freshly cut ear. Going to get the first aid kit would have given Redbear another chance to get near Boose.

"Yet another thing duct tape can fix," Boose said cheerfully. The others ignored him. Blood seeped to the corner of the duct tape and dripped to the floor, slow, one solitary drop at a time.

"She's right about the keys," Esbeth said. "They don't belong to her. No bank would let her waltz in and open the boxes. She'd need the owner along for that."

Mook's head swung like a fox in the hen house and his eyes narrowed at Esbeth.

"We can tell you where to find the man, too," Esbeth said. Normally she would have never put another human being in harm's way if she could at all help it. All Esbeth was after now was time, just a few more breaths of it. She had a shimmering idea for the first time of why those folks in the rest home don't just roll over and pass along, but stay grasping at each moment left in their lives with such persistence even when each day is no longer one spent at the beach.

"Don't tell him, Esbeth. They'll just kill us." Silky strained and struggled against the tape that held her to her chair.

Gardner watched Esbeth with a look that could be fascination or could as well be astonishment at her giving in so readily. Boose's head moved back and forth from the speakers with the interest he would give a mediocre Ping-Pong match. The only time he showed anything was when he glanced at Adele, and Esbeth did not know what to make of that look. He might want either to kiss her or bite her.

Esbeth looked up to find Mook standing over her. His clothes were crusted in mud, and he should have been uncomfortable, but that looked like the last thing on his mind. Redbear's clothes didn't look any better, and he had the one leg in a splint. The two of them had been through the mill. Their eyes were bloodshot, from anger or being up this late, and neither looked liked he had been all that rational in the first place.

Mook turned back to Silky. "Where is he? The one who these keys belong to."

"I don't know. That's one of the only reasons I was tagging along with the likes of these two. They know where he is, and he's the only one able to open those boxes."

Hmmm. Esbeth mulled that over. One minute Silky doesn't want her to tell, the next she prods Mook right at her. That is one manipulative broad. Esbeth didn't have long with her thoughts. Mook was back and towered over her.

"The Hampton Inn," she said. There was no use dragging it out. "I don't know what name he's using. Almost certainly not his own, though Silky there says it's James Calloway. But he's driving a Lincoln Town Car. I know that much."

Redbear looked eager for the first time, even with Adele still near him with her skillet.

"We don't have time for any of that. We'd better bring one with us, the one most likely to do us some good." He pointed to Silky. "And I think you're it."

"No. Take me." Adele surprised them all. "I'm the only one strong enough to help get Redbear to the car, and taking me will keep the others from going to the law. Besides, the law can have her if they need it. That's all any of the others wanted."

Mook stood over Esbeth. "Tell me why I shouldn't just kill you all right now."

Esbeth said, "For one, if this turns into a dead end for you we're the only place you have to start over."

For a minute he tilted his head and seemed to think. "Nope. It's not enough."

"Keep an eye on all of them," he told Redbear. "And you keep an eye on Redbear," he said to Adele. He shoved his gun into his belt and went out of the house the back way. There was a tense five-minute wait before he returned with two cans of gas and some other odds and ends he had rounded up out in the barn.

He placed a can of gas on either side of Boose's microwave and began mixing the other ingredients. Esbeth watched him pour some of the gasoline into a clear Mason jar, then use a knife to open a handful of shotgun shells he had gotten from Boose's supplies that still remained, even though they had tossed the guns out. He put a single small nail into a wad of paraffin he took off a jar of preserves and folded the waxy stuff tight around the nail.

Gardner glanced Esbeth's way. She knew he had to know what it took to make a bomb, and he just nodded in a farewell sort of way—that "it's been swell knowing you" sort of nod Esbeth would just as soon have not received, not only because it spoke of an emotion with which she wasn't ready to deal, but because it meant the end, not a dress rehearsal, the end.

Mook finished and slipped the jar inside the microwave and twisted the dial. "Let's get out of here. Cheap ass microwave's only giving us fifteen minutes."

They rolled Redbear out of the kitchen toward the front door, and as she slipped out of sight Esbeth caught Adele's glance toward Boose. The ticking grind of the microwave's clock was the only sound in the kitchen. She didn't know what to make of Adele, but at the second it didn't matter a whole hell of a lot.

James Calloway had had a bad evening all around. A sour taste hung in his mouth he had not been able to brush away and he woke from the restless sort of anxiety dream he had not experienced for years, of going to buy something and reaching in his pocket to find nothing, no money at all. It was worse than the dream of being naked on a bus, or of falling, or of the need to get to an urgent appointment and being lost. He woke, tried to turn and go back to sleep, then realized he needed to take a trip to the bathroom. He kicked off the sheet and bedcovers and sat on the side of the bed for a moment.

First there had been dinner, where he found that the Flamingo's Smile's ownership had changed hands. That led to both a fish entrée that had been underdone—snapper with a pecan crust—and his irritation at incompetence. In a rare departure from gin, he had tried a half bottle of wine, a Cabernet Sauvignon that had been tannic when poured and lifeless once it had aired. On the way back the only classical station he could get on the car radio had been having a night of PDQ Bach, one of those irritating ironies in life. Only those with enough musical background to understand great music could get the dry humor and musical jokes of that damned Peter

Schickele, but that still did not make it good classical music in his opinion. All of that had only pointed out to him how petty he had become, that there was a more pressing crisis. Then he had been checking the motels for Silky when he had had to cut and run. Everything conspired to thwart and enrage him until he got his hands on Silky and those keys. Still, he had a good idea where she was staying now, but he needed to wait until morning to try again. He could go and try in the middle of the night, though he still did not know which room.

Stepping into his slippers he was halfway to the bathroom when the phone rang. He glanced at his Patek Philippe watch face. Three a.m. Now who in the devil could that be? On top of everything else he had half a mind not to answer. But he went across the room and picked up the receiver. It was the night desk clerk.

"My car is being towed?" Calloway shouted.

"I only know what the rental company said, that they were sending a truck over to tow away a Lincoln Town Car, and yours is the only one I know of in the lot." The night clerk's voice was low, careful at this hour to not wake so much as the mouse in the next room.

"But why?"

"I have no idea. That's for you to straighten out with your rental company. I'm just letting you know as a courtesy, that's all. I apologize for the late hour of the call."

Calloway slammed the receiver back onto its hook not caring if he woke anyone else or not. He went over and pulled open the drape. Damn. He had gotten a room on the lake side. As a result he could not see the parking lot. He went and used the bathroom, ran a brush through his hair, and flipped on the lights as he went back into the room. He pulled on his clothes. Three a.m. for cripe's sake. At least it looked like the damn rain had stopped out there, so he did not grab the umbrella that was

still open and drying beside the door as he rushed out into the hallway. But he did think to grab the Glock .9mm and his fake FBI identification. He did not know what to expect, but it was best to be prepared.

Downstairs he slipped out the side door so he would not have to deal with any sympathetic looks from the damned night clerk. The parking lot was slick with puddles from the recent deluge that had finally stopped, but he had to trek across the entire lot to get to the car. Leave it to him to park as far from the motel as possible, though he had always done so since having to skip out a time or two in the night just ahead of an enraged mark who had seen through a scam too soon.

When he got to the car no one was around. He had the car keys in his hand. Maybe if he just drove it off the lot and left it down the street, maybe in some alley behind one of the downtown stores, he could straighten out the whole mess in the morning. There shouldn't be a problem. He had left a cash deposit. As he reached for the car's door a man in a dark blue rain jacket slipped out from behind a pickup truck parked three spaces away and walked toward him with a gun pointed at his stomach.

"Where you think you're going, fat boy?"

Calloway played through a dozen responses he could use under normal circumstances, ranging from outrage to trying to work something out. The gun threw all that out the window. He stood and waited, feeling sick bile rise up in his throat.

Each step plodded after the other, slower each time until the gun poked into the soft flesh covering his back ribs. A hand patted him down and took away his gun and the badge holder.

"Are you sure you want to mess with a federal agent?" Calloway tried.

"You're as much an agent as I'm a hootchy-coo dancer. Now, get moving. Over there."

The man nudged him toward a car. As they got closer a couple of heads popped up. Neither of them looked happy to see him.

Carson Billings stared through the night-vision goggles. He had his window open. The rain had stopped except for sporadic drops falling from soaked tree limbs onto the roof of the car. He hadn't seen a thing since the car with Esbeth, Gardner, and Silky Baron had pulled up. If they had stayed a moment longer at the car he would have gone over and tried to find out what they were up to. But they had shot off into the thick of the woods where the cast of characters was getting more interesting by the moment.

He was torn about what to do. Out on his own like this he was supposed to stay in the car, be there if anything happened. It was hard to tell what was or wasn't happening. He gave it only another minute before he reached for his trench coat from the backseat and took out his pocket penlight. He sure enough couldn't see anything sitting out here. He eased the door open and pressed it slowly closed before heading down the road toward the mailbox and cars that marked the beginning of the path into the woods.

The steps the others had taken wove through the thick growth, pointed out the way. He wondered why their steps wove all over the damn place until he tried to step off their tracks and spotted his first trip wire, about the same time one of the rattlesnakes popped up and rattled at him. Common sense said a snake wouldn't be active on a cool, rainy night, but he nearly had to head back for fresh underwear the first time one rattled.

He backed away from the trip wire and stayed on the trail, making slow time, bent forward as he was following the needle of light through the wet, sticker-covered brush when he heard voices. They were coming his way. Well, damn.

He crawdadded back up the trail as fast as he could without making noise, and heard a man's voice and that of a woman head toward him. As soon as he got to the road he sprinted over to his car, got inside, and tugged on the night-vision goggles. A man and woman came out of the woods with another man between them who they helped. Well, well. There was the missing Adele Kilgore, and she was helping Mook Jackson ease Fred Redbear into the backseat. Now, wasn't that cozy, even if it did not make a great deal of sense. Mook had been carrying some sort of secretary's chair under one arm and he popped that into the trunk.

When they were inside and the car took off Carson had another decision to make—check the house or follow them and see what they were up to. He didn't have to wrestle with that one long. As soon as the car was out of sight he fired up his car, but left the lights off and slipped the night-vision goggles back on.

He had driven using night-vision goggles this way before, as practice. It took concentration to keep the taillights ahead in sight at this pace. There was no moon nor were there stars because of the thick cloud cover, so he had to strain to catch every curve of the wet road. More than once he heard and felt the crunch of gravel beneath the tires on one side or another. All he needed now was the headlights of a vehicle coming the other direction to blind him for sure, but they had the road to themselves until they came into the night glow of the sleeping small town of Fearing.

He slipped the goggles off and stayed back, flipped on his lights only when he was far enough away he wouldn't attract attention. There wasn't much traffic. A solitary car here and there eased out of one street and turned down another. The car pulled into a convenience store just long enough for Mook to make a quick call at one of three outdoor pay phones. Carson went around the block and waited far enough down a side street to see the car as Mook got in and it pulled away.

A pickup truck eased out of the 24-hour convenience store. Far down the street a patrol car turned off onto a side street in its plodding vigil. Tillis Macrory had cautioned him about the local police, that there were one or two good ones, but the rest had not graduated at the top of their police academy classes, if they had gone at all. Tillis had witnessed one of them stop an elderly man who walked along a street and take away his cane because the cop said it was too heavy and could be a weapon. Before the policeman had walked away from the bewildered older gentleman he had asked if he had any more weapons. It was that dazzling display of police work that had made Tillis wonder out loud if Fearing's finest ought to be allowed to carry guns.

The car he followed slowed as it wound down a side street and got nearer to the lake. Carson slowed as well, pulled over and waited while the car turned into the parking lot of the Hampton Inn. How was that for coincidence? If Carson wanted to he could go on inside where he had a room. But the evening had just started to get interesting.

The car pulled up a few spaces away from the Lincoln Town Car Carson had seen pass by the Kilgore residence earlier. He sunk lower in his seat while the car settled into place. Then he sat upright and put the night-vision goggles back on. The Town Car's driver had been the least known commodity for Carson. He knew what Silky Baron wanted, the insurance million. He had Tony Two Chins' two goons figured as well. But the Town Car driver had been a new player, which is why he had sent off that digital copy of the photo he had taken to Virginia while he changed into dry clothes earlier. Carson had a name to go with the face now after getting an E-mail back. The Bu files on James Calloway sketched him as a con man, but there had never been enough to hang a case on him, though he sure seemed to be in the middle of something now.

At the car, one of the men got out, Mook Jackson. He headed toward a pickup truck near the Lincoln Town Car and crouched low behind it. Billings swung the goggles back toward the now silent car. The other two were in the backseat. It made an interesting combination.

In less than five minutes a short, round profile scurried across the parking lot between the rows of cars with mad, quick steps across the damp asphalt, right through puddles in a beeline toward the Town Car. Well, well. Jimmy Calloway, himself, all fluffed up and as mad as a wet hen.

Calloway had barely gotten to the car when Mook came out from behind the pickup truck. He pointed a gun at the con man, and used it to head him into the backseat. Adele slid over so she was next to Redbear and between him and Calloway, all three in the backseat. That looked even more cozy. Then the car pulled out of the parking lot and headed out the street that led to the highway.

To keep close in the early going, Carson didn't turn on his headlights, and left the night-vision goggles on so he could see where they were headed. The streetlights and the goggles lit the wet streets enough for him to see to steer by. They had barely gone three blocks when lights blasted white hot in his rearview mirror and red and blue swirls lit up the street around him. He yanked off the goggles and blinked. A police car had pulled up close behind him. He thought of making a dash for it, but that would just tip off Mook and the others. He pulled over and gave the policeman time to get out and come up to his car, one hand on his pistol and the other flashing a light right into Carson's eyes before the light swung to the FBI credentials he was holding out.

The policeman looked about sixteen years old and was five

foot five, maybe five foot six. Carson wanted to pound the steering wheel, or yell at the young man. But it would have all been a waste.

"Oh," the cop said. "Hope I didn't mess up anything."

Carson looked ahead, but he couldn't see the car he had been following anywhere.

CHAPTER FIFTEEN

"We have at least fifteen minutes to collect our thoughts in our final minutes, don't we?" Esbeth couldn't help staring at the darkened small window of the ticking microwave.

"No," Gardner said. "That thing could go off at any second. Don't count on what you might have seen in movies. Why do you think the three of them hustled out of here the way they did? Well, I suppose we should be glad for the chance to get off our feet after all we've been through this evening."

Esbeth snapped at him. "Can you please stop looking for the half-full glass for a ding-dong minute? We're in serious do-do here. It's okay to panic for a change. Shout a bit in anger if you'd like."

"What good would that do?"

"It'd help me know you're human," she grumped. Her glance toward Silky Baron caught beads of sweat forming on that smooth forehead as she stared in fixed horror at the microwave.

"You might could spin one of those yarns of yours, Gardner, about perception fixing to outweigh what's real," Boose muttered. He struggled with the bonds that held his wrists behind him.

"Boose Hargate, now don't you go getting him going on that at this of all times."

"You know, Esbeth, we may not have a lot of time left here," Gardner's voice was low and full of a warmth Esbeth found chilling somehow. "There's something I'd like to say to you."

"I'd hold onto that thought if I was you," Boose said. He shook his hands free from behind him and reached down to start a tear in each stretch of silver tape holding his legs to the chair. "You're liable to slip on a pair of pants you'll have to wear for a spell."

Boose tugged off the final bit of tape and rushed across the room and yanked open the door of the microwave with his head turned away from it.

Nothing blew.

He cautiously lifted the gasoline cans off the counter and lowered them to the floor, then reached inside and picked up the jar. He held it at arm's length as he scurried to the back door, opened it, and threw the jar out into the damp woods.

Esbeth realized she had stopped breathing. Her head started to spin, so she sucked in a big gulp of air. Boose came back in and grabbed the kitchen paring knife off the counter that Mook had used to open the shotgun shells. He rushed over, cut the tape that bound Gardner's wrists and handed him the knife.

"How did you manage that, Boose? Did Adele cut the tape on your wrists?" Esbeth said. Gardner got his legs free and went over to cut Esbeth's bonds.

"No. But I figured if that Vance fella got himself clear then I could. I dint wanna believe I couldn't do as well or better'n that lightweight."

"His name is Van," Silky shouted. It was the first thing she had said in quite a while, and her mouth snapped shut again this time as soon as she had said it.

Boose ignored her and dashed through the room into his bedroom. He came out carrying a fairly new ax handle. He had slipped on a white T-shirt over his bandaged chest.

"You keep that in your bedroom?" Gardner asked, and nodded at the piece of oak Boose carried. He knelt beside Esbeth's chair to cut her free.

"It ain't no marital aid device, if that's what you're thinkin'. Don't take no batteries neither. Since they throwed out my guns it's all I got." He moved briskly across the room.

"Boose, let us call someone," Esbeth said.

"With what?" Gardner said. "We watched them cut the phone lines."

"You've been shot," Esbeth reminded Boose.

"Yeah, I'm hurt a bit. But I ain't near crippled enough, though." He gripped the ax handle tight and shot out the back door with a bang.

"Do you think he's off to a rescue?" Gardner asked Esbeth.

"Something like that," she muttered. She rubbed her wrists to get the adhesive off.

Gardner moved over to cut Silky's duct-tape bindings.

"I've had just about all of this I care to experience," Silky said. "If you two could just take me to my car I think I'm done with this little part of the world for good."

"It remains to be seen if it's done with you, though," Gardner said.

Esbeth looked around the counters and in the kitchen drawers. There was just the one flashlight from her car the others had left behind. She looked up from a drawer that had a couple of packs of batteries but not another flashlight and saw Silky's eyes dart around the room and take in every detail. There was a woman whose mind was always on the go. Silky went over to her open purse from which the men had taken the cash and the deposit keys.

"Is that it?" Gardner said.

"It'll have to do. If we stick close together we should be able to make it out to the car."

"Are you sure you still have your keys?" Silky asked. She slipped her long purse strap over her shoulder and came over to the two of them. The alert glitter in her eyes should have tipped

Esbeth off, but didn't, tired as she was.

"Sure, they're right. . . ." Esbeth had hardly gotten them out of the tight pocket of her jeans when they were snatched from her fingers. Silky shoved Gardner to one side and ran to the front door. She shot out it and off into the night by the time Esbeth and Gardner got into the living room.

Gardner ran across the room and looked out the open front door. He panted, even after such a short sprint. "There are sure a lot of things," he gasped, "I don't like about getting old, and being slower than just about anyone who's younger is one of them."

Esbeth was about as tired as she ever recalled being, and now she felt even more so knowing they were probably trapped at the house. There wasn't even much comfort from the place having not blown up or burned down. She felt as hollow and as rattled inside as a worn set of painted gourd maracas from a not particularly good mariachi band. If it was up to her she would lay right down on the hardwood floor here and go to sleep. But there was still a lot to do.

"You clasp a snake to your bosom it's best not to believe you made it a loyal friend," Gardner said.

Esbeth sighed. She didn't have the strength to roll her eyes, so she turned and checked all the rooms for another flashlight. Tired as she was she didn't quit until she found a 12-volt hand lantern out at Boose's workbench in the barn.

Together they started up the winding trail through the maze of traps Boose had set, several times slowing to make sure they were on safe ground. Each time one of the rattlesnakes reared up to bare its fangs and rattle at them Esbeth cursed her own lousy sense of the comedic for having suggested that Boose get the damned things. The bushes where wet and full of stickers, and drops of cold water fell on them from the still-dripping trees. In time they pushed out of the woods beside Boose's mailbox, and Esbeth was startled to see that her car still sat there. Before they had time to go and see if the keys were in it, headlights turned the corner and nearly blinded them as a car pulled up.

A door opened and she heard Tillis Macrory's voice. "Well, don't you two look like something that's been rolled sideways down a wet hill. I wondered why you didn't show to bask in the moment back there." He had his gun out and down at his side, as did Carson Billings, the FBI agent who had slid out the driver's side door by now.

"Anyone still back at the house?"

"Those two fellows, Jackson and Redbear, took off with Adele some time ago," Esbeth said. "Boose hightailed it after them not too much later. It's just us, though we seem to have lost that Silky Baron somewhere between here and the house. She got the jump on us, but we ended up making it to my car first, though she has the keys."

"Any idea where Mook and that crew went?" Carson asked, sliding his gun back into its holster.

"No," Gardner said.

"Yes," Esbeth said.

Gardner's wide-open eyes swung to her.

"You know the old Sutton place out off the highway that heads to Austin? Has a unicorn on the stone gate." She looked at Tillis.

"Yeah."

"I think that's where they must have worked over Kilgore, where they may head if they get their hands on that Calloway fellow."

"They have him, sure enough," the agent said. "You'd better call the sheriff and have him send men over there. It is in the county, isn't it?"

"Yeah, but we're closer than he or any of his men are just

now. They're all across town at the funeral parlor grounds still."

"Then we'd better roll, though I wonder if we're doing the world good or harm saving the likes of a con artist like that. Speaking of which, where exactly is Silky Baron? I had her figured for Calloway's partner."

"Like I said, we were wondering that ourselves."

"Give me a minute." Tillis reached for Esbeth's light.

"I'd better go with you. There're booby traps and fake rattlesnakes like mice in there. It'll go quicker if someone knows the way. Trust me."

Tillis looked to Gardner who nodded a confirmation.

"I'd better go," Carson said to Tillis, "while you get some of the sheriff's men headed to the right place." He turned to Esbeth and said, "Lead the way."

Once more Esbeth slogged through the woods, dragging feet that might as well have been made of lead.

At the first rattlesnake to pop up and threaten them, the agent paused, and when Esbeth stopped and looked back at him he said, "Somehow I knew you weren't kidding, but the first one is always a jolt."

They stepped around the large steel cage that had fallen across the path when Esbeth heard a soft, "Hey. Over here."

"Watch your step," Esbeth suggested, and led Carson off the trail to where a rope was tied to a tree on one end and coiled in a white lump on the ground. Esbeth held out a hand to keep Carson from stepping further. Her light beam swept down the wet mud wall of the deep pit and stopped when it spotlighted Silky Baron, whose normal suave bearing was diminished somewhat by the mud that covered most of her, and by the rifle she pointed up at Esbeth and Carson.

"Throw a rope down here," she snarled.

The agent yanked his gun out and his trigger hand was squeezing tight when Esbeth snapped up a hand to stop him.

"I don't think so," Esbeth said, "unless you think you can throw that at us from there." Silky had not been able to put her finger through the trigger guard because of the lock Boose had put there.

The FBI agent still had his gun out, but Esbeth glanced his way and told him, "Oh, you won't need that."

"We'd better get her out and take her with us."

"Why? She'll keep just fine right where she is until you can come back and get her. We have more pressing business, don't we?"

The agent holstered his gun. "I guess we do."

"Redbear. Remember, we gotta turn this car in. So let's ax Mr. Calloway our questions when we get there. You got it?"

This was one of the tensest, if not longest rides Adele had ever been on. To Adele's left the Indian stared across her at the con man. One hand rested on the sheath of his knife. From her right the cold smell of raw fear wafted past the light manly cologne Calloway wore. The way his eyes darted to the window made her certain he weighed his chances of opening and rolling out the door, even though they were going seventy miles an hour.

The sky grew lighter to the east, but there didn't look to be much hope the sun would make it out today. What Adele could see of the world as they whooshed up the highway was dreary and damp, like some swamp in the process of being drained.

"What's this about?" If Calloway tried for a calm, controlled tone he missed it by a mouse-squeak mile. Still, he had been a con man all his life and had to believe he could talk his way out of anything, and he had to know that the minute he showed any weakness he was through. He would act as calm as he could and hope for a chance to get clear. He avoided looking in Red-bear's direction since the man glared in a fierce, hungry way at

219

him, and even the frying pan Adele still clutched might not be enough to stop him.

Adele had a hard time taking her eyes off Calloway. He was a real piece of work. At first he had been all bluster and swagger, once put in the car at gunpoint he had gone mouse or rabbit. Watching him was like flipping though the channels of a television. He seemed to be deciding what to be next, what would work best. Years of manipulating people hadn't taught him the right approach to a situation like this. She watched as the rabbit-like twitching and furtive look evolved into one of confidence and indignation. So that's the way he was going to play it. Bad choice, she thought, but said nothing.

In one way, she could relate to Calloway's desperate nothing-to-lose recklessness. Back at Boose's place it had been one thing for her to volunteer to replace Silky. The others were all dead now. So it hadn't been the worst choice. But she was far from in a perfect situation herself. These were two cold killers, and even though she had patched up Redbear he showed no appreciation or intention to return any favors. These were very bad men. She could feel Calloway quiver beside her, even as he sought to act and sound calm, confident.

"If you agree to open some safety deposit boxes for us, we have no issues whatsoever," Mook said without a glance back.

"I don't even know what you're talking about, so that's not very bloody likely."

Adele could feel Calloway shake even harder as he said it, as if he had shifted up a gear. He may be smooth as they come, but he would never pass a lie detector test. It didn't look like he passed with Mook, either, and Redbear grinned now and stroked the leather of his knife sheath.

This didn't look good for Calloway, whose fine clothes and round figure spoke of a life of spoiling himself. It was all about to take an ugly turn for him. There was no way he could win.

him, and even the frying pan Adele still clutched might not be enough to stop him.

Adele had a hard time taking her eyes off Calloway. He was a real piece of work. At first he had been all bluster and swagger, once put in the car at gunpoint he had gone mouse or rabbit. Watching him was like flipping though the channels of a television. He seemed to be deciding what to be next, what would work best. Years of manipulating people hadn't taught him the right approach to a situation like this. She watched as the rabbit-like twitching and furtive look evolved into one of confidence and indignation. So that's the way he was going to play it. Bad choice, she thought, but said nothing.

In one way, she could relate to Calloway's desperate nothing-to-lose recklessness. Back at Boose's place it had been one thing for her to volunteer to replace Silky. The others were all dead now. So it hadn't been the worst choice. But she was far from in a perfect situation herself. These were two cold killers, and even though she had patched up Redbear he showed no appreciation or intention to return any favors. These were very bad men. She could feel Calloway quiver beside her, even as he sought to act and sound calm, confident.

"If you agree to open some safety deposit boxes for us, we have no issues whatsoever," Mook said without a glance back.

"I don't even know what you're talking about, so that's not very bloody likely."

Adele could feel Calloway shake even harder as he said it, as if he had shifted up a gear. He may be smooth as they come, but he would never pass a lie detector test. It didn't look like he passed with Mook, either, and Redbear grinned now and stroked the leather of his knife sheath.

This didn't look good for Calloway, whose fine clothes and round figure spoke of a life of spoiling himself. It was all about to take an ugly turn for him. There was no way he could win.

"I don't think so," Esbeth said, "unless you think you can throw that at us from there." Silky had not been able to put her finger through the trigger guard because of the lock Boose had put there.

The FBI agent still had his gun out, but Esbeth glanced his way and told him, "Oh, you won't need that."

"We'd better get her out and take her with us."

"Why? She'll keep just fine right where she is until you can come back and get her. We have more pressing business, don't we?"

The agent holstered his gun. "I guess we do."

"Redbear. Remember, we gotta turn this car in. So let's ax Mr. Calloway our questions when we get there. You got it?"

This was one of the tensest, if not longest rides Adele had ever been on. To Adele's left the Indian stared across her at the con man. One hand rested on the sheath of his knife. From her right the cold smell of raw fear wafted past the light manly cologne Calloway wore. The way his eyes darted to the window made her certain he weighed his chances of opening and rolling out the door, even though they were going seventy miles an hour.

The sky grew lighter to the east, but there didn't look to be much hope the sun would make it out today. What Adele could see of the world as they whooshed up the highway was dreary and damp, like some swamp in the process of being drained.

"What's this about?" If Calloway tried for a calm, controlled tone he missed it by a mouse-squeak mile. Still, he had been a con man all his life and had to believe he could talk his way out of anything, and he had to know that the minute he showed any weakness he was through. He would act as calm as he could and hope for a chance to get clear. He avoided looking in Redbear's direction since the man glared in a fierce, hungry way at

Either way they would probably kill him. The only satisfaction he might get was by not cooperating, but he would be just as dead in the end. She didn't much care for her own chances now, either. She would be extra baggage too, and real soon.

Mook turned off the highway and passed through a yellowed rock arch that had a unicorn's head sticking out. Almost every ranch had some kind of grand gate, a few of the newer ones had solar-powered electric barred gates. This one had no inner iron bar grating and had been let run down over the years. The long lane back took a right curve to wind around behind a half-crumbled old house that showed three different kinds of stone to its various stages that had been built years apart. The lane gave out at a flat, scorched area where once there must have been a wooden barn or some other structure that had not lasted as long as the house.

As soon as the car stopped Calloway's door flew open and he made a dash for it. Mook was out his door at the same time and Calloway had tucked in far too many crème brûlées to ever aspire to be a marathon runner at this point in his life. As Adele got out, Mook dragged Calloway back toward the house, and Calloway whimpered and pleaded.

"Get that roll of tape we brought," Mook said to her. When she hesitated, he said, "Take it easy. Just do it."

It was on the front seat. Redbear sat in the backseat waiting to be helped onto the rolling chair they had tucked into the trunk. She glanced his way, and wished she hadn't. He winked at her.

Ice surged in excited charges up and down her veins as she took the roll of tape over to Mook and handed it to him, careful to avoid looking directly at Calloway, who sobbed. Her eyes were drawn instead to a wooden set of steps that led up over a low stone wall in what would have been the house's backyard. Bits of silver tape showed on the ladder, at the same strategic spots where Mook was binding Calloway into place. Now she did look at Calloway's face and found it flushed red and wet. He kept trying to blink his eyes open but they snapped closed again as if on their own. The thing that hit Adele like a punch in the stomach was that this was the exact spot where these men had tied up her own husband, Vance, where they had tortured him. What kind of man brings you to the place where they tortured and cut on your husband in a way that led to his death and then tells you to "Take it easy"?

Her knees nearly buckled. With everything in her she forced herself to stay upright. She began to look around for a stick, a rock, anything, a weapon of any kind. She kept her breath steady as she looked around. If she ran, where to? There was no place she could go they could not catch her, at least Mook. Over by those trees along the creek? No.

"Give me a hand with Redbear," Mook said.

Calloway was stretched in an uncomfortable lean, and he twisted hard against the tape but got nowhere. They went over to the car and got the rolling chair out of the trunk. As soon as he was on it, Redbear began pushing with his good leg. He had his knife out of its sheath.

"Now, remember, Fred." Mook leaned and helped push the chair toward where Calloway was stretched in the growing light. "We need information first. Okay? Just tease him a bit." He took a pair of plastic surgical gloves out of one pocket and handed another set to Redbear. They both slipped them on. The stark white of their hands seemed even more menacing.

Adele couldn't move. Now, her head screamed. While they are busy. But she had seen Mook effortlessly run down Calloway, and she doubted if she could run much faster, especially after the night she had had so far.

Redbear rolled up close to Calloway. Mook stayed close, bent over the back of the chair, where he could see, and perhaps spots where Mook was binding Calloway into place. Now she did look at Calloway's face and found it flushed red and wet. He kept trying to blink his eyes open but they snapped closed again as if on their own. The thing that hit Adele like a punch in the stomach was that this was the exact spot where these men had tied up her own husband, Vance, where they had tortured him. What kind of man brings you to the place where they tortured and cut on your husband in a way that led to his death and then tells you to "Take it easy"?

Her knees nearly buckled. With everything in her she forced herself to stay upright. She began to look around for a stick, a rock, anything, a weapon of any kind. She kept her breath steady as she looked around. If she ran, where to? There was no place she could go they could not catch her, at least Mook. Over by those trees along the creek? No.

"Give me a hand with Redbear," Mook said.

Calloway was stretched in an uncomfortable lean, and he twisted hard against the tape but got nowhere. They went over to the car and got the rolling chair out of the trunk. As soon as he was on it, Redbear began pushing with his good leg. He had his knife out of its sheath.

"Now, remember, Fred." Mook leaned and helped push the chair toward where Calloway was stretched in the growing light. "We need information first. Okay? Just tease him a bit." He took a pair of plastic surgical gloves out of one pocket and handed another set to Redbear. They both slipped them on. The stark white of their hands seemed even more menacing.

Adele couldn't move. Now, her head screamed. While they are busy. But she had seen Mook effortlessly run down Calloway, and she doubted if she could run much faster, especially after the night she had had so far.

Redbear rolled up close to Calloway. Mook stayed close, bent over the back of the chair, where he could see, and perhaps

Either way they would probably kill him. The only satisfaction he might get was by not cooperating, but he would be just as dead in the end. She didn't much care for her own chances now, either. She would be extra baggage too, and real soon.

Mook turned off the highway and passed through a yellowed rock arch that had a unicorn's head sticking out. Almost every ranch had some kind of grand gate, a few of the newer ones had solar-powered electric barred gates. This one had no inner iron bar grating and had been let run down over the years. The long lane back took a right curve to wind around behind a half-crumbled old house that showed three different kinds of stone to its various stages that had been built years apart. The lane gave out at a flat, scorched area where once there must have been a wooden barn or some other structure that had not lasted as long as the house.

As soon as the car stopped Calloway's door flew open and he made a dash for it. Mook was out his door at the same time and Calloway had tucked in far too many crème brûlées to ever aspire to be a marathon runner at this point in his life. As Adele got out, Mook dragged Calloway back toward the house, and Calloway whimpered and pleaded.

"Get that roll of tape we brought," Mook said to her. When she hesitated, he said, "Take it easy. Just do it."

It was on the front seat. Redbear sat in the backseat waiting to be helped onto the rolling chair they had tucked into the trunk. She glanced his way, and wished she hadn't. He winked at her.

Ice surged in excited charges up and down her veins as she took the roll of tape over to Mook and handed it to him, careful to avoid looking directly at Calloway, who sobbed. Her eyes were drawn instead to a wooden set of steps that led up over a low stone wall in what would have been the house's backyard. Bits of silver tape showed on the ladder, at the same strategic grab Redbear if he started to go too far.

The knife blade flashed silver in the dim light as an arm lifted and a button flew off Calloway's shirt. Then the next button, one after the other until Redbear reached up to rip open the front of the shirt to bare a rounded, pale chest. Calloway quivered and tried to press back. But there was nowhere to go.

Mook shoved the gun he held down into the front of his pants where it was held in place by his belt and he reached in his jacket pocket and pulled out a tube of ointment. "Are you thinking about helping us now? All it would take would be a few trips to the right banks and we'd split with you, wouldn't we, Fred?"

Redbear didn't nod or otherwise agree. He seemed eager for Calloway to say no.

The con man's eyes flitted about like a rabbit's in a cage, settled on Adele as if pleading, but there was nothing she could do.

"This stuff here, it's lidocaine, a pain killer. You think hard and you think fast, Calloway. If you're cooperative, I'll rub some on you. Otherwise, some of this is liable to sting like dammit."

Calloway's expression fixed somewhere between petulance and indignation. He was still not a full subscriber to the program. Adele could have told him to cooperate, but she didn't get time. "Right, Fred?" Mook said.

That was a sign. Redbear leaned forward, his knife blade glittered silver, and Adele watched the expression on Calloway's face shift from scorn to belief. "Wait. Wait. Wait. Wait."

"What?" Mook asked, leaning closer as if he couldn't hear him.

"I'll help."

"I'm sure you will. But you have to feel just a bit more so you understand the importance of obeying. Understand?"

It was another sign. Faster than she could imagine the knife blade flickered and a red spot blossomed and began to well and drip from where one of Calloway's nipples had been. A trickle of wet, dark red ran down the pale, rounded barrel of a chest.

Mook squeezed out a sizeable dollop of the lidocaine onto the fingers of one gloved hand. He dabbed the lotion onto the open wound and slapped a short stretch of silver duct tape on top of that. Adele didn't doubt it was the same technique they had used on Vance.

From his pocket Mook took out a small vial of clear liquid in a prescription bottle on which Adele could see part of her husband's name. "I've got the liquid form of lidocaine too and will inject some if you're a good boy." Adele hadn't seen any syringe and doubted any genuine compassion in Mook's words. But none of that mattered. The stuff they had already used should have reduced Calloway's shock and pain, but it didn't seem to work quickly enough.

Calloway's eyes rolled back and he shuddered into a slump.

"Well, damn, Fred. Ain't this one the delicate flower. Give him time to come to before we start again. No sense wasting your science on him just now. Maybe we'd best tend to Adele."

The chair pivoted on the flagstones of the old patio and Redbear's eyes narrowed at her. Mook turned and started toward her, too.

She took a few seconds to gulp and try to take in her last glimpse of the day, such as it was. Then she turned and ran close along the side of the house. Fast as she was going she could hear the pounding steps behind her gain on her. The ground was covered with thick, tall grass that had been bent by the rain into clumps. Twice she nearly tripped, but panting hard she rounded the corner of the house with Mook almost to her. He ran hard while he tugged the gun out from under his belt. As Adele rounded the corner she saw a blur of white and heard a *thunk* that sounded like a line drive out of the stadium. She risked a glance back and saw Mook fall to the ground into a crumpled heap. Over him stood Boose, who wore a white T-shirt and jeans and held an ax handle.

She slowed to a halt and bent, held her knees while she caught her breath, and looked up at him. "Now aren't you just the knight in tarnished armor."

"Well, there wasn't nothin' good on television so I thought I'd see what was up with you. Where's the other one?"

She nodded toward the back of the house. Boose took off in that direction in a jog. She thought to yell to him that Redbear had a gun, Boose's .45, but she figured he knew that. She didn't want to risk a yell and alert him that Boose was coming.

She shouldn't have worried. By the time she got to the back of the house where she could poke her head around, Boose was almost to Redbear. The bleeding on Calloway's chest seemed much worse. In fact, there was a lot more blood. At the sound of Boose's running footsteps the Indian spun his chair as fast as he could, held the bloody knife with one hand and reached for the automatic in his belt with the other.

Boose swung for the elbow of the gun hand and Adele heard the crack as he connected. With his knife hand extended, Redbear lunged toward Boose, who whipped the ax handle back the other direction and caught the knife hand, sending it whipping up past Redbear's face. The most surprised look appeared on Redbear's face, and Boose jumped back as a red fountain shot out in a gush more than a foot and a half from his neck where Redbear had nicked himself with his own sharp knife.

"Well, damn," Boose said. "I didn't intend that."

Redbear slumped off the chair and fell to the ground. Boose yanked off his T-shirt and dropped down beside him, tried to wrap it around the neck enough to slow the bleeding without strangling him when the growl of tires on gravel sounded from another car. It screeched to a halt and the front doors swung open. Carson Billings and Tillis Macrory came running, both with their guns drawn.

"This one's out of it and the other's up front. You'd better call an ambulance or something," Boose called back to them. He didn't take his hands off the shirt that was now soaked through with blood.

Tillis pulled out a pair of handcuffs and tossed them to Carson who took off for the front of the house. He came closer, slid his gun into his holster as he did. "What happened, Boose?"

"I guess you ain't gonna believe he cut himself shaving."

"We don't have time for that, Boose."

"I was just disarming him. He cut his own damn self."

"That's right," Adele said. "This is the spot where these same two guys worked over Vance."

Tillis leaned close and took a brief glance at Redbear before giving a shake of his head and straightening again. He went over to where Calloway hung in a slump where he had been taped in place.

"That one need an ambulance, too?" Esbeth said. She and Gardner clambered out of the back of the car and stood next to Adele, leery about getting any closer. Both looked about as tired as Adele had ever seen two human beings look.

"I'm afraid neither of these men do. They're probably going to leave in bags. This one's had a heart attack. Don't anybody touch anything."

The two-car-wide garage door rolled up and a stealth gray Hummer H2 with brown leather interior began to ease back down the driveway from the brick and white stone three-story, thirty-thousand-square-foot home. The back of the SUV was crowded with matching Louis Vuitton bags with one larger matching trunk strapped in place on the aluminum crossbar rack on top. Behind the wheel Torrence Furlong drove while engaged in an intense conversation with his wife in the passenger seat—well, argument really—which is why he nearly ran into the brown and copper patrol car that pulled up on the street and blocked the end of his drive.

The brake lights flashed on and Furlong opened his door and lurched out with an outraged "How dare you?" poised to spring from his lips when he saw the quiet, serious sheriff as he got out of the driver's side of the patrol car. Chunk Philips, the deputy, got out the other side and stared in an insolent way at Furlong that could not mean anything good.

"Going somewhere?" Sheriff Gonzalez asked. He came forward to stand within a foot of Furlong, who was dressed in khaki slacks, cordovan loafers without socks, and a polo shirt under a navy blue golf windbreaker. Gonzalez had to look up at Furlong from under the brim of his hat, but he did not let that intimidate him any.

"My wife and I are off to a previously scheduled trip to Bermuda," Furlong said. "Though that's no business of yours. Will you get out of my way so we can get to the airport on time? We're already cutting it close."

"You made the reservations last night, and it's a spur of the minute trip that meant you had to cancel half a dozen appointments for today. Besides which, the tickets aren't just to Bermuda; the next leg's to Rio if you choose to take it, and it's not Carnival season there." Gonzalez glanced toward the sun that was barely an hour up over the horizon.

"None of what's been going on has anything to do with me. I hope you're not trying to tell me I can't take a trip if I choose to."

"I'm not trying to tell you anything. I have a bench warrant for you since you've been judged to be a flight risk."

"Fly from what? I haven't done anything."

"Then you won't mind staying and answering some questions."

"I do mind, and I won't do it."

Gonzalez shrugged and nodded to Chunk, who stepped around behind Furlong and began to put on the handcuffs.

"I can't believe this. You have nothing."

"We have Karl Williams, and he was casting around on how he might make a deal. That led to your place, and you offered up Melba Jean, and would you believe it? She wants to make a deal, too. The autopsies show a pattern, as do all the records that Melba Jean conveniently kept copies of at her home. All this happened under your watch, and with your full knowledge."

"I told you to make a deal before they did," Furlong's wife yelled from the passenger seat window.

"Shut up. Will you? You stupid. . . ."

"You'll have plenty of time for that later," the sheriff said.

"I won't take that from the likes of you, either," Furlong snarled at the sheriff.

"Yes, I do recall now you suggested I was a *cabron* when you openly supported the man who ran against me last election. We'll see how you feel about that after a judge and jury get their chance at you."

Furlong's wife opened her door and got out of the Hummer, in slow dawning awareness they were not going anywhere after all. She had long blond hair and wore a red cashmere sweater over tight brown slacks and open-toed sandals. She blinked at her husband as if getting a clear look at him for the first time, but she didn't rush to him even though she was twenty years his junior and could have made the sprint without effort. Instead she looked like the princess just as the prince turned back into a frog. The house, the car, the luggage all spoke of a different way of living in a small town like this, a way that had until this second been a cut above the rest, and she looked dazed.

"You'll have a hard time proving anything. You have nothing. I'm saying nothing more until I speak with my lawyer."

"That would be preferred, Mr. Furlong." Gonzalez was all politeness while Chunk loaded the rest home director into the backseat.

Across the street a man and his wife had come out onto their lawn to get a paper they left lay while they stared at the scene across the street. The paperboy had stopped on his bike to watch, too.

"What d'ya say we run in with lights and siren going, Johnny?" Chunk said as he opened the front door on his side.

"If that makes you happy, Chunk, why that's just what we'll do."

Mrs. Furlong stepped away from the car and glared angrily at the backseat of the patrol car. The sheriff shook his head and climbed into the driver's seat. He flipped on the lights and siren and pulled away. The kid on the bicycle waved, as if a parade was going by.

Tillis arrived ten minutes late at the Bluebonnet Café, but they had saved him a seat at the big, round granite table in the corner. It felt warm and cozy inside the restaurant. A week into November, it was the first chance the ranger had gotten to meet and sit down in a group with any of them. Outside, what Texans call a "snap" had taken the temperature down into the 40s, but locals were no doubt bravely burning the furniture to stay alive while up in Montana plows were working on more than twenty inches of fresh snow in subzero temperatures.

Esbeth had already started on her pot roast and deep-fried okra and Gardner on a plate of catfish and fries. Adele had a salad and Boose worked on a plate of liver and onions. They waited until the ranger got his hat hung, settled in his seat, and his order placed with the waitress, Thelma Sue, before they started in on him with the questions.

"Did that federal agent fella get that Two Chins guy he was after?" Boose asked.

"I can't tell you everything, but Tony Petralia is in custody, and Mook has said enough to keep him there probably. I doubt if Mook gets to be his cellmate, though. The ears are sure healing nicely, Boose."

"Yeah. I think it makes me faster. I ain't timed myself yet, but the other day I just about outran Spook Daddy to the mailbox. It's kinda like bein' streamlined." Fresh bandages covered the lower half of each ear, but he would always look like some lower order of elf, even when they healed all the way, but he was not the sort to worry over that.

"I'm glad you cleared out all those devious traps of yours so you can enjoy that sport."

"Don't know why I didn't get to keep that Silky lady. I caught her fair and square." Boose tried to act serious while he suppressed a grin.

"She's locked up, too, and won't be anyone's gal for a while, unless she has a very friendly cellmate. But you don't need her. Aren't you and Adele still an item?"

Boose started to speak, but Adele put a hand on his forearm and said to the ranger, "We've agreed to disagree, to be friends and stay away from each other."

"Yeah, I sooner or later rub even myself the wrong way sometimes, so it's just as well." Boose cut off a piece of liver and forked it toward his mouth.

Thelma Sue brought Tillis' plate of meatloaf and mashed potatoes and put it down in front of him, and with the other hand she topped off his coffee before she shot off as quiet and as quick as she had come.

"Adele was kind enough to replace the sixty-four thousand dollars Boose's mother had swindled away by the Baron woman and Calloway, though," Esbeth said. "She's in a rest home again, though certainly not the Oakline Hills Rest Home."

"There's talk it may open again," Tillis said. "Torrence Furlong sure won't be running it. He's still trying to put all the blame on Melba Jean, but when she rolled over on him she did it hard. Turned out she knew far more about how he ran his operation than he'd expected. Plus she'd kept that duplicate set of records at her home. Furlong trying to take off the way he did won't help his situation, either. Case won't come up for another month or two, but the DA doesn't have any doubts about it." He turned to Adele. "I'm sorry you didn't get the increased insurance, though. Vance's death stayed ruled a suicide, however he was driven to it. You could probably fight that if you wanted, since there were circumstances."

"Oh, I'm okay. All I wanted really was the satisfaction of knowing what really happened, which just shows you've got to be careful what you wish for."

She glanced Boose's way again, and Esbeth noticed, not for the first time, that there was a revitalized glow to Adele's smile.

"I gotta hand it to ol' Esbeth, though," Boose said. He chewed a partial mouthful of food and washed that down with a sip of coffee. "She did what no one else could do—collared two con artists and solved the details leading to a death that no one else could figure out. Though in her way of doin' it she sure gave a whole new meaning to sweating with the oldies."

"Gee, thanks, Boose," Esbeth said with little sincerity.

"How much of it was being lucky?" Tillis looked up at her from applying a liberal dose of pepper to his mashed potatoes.

"I sure enough don't feel lucky about any of it," Esbeth admitted, "coming as close to being blown off the face of the earth the way a few of us here almost were."

Gardner cleared his throat, and for a hushed second Esbeth was afraid he was going to launch into one of his instructive tales again. But he said, "In life you have to work with the cards you're dealt or the set the pieces take after the first several moves on a chessboard. Sometimes winning is coming out the other end at all with whatever scraps of grace and dignity remain."

No one had anything to add to that for a minute, until the Texas Ranger broke the silence.

"What about you, Gardner? Find a place to live yet?"

"Well . . . um . . . yes, I did."

"Yeah," Boose chipped in. "Seems there was a house for rent just half a block down the street from Esbeth's place—one of them coinqidinks Esbeth talks about. They can visit each other without getting in each other's hair too much, and Gardner don't have to go back to that place where he had to pretend his cornbread wasn't all the way baked in the middle."

"Being near friends is good," Gardner said. "Folks our age really only know how to fall in love with a pair of shoes that fit right and feel good."

"Or a chair," Esbeth added.

"Well, yes. There's that."

"And you, Esbeth," Tillis said. "Are you satisfied?"

She sighed and lowered the piece of deep-fried okra that was poised on her fork near her mouth. "I suppose it's not a perfect world, or I wouldn't be the busybody I am. I feel bad when anyone dies, no matter how bad they might be, though people going to prison for being low-life mean to others won't cost me as much sleep. But if it was up to me there would be a quicker and easier way to get money back to the ones who were ripped off by people like con artists, though the ones treated ill by a rare rest home that's just in it for the money deserve attention, too, and there's not a whole lot can be done there at all, is there?"

"You know, Esbeth," Tillis said, "the official stand on

vigilantism, or being a busybody, if you prefer, is to discourage it. But I suppose it's a good thing there are still a few people with convictions who care and have the brass to live up to them."

"Oh, she's got ever bit as much brass as the courthouse lawn cannon," Boose said.

Esbeth's brow wrinkled and her mouth tightened at Boose before she turned back to Tillis. "Well, I'm sure not going anywhere soon, if that's what you are jawing about. I expect to be around a while. If that cramps anyone's style they'll just have to get over it all on their ding-dong own."

ABOUT THE AUTHOR

Russ Hall lives in rustic splendor on a lake in Central Texas Hill Country. He has had ten books and numerous short stories published. He won the Nancy Pickard Mystery Fiction Award. A veteran of over twenty years in the publishing industry, he now spends as much of his time as he can hiking, fishing, and writing.